GHOSTS

of

BERGEN

COUNTY

GHOSTS

of

BERGEN COUNTY

Dana Cann

 TIN HOUSE BOOKS / Portland, Oregon & Brooklyn, New York

Published by Tin House Books, Portland, Oregon, and Brooklyn,
New York

Distributed by W. W. Norton & Company

Library of Congress Cataloging-in-Publication Data

Names: Cann, Dana, author.
Title: Ghosts of Bergen County / by Dana Cann.
Description: Portland, Or. : Tin House Books ; New York : Distrib-
    uted to the trade by WW Norton and Company, 2016. | Includes
    bibliographical references and index.
Identifiers: LCCN 2015041609 (print) | LCCN 2015048372 (ebook)
    | ISBN 9781941040270 (pbk. : alk. paper) | ISBN 9781941040287
    (e-book) | ISBN 9781941040256
Subjects: LCSH: Accidents—Fiction. | Fate and fatalism—Fiction. |
    Drug addiction—Fiction. | Visions—Fiction. | Bergen County
    (N.J.)—Fiction. | New York (N.Y.)—Fiction. | Psychological fiction. |
    GSAFD: Mystery fiction.
Classification: LCC PS3603.C36 G56 2016 (print) | LCC PS3603.
    C36 (ebook) | DDC 813/.6—dc23
LC record available at http://lccn.loc.gov/2015041609

First US edition 2016
Printed in the USA
Interior design by Jakob Vala

www.tinhouse.com

For Alice, Brigit, and Travis

Fate is the mistake that was meant to happen.

—MICHAEL MEADE

PROLOGUE

There were no witnesses except the woman who'd been up all night, had consumed two beers and three vodka tonics before switching to (and sharing) the playwright's Scotch, and she (the witness) could remember the morning only in snatches, like the digital stills and clips that cycled through her computer's screen saver. There was the club where she'd met the playwright. There were her friends leaving the club. There was the playwright tucking his loose curls behind his ear. There was the playwright in the stairwell of his building. There were the vents, condensers, and fans, the mechanical infrastructure on the roof, looming like the lunar module on the surface of the moon. There was the sun coming up over Chelsea. There was the playwright on the pavement below. And one other im-age, which came to her in the early afternoon, when she woke in her bed, naked, her dress and underwear bunched on the floor: the playwright, leaping from the gravel rooftop to the parapet that framed it, gilded and smooth and almost shining in the morning light, leap-ing the way an acrobat leaps from one tightrope to a higher tightrope, arms spread, for balance not flight. And it was this last image she trusted least, because it was the clearest and sharpest, as though it had never actually happened, as though she remembered it only from the dream she'd just dreamed.

PART I
JUNE 2007

CHAPTER ONE

Gil Ferko sat in a conference room on the fiftieth floor, arranging business cards before him according to who sat where across the table—a narrow oval, with eight chairs on each side. Ferko's chair wasn't in the middle; nor was it on the end. He was a bishop, an important enough guy, strategic to a point, comfortable in his role, able to take a piece or two if such an opportunity presented itself. He had the king's ear; though, more accurately, the king had Ferko's ear.

The king in this case was William Prauer, a founding partner at Riverfront Capital. He was thirty-five, two years younger than Ferko, and worth a few hundred million, rumor had it. Prauer had worked at Goldman, then at age twenty-nine launched Riverfront in a

Midtown office a half-dozen blocks from either river. Since then, Prauer had timed metals, then automotive, buying at the trough and holding, sometimes selling, always higher, while the rich guys from Europe and the Mideast and the pension funds in the US kept betting with him, pouring billions into his funds. Now he was on to retail, and posted up, in the corner of the conference room, with Roy Grove, the controlling shareholder of Grove Department Stores, with sixty stores operating in eleven states that once comprised the Confederacy. It didn't make sense to Ferko—this push for Grove, a brand beaten down figuratively and literally, as lately, it seemed, the paths of hurricanes crossed the nearest Grove store with alarming precision. Three roofs blown off last season alone. It didn't make sense that Prauer and Grove were doing their little dance in the corner, lips to ears, practically holding hands. Prauer had friends in media, rich friends who bought his funds and were conflicted enough to deliver bad news on a company like Grove, with closely held equity and publicly held debt. If Prauer couldn't buy the equity from the Grove family, he could buy the debt in the market. He had plenty of time. Ferko had watched Prauer do it before—buy bonds on the cheap and convert them to equity. He had a reputation as a shark because he was one. Now Ferko watched his boss with Roy Grove. Was Prauer threatening the man? Win-win was a myth, a platitude the losers consoled themselves with each time they lost. Ferko had been with the losers. He could hardly believe his luck now. He hadn't gone to the right schools. He'd never paid his dues, working sixty to eighty hours a week on the lower rungs. He was sure that one day he'd be discovered, banished to some faceless box in an industrial park in Parsippany or outside of the Oranges, where his former classmates— the MBAs who, like Ferko, had completed their degrees at night, part-time—compared monthly budgets with actual results and noted variances on a spreadsheet. Was Ferko really better than them?

"Do you know any of these guys?" Lisa Becker whispered into his ear, indicating the business cards Ferko had arranged before him. She sat to his left, the knight to Ferko's bishop, the nimble piece that was brought out early and arguably worked the hardest. She was thirty-one, unmarried and unattached, though Ferko suspected she was seeing George Cosler, a managing director, another bishop, who oversaw automotive for Prauer. Ferko wondered if that relationship had brought Lisa to this meeting, this conference table, at Ferko's elbow. The toe of her shoe touched his ankle.

And again. She played guard for a women's basketball team in some city league.

Ferko shook his head no. Grove was represented by a new firm started by a couple of guys from New York who collected some bankers from California and called themselves, not so cleverly, EastWest Partners. This was their first transaction, as far as Ferko knew. But then he read the name on the business card he was holding: GREGORY A. FLETCHER, PARTNER, EASTWEST. Ferko glanced up and found Greg sitting directly across the table—the right age, late thirties, with a full head of hair the color of sand. But this Greg Fletcher had sleepy eyes, half slits. Ferko thought of those mailings you sometimes get with photographs of missing kids and computer-generated age progressions of what they might look like now. Greg had been thirteen when he left Edgefield Junior High. Then Ferko saw it—the sideways grin, directed at an associate, then across the table at him.

"Gaylord Ferko," Greg Fletcher said.

Here's what happened to those guys who tormented you growing up: they became investment bankers and private equity kings.

Not the bullies, the ones who frightened you physically. The other guys—the ones you envied, because they were popular. Years ago, they came up with stupid names to call you, like Gaylord, which stuck, because Greg Fletcher could hit a baseball and throw a football and shoot a basketball better than anyone else in fourth grade. Back then Ferko hadn't known what to make of Greg Fletcher's sudden interest, even as Ferko understood it was merely for ridicule. Still, he went with it. First because he had no choice, but then because Greg Fletcher was actually talking to Ferko. Which became a bigger deal in fifth grade and bigger still in sixth, when Greg advanced to the regional finals of the Punt, Pass, and Kick competition, and everyone watched during halftime of the Giants-Cardinals game, at home, on their TV sets, as Greg was introduced in a Giants uniform, number one, along with the other shaggy-haired kids, the other Greg Fletchers of New Jersey and New York, with a ball in one hand and a helmet in the other, standing along the home sideline at Giants Stadium. Ferko cheered. He waited. Then Greg proved he was human. His punt was not the best. His pass wobbled and fell outside the hash marks. His kick knuckled and died. And he didn't advance. No Hawaii. No Pro Bowl. He remained a local hero until seventh grade, when his locker was next to Ferko's. Then Greg moved to California.

Now Ferko stood at the far end of the conference table, by the window that faced east, where a tugboat pushed up the East River, and shook Greg Fletcher's hand.

"This is weird, man," Greg said. "Like déjà vu, you know?"

"Like memory," Ferko said.

"Dude, I know the difference. I was just *thinking* about you the other day."

"*Really?*"

"Sure, man." His hair was actually longer than it had been in seventh grade. He swept it out of his eyes with his tanned fingers. "I've been back east a year or so. I ran into Jen Yoder. She trades metals for Deveraux, so she's interested in our world."

Ferko was unsure whether *our world* included him.

"We get together every now and then," Greg said. "We'll loop you in. She's still very cool."

"That's cool," Ferko said, like a parrot. Jen Yoder had been untouchable in high school. She'd walked the halls on a raised dais, it seemed, in her white cheerleader uniform on game days, her black hair spilling down her back, her face freckled, light-complexioned. Was she even pretty? He remembered her perched on the back of a convertible, with an armful of lilies, cruising laps around the track that circled the football field, where Greg Fletcher's old buddies—who could never throw or kick the football as far as Greg, but that year, Ferko's senior year, were on their way to the state finals—stood and applauded along with those in the bleachers, the parents and the students, including Ferko, who'd realized years before, when he'd first been called Gaylord, the benefits of invisibility, of blending in. So much so that now he couldn't be sure he had actually been there that day, standing in the bleachers, when Jen Yoder was named homecoming queen. Maybe it was a picture in the yearbook he remembered, the victory lap in the convertible from some movie he once saw. He couldn't remember a single conversation with her. He imagined Greg calling her later, telling her he ran into Ferko, and Jen saying, "Who?" "Gaylord," Greg would say, and Jen would say, "*Who?*"

She'd had a party at her house the night of graduation, smack in the middle of the two-week window that marked the end of high school and the start of the next stage, when the spirit of achievement trumped the cliques and their laws of exclusion. Ferko swam in the pool in Jen Yoder's backyard. He drank beer from the coolers that had been stashed beyond the hibiscus, away from the lights of the pool deck and the patio and

the imposing house, in the dark part of the yard, where
the leaves on the trees cast shadows in the moonlight,
and where, later, as Ferko left, faceless couples sat along
the stone wall, making out. He walked home alone in
the moonlight, his hair, which he wore long then, still
damp from his swim in Jen Yoder's pool.

"You're married," Greg Fletcher said now. His
thumb and forefinger touched his own bare ring finger
like pincers.

Ferko looked at his gold band and shrugged. It was
a symbol, sure, an asset even. It defined men; those
pushing forty who lacked one began to exude an air
of damage, despite the feigned envy of their peers.
He supposed his ring scored him one up on Greg. It
was, perhaps, the first time Ferko had had anything on
Greg. Though he remembered Mary Beth, at home in
their dark room, the heavy curtains drawn to proscribe
the fine day. The truth was something else.

Ferko prepared himself for the logical follow-up,
the one about kids. He'd come up with an answer some
months ago that had proved useful in deflecting the
question: *We don't.* Vague enough, casual enough, *true*
enough. The answer defeated the question, conquered
it, rendered it as inconsequential as the asker had in-
tended.

But Greg didn't ask the logical follow-up, which left a void in the small talk, one Ferko was eager to fill: "And you?"

"My sweetheart and I cohabitate." Somehow Greg managed this proclamation without a whiff of irony. He glanced toward the window, where Prauer and Grove had parted. They took their seats—the black king and the white king, facing each other. The tug on the river had motored out of view.

"Game face." Greg touched his chin and the smile he'd worn since the instant of recognition vanished, replaced by the intimidating, blank look of a boxer at a weigh-in—eyes small, mouth drawn to a frown.

And then he was gone, back to his seat, and Ferko took his, across from Greg's. The toe of Lisa's shoe, suspended from her crossed leg, touched Ferko's ankle. She leaned over and picked up his pen and wrote in his notebook, *You know a lot of people!* She dropped the pen, hesitated, then picked it up again and underlined the words *a lot*.

Ferko crossed it out and wrote at the top, *Initial Meeting w/ Grove*, along with the date. She was flirting, sucking up, or it was simply her way. It was difficult to distinguish the sincere from the bullshit, especially when the sincere traversed such a wide moral spectrum.

The fortunes of associates like Lisa were tied to those on the higher rungs—the Ferkos and Coslers—for the slather from the annual bonus and the juice from the next assignment. She had to play nice, right? Though it was true that each time they'd worked together (there'd been only three instances) he'd known *someone* on the other side. Maybe she was right—he knew a lot of people. And maybe his value to Prauer was ripening. Promise sparked like a flash on a camera, blinding him for an instant before the table was revealed, the conference room, the bank of windows, the haze between here and Queens, and Scott Horowitz, Grove's attorney, the meeting's host, who sat to the left of his client and began to speak, a preamble of how the parties got here. It was a speech Ferko had heard a hundred times at the start of as many different pitches. He could deliver it himself if pressed. He knew the words. He knew the punch line: the company was for sale! He leaned back and soaked up the lack of pressure. He was making good money to sit here and listen.

Greg Fletcher's sleepy eyes dimmed. His face was still boyish, his hair unkempt. He listened to the preamble with an indifference to match Ferko's. They were peers, right? They would go one-on-one—valuation, strategy, negotiation. It was no longer about brawn, about arm strength or foot speed. It was about creativity, intellectual agility, collaboration. And names couldn't hurt Ferko any longer.

The toe of Lisa's shoe brushed his ankle. He nudged her elbow with his. He would speak with Greg, his once-tormentor, at the meeting's conclusion. There was this deal. There were others. And Jen Yoder, the homecoming queen. Beyond Greg Fletcher's sleepy head, beyond the glass that separated meeting from sky, the day was as bright as that.

CHAPTER TWO

Jen Yoder hadn't planned a detour when she mounted
her bike on the sidewalk outside of the Deveraux office building, pushed off, and headed south down Fifth
Avenue, but then the traffic stopped at Thirty-Fourth
and the only direction things were moving was west, so
she took that as a sign and followed the cars and imagined a route that took her all the way to the Hudson,
then south around the tip of the island and up the East
River to Tenth Street. She lived in the East Village. It
would be an adventure—part pilgrimage, part distrac-
tion. She'd call it the West Side loop. She was trying
to find new things to do, take on new challenges, and
here was one: a circuitous route home. The bike paths
along the rivers were used by cyclists in sleek clothes

on sleek bikes, often going faster than the cars on the adjacent expressways. Jen rode a beach cruiser, a one-speed with a foot brake and too-wide handlebars, with which she'd clipped, over the years, more than a few side-view mirrors on parked cars. She wasn't a fast cyclist, but she figured this diversion was only eight or so miles, something she could do in a little over an hour.

Plus, it was a beautiful afternoon, a rarity in summer. The fierce heat had yet to arrive. She pedaled with the traffic along Thirty-Fourth, the breeze in her face, then turned left onto Seventh and followed the one-way south to Twenty-Fifth, where she turned right and dismounted. This was the pilgrimage part. Chelsea. The playwright, Felix DeGrass. She'd done the pilgrimage before but it had been years. She walked her bike along the road, chin raised, eyes on the looming rooftop over a dozen floors up, and imagined the fall. She hadn't seen it at the time. She didn't think so, anyway. But now she did clearly, from this angle, from the street below—a man, limbs churning the way one turns pedals on a bicycle, his speed accelerating until he hit the pavement.

She closed her eyes a moment, then reopened them. It was just a streetscape. People in summer clothes. She waited for a car to pass, then crossed Twenty-Fifth and pushed her bike up the curb and onto the sidewalk and stood on a square about thirty feet from the corner where Twenty-Fifth met Eighth. *This place?* she wondered, picturing the approximate spot on the sidewalk where the body was when she'd peered over the edge of the rooftop. Eight years ago. Now nothing marked the sidewalk, and people went about their business, circumventing her as she took up too much space with her bike and its wide handlebars, gazing down at the sidewalk and up at the rooftop, and again came the image of the man falling toward her—so clearly that she braced for the impact. Was this a ghost? According to Jen's father, who wrote books about ghosts, they inhabited the places where they lived and died. Felix DeGrass had lived here, in this building. He'd died here, on this sidewalk. *Inhabited*—that was the word Jen's dad used in his books—not *haunted.* Jen wasn't sure she understood the distinction. But while she might have felt haunted by the image of the man falling off the roof of the building, there was no ghost of Felix DeGrass. Not here. Not now. The image was just her mind doing what she commanded of it. Twenty-Fifth Street and Eighth Avenue were peopled with the living, walking and driving and cycling east and west, north and south, except Jen Yoder, standing on a square of concrete,

surveying the scene, when something caught her eye—
a flyer stapled to a telephone pole: AUDITIONS! the
flyer said. Someone was putting on a play.

She'd acted in college, at Columbia. She played a clos-
eted lesbian in a production called *Tri*. There were
three characters—all women—who shared a house in
Brooklyn. Jen played Gail, a recent dropout from NYU.
The other housemates were Frances and Lana, sorority
sisters and recent graduates of an unnamed (and presumably small) liberal arts college upstate. There was
a fourth character, too, a man named Jonah, though
he never made a physical appearance on the stage. But
his presence in the three women's lives informed every
scene. Jen's Gail had crushes (to varying degrees and
against her better judgment) on each of her housemates, while each of her housemates had fallen (to varying degrees and against her better judgment) for Jonah,
who had developed a crush on Gail. The housemates
lived their lives in and out of the house in Brooklyn
(though the living room was the production's only set),
while Jonah phoned from time to time, and the one-
sided conversations with whoever happened to answer
revealed the relationships of the characters as much as
those scenes when the women were hanging out, either

all together or in one of three combinations of two. Jen loved the geometry of the script, which she thought of as a kaleidoscope of triangles. In New Jersey she'd been a cheerleader, our team against yours. The world was more complicated than that.

Yet, despite her experience in *Tri*, she convinced herself that she'd done the play only as a lark. She convinced herself that she didn't have the discipline of the other actors—those majoring in theater arts. And so she majored in history, which, to Jen, meant she'd had few ambitions, a quandary that hadn't seemed to vex her father.

Then, years later, the playwright of *Tri*, another student at Columbia Jen once counted as a friend, became somewhat famous—first in theater and then in films—which gave Jen hope that there was still an avenue in. This hope lingered until the other playwright, Felix De-Grass, was with her one night and then was gone and she slid down the slide and never bothered to climb back up.

Until now, finding this flyer in the approximate spot where Felix had died. It meant something, it had to, and, in addition to riding her bicycle home this afternoon via the Hudson River Greenway, Battery Park, and the East River Bikeway, she would also call the number that had been written multiple times across the bottom of the flyer and cut with scissors into two-inch strips. There

were only three tabs left, and Jen tore one off, unshoul-
dered and unzipped her bag, and found the smallest inside pocket, one so small that all she kept inside was a
book of postage stamps. And now this phone number.
She slipped it inside and zipped the pocket. Then recon-
sidered. She should call it now before she forgot and,
months later, found the number in the tiny pocket only
to realize it was too late for it to be of any use, or worse,
have no recollection of what the number was even for.
She was that sort of a fuck-up. She dug in her bag for her
phone just as it rang, which startled her, and she wondered, during a brief, confused interlude between the
first and second rings, whether the persons holding the
auditions had somehow called her. But of course they
hadn't. Her phone told her it was Greg Fletcher.

"Hey!" she answered.

"Long time," he said, which must have been a joke.
They'd seen each other last week, when she'd bumped
into him at Lexington and Eighteenth and they hung
out in a bar nearby.

"Guess who I ran into today?"

"I'm supposed to guess?"

"Gil Ferko." He paused a moment, presumably to
give her a chance to react. When she didn't he asked,
"Do you remember him?"

She thought she knew the name. "From Edgefield?"

"He lived on Holt," Greg said.

Jen knew Holt. The houses were newer than where she grew up, near the high school. "Skinny kid?" she asked, because a blurry image had formed in her mind.

"That's him. Black hair that stuck straight up. Crooked teeth."

And with that the image was complete. Gil Ferko had been a quiet kid. She remembered him in kindergarten and she remembered him in high school. Thirteen years. How did she never get to know him?

"I think his teeth got fixed," she said, remembering the high school version.

"They did indeed," Greg said. "His hair doesn't stick up anymore, either."

"How was I supposed to guess Gil Ferko, Fletcher?"

"It's just a saying, a way to start a conversation, to introduce a new concept. You're always running into people you know. You said so yourself."

"I know a lot of people."

"Well, I know some, too."

She read the phone number from the flyer. She'd call it once this call ended. She wished to improve herself. Taking up acting again was one way, and here was another: "Do I brag," she asked, "about all the people I know?"

"A little." Greg's voice was sweeter than she'd expected.

"Seriously," she said, "am I *tiresome?*"

"Of course not. Besides, it's true: you know a lot of people. And I need to know more."

The bar off Lexington had been in a basement, a place so nondescript its name hadn't registered. She wasn't even sure how they'd found it, how she'd known it existed. Down a set of narrow, concrete stairs, the walls were wood-paneled, the floor linoleum. A wood bar stood to one side, with mismatched stools, across from a pool table that took quarters. In between were metal tables and chairs, arranged without pattern. Someone's playlist spilled from speakers mounted on corner brackets. There was no TV. Everyone knew each other—including Jen, who chatted up a couple of guys from Sons of Squirrel, just back from a two-week tour in a borrowed van that had taken them as far west as Columbus, Ohio. It was like hanging out in someone's basement. Later, when it was time to close, they merely locked the doors and lit a joint and passed it around. Then another. The thin crowd thinned further. Jen and Greg sat in a corner more or less by themselves. It felt like a dream, where your past collides with your present in a surreal setting. Here was the first boy she'd ever kissed. The summer after seventh grade. That part was real. She told him her recurring dream, where she broke into people's houses, sometimes those of her neighbors growing up in Edgefield, and hung out in their basements until she was discovered and fled. And he told her his recurring dream, where he committed a crime and set about destroying the evidence until it was too small to be seen by the naked eye. His were glassy in the bar's dim light. She imagined the dream version of Greg Fletcher in a conference room, shredding reams of paper as the FBI closed in.

"Are you free this Friday?" he asked her now, over the phone. "Lunch?"

"I think so."

"With me and Ferko. He's the man."

"The skinny kid is the man?"

"Well, his boss is the man. William Prauer. Have you heard of him?"

"No."

"Read the paper. The dude's *acquisitive.*"

"That's a good thing?"

"Which makes the skinny kid the man by association," Greg said, then paused. "I used to call him *Gaylord.* I came up with that nickname. Do you remember that? It stuck, at least for a while."

Jen didn't remember the skinny kid having a nickname.

"I need to make up for that," Greg said, his voice
infused, to Jen's ear, with genuine remorse.

Still, she couldn't help herself. "To do more deals?"
she asked.

"Well, I feel bad about all that stuff, but, yes, to do
more deals."

Jen sighed. "I get off at two. Send me a text where
you want to meet. Just make sure there's a bar."

"A bar."

"It's Friday."

"Of course."

They said their goodbyes, and she held her phone
and regarded the numbers on the scrap of paper, then
keyed them and put the earpiece to her ear. The phone
on the other end rang until voice mail picked up. There
was nothing in the message about auditions—just a
woman with a Brooklyn accent repeating the numbers
Jen had dialed and inviting her to leave a message,
which she did:

"Hello," she said, conscious of her cadence, of slowing down her delivery and using her best stage voice.
The audition started with this message, she told herself. "My name is Jennifer Yoder." (She'd used her full

name—Jennifer Yoder—when she'd performed in *Tri*. That was the name listed on the playbill.) "I saw your flyer in Chelsea and I'm calling about the auditions. Please call me. I'd love to hear about your production." She left her phone number.

It was a simple thing—leaving a phone message. People did it all the time. Yet she felt especially good about this message, with no *um*s or *uh*s, no awkward pauses. She used a clear voice, a smooth stream of words in the correct order. She closed her phone and zippered the bag, then chanced a last look at Felix De-Grass's rooftop, allowing the image of the falling man to plunge toward her once more before she pushed her bicycle into the street and mounted it and continued west, down the hill, toward the Hudson and the bike path that followed the river south.

CHAPTER THREE

It was still light when Ferko arrived home. The house was quiet, the mail strewn on the dining table. "Hello," he said, under his breath, to no one. There were catalogs and cheap envelopes with cheap printing, windows through which his name was misspelled, glossy postcards from realtors and remodeling contractors. He placed it all in the recycling bin that held paper. The bin was full, so he took it out the front door to the barrel beside the porch, half hidden by the hemlock.

The house was new, a Cape, wood-framed, with cement siding and a porch with gray planks and white columns and a wood swing that hung from chains, affixed to the beadboard ceiling with hooks like small anchors. Mary Beth had loved the porch the moment they'd first parked at the curb on a May afternoon, in front of the lone remaining tall oak from the woods Woodberry Road had replaced. She'd wanted an older house—pre–World War II—but this one did the trick. She sat on the swing and made room for him, and he joined her and swung, their feet drawn up off the floor, while their agent fiddled with the lockbox and then with the key.

Now the bench was empty. He sat on it, then regretted doing so. He should be inside, saying a proper hello. The porch was his after dark, after Mary Beth had gone to sleep. He'd sit in the shadows, with the porch lights out and two bottles of beer in a bucket of ice. He'd sip the beers over the course of an hour, while the evening bugs sang and the occasional car coasted past, its radio muffled, while dogs walked up and down the sidewalks on leashes, their masters mostly silent, though sometimes coaxing, the way a parent might coax a child.

He was comfortable by himself, drawn to the quiet. So was she. It was a bad recipe, they'd joked when they first got together and recognized how alike they were. They'd met through mutual friends—party folk, a core group of extroverts who'd gone to Yale and functioned, in those days, in New York City in Y2K, like a star, throwing off heat, pulling others into their orbit. Neither Ferko nor Mary Beth were extroverts or had gone to Yale, yet here they were, attending the same rooftop party in the West Village. Later they adjourned to a corner bar, where Ferko, feeling magnanimous and tipsy, bought a round for the denizens, a couple dozen or so at that wee hour, including the complete strangers who happened to be there, and this discreet bit of generosity—buying a round for the bar—pulled these strangers, in that moment and for the next hour or two, into their orbit as well. Truth be told, Ferko had always wanted to stand beside a bar and announce loudly that the next round was on him, to receive the backslaps and the glasses clinking against his own, and he'd done a quick estimate, before committing, of the numbers in the narrow room and figured this was as good a time as any. He hadn't yet spoken with Mary Beth at this point, but he'd noticed her, a new face, and if Mary Beth hadn't yet noticed Ferko, she did so now. She told him weeks later, when they were alone together for the first time, shoulders touching in the back of a cab between one party and the next, his gesture was generous. She was impressed.

It was a risk, they both knew, given their introspective natures; they needed others. When their others moved to different cities and suburbs, Mary Beth and

Ferko moved here, to start a family, a new star, a new orbit.

He stood and steadied the porch swing and went to see if she was asleep or awake.

The next morning he woke to find the girl standing in the hallway outside their bedroom. The light was gray through the white curtains. It was dawn. He didn't wish to turn from the girl to check the time. It had been some weeks, maybe a month, since he'd seen her last. She wore a striped shirt and shorts, like usual. She was barefoot. Five years old, maybe. He propped himself on his elbow. Her pigtails fell in messy braids, the color of the clay Mary Beth had turned over their first year in the house, before the accident that killed Catherine, before the girl with the pigtails appeared, before Mary Beth neglected the garden and it was reclaimed by weeds that he mowed each week this time of year. The girl's bangs fell in her eyes. She was looking at him. Or maybe not. Maybe she was studying Mary Beth, who slept on her back, her mouth open, and in that moment of Ferko's doubt, the girl vanished.

He blinked, then brought his legs out from under the sheets, careful not to disturb Mary Beth. He went to the place where the girl had stood. He checked around the corners, down the stairwell. He poked his head into the guest room, his home office, and, finally, into the nursery, which was void of furniture except a dresser, where Mary Beth kept her off-season clothes, and a toy box that had once belonged to Mary Beth's grandmother. It was a wood crate, lacquered, and painted with circus seals and elephants and the sorts of clowns that gave children nightmares.

He opened it, half expecting to find the girl curled up inside, but all he found were papers and photographs, a stuffed caterpillar and a green plastic cup.

There were holes in the back of the box. Mary Beth had insisted he drill them. "For breathing," she'd said.

He'd looked at her.

"I used to hide in it," she'd said, "when I was a girl. The lid is heavy."

"We'll fill it with toys."

"We'll drill air holes in the back first."

Now he closed the lid and went back to where the girl had stood, outside the bedroom door. He placed his palm on the runner. There was no heat. He put his nose to it. Mary Beth slept. He felt less alone, more hopeful. Once he'd been afraid. But the girl was calm, serene. He wished to know what she wanted. His clock said it was 6:28, time to shower, dress, and go to work.

CHAPTER FOUR

There was a voice mail message waiting when he arrived. "Gil," Greg Fletcher said. "Spoke with Jen. You, her, me. Friday, lunch. Two o'clock. I'll charge it to Roy Grove. She'll be done with work. She wants beverages, is excited to see you, buddy. Call me."

Ferko hung up the phone. Something stirred inside of him—part hope, part nausea. It was inexplicable, really, that Jen Yoder wanted to see him. Such was the lure of nostalgia, perhaps. It blinded you to the facts—like, for instance, you'd spent the better part of your youth ignoring boys like Gil Ferko. He wondered whether it was some elaborate plot to embarrass him, to dominate him the way Greg once had when they were kids. Maybe Greg would somehow parlay this

dominance into concessions on the Grove deal, forever
diminishing Ferko's worth to Prauer, boosting Greg's
fortunes and options. Or maybe they'd simply grown
up, and the cliques no longer mattered. Maybe it was
no more complicated than that.

Lisa sent him the notes from the Grove meeting,
and, in the days that followed, they worked together on
an action plan and an information request, they pulled
research reports on retail and Grove's competitors, they
scratched out the bones of a database, compiled the
trading values and market statistics for comparable
companies, and all the while Ferko counted down the
days from Tuesday to Friday, back and forth on the
train, while Mary Beth remained in bed and the apparition failed to appear. The lawyers exchanged con-
fidentiality agreements, and Ferko realized, as he did
at the end of every week, that weeks were finite, that
something, if only endurance, had been achieved. This
week retained an energy that Mary Beth's melancholy
could not dispirit. As things happened with anticipated
events, the day approached like a ship at sea.

The restaurant was more a bar, with high tables in
front and booths in back. A pub. He'd have a burg-
er, maybe, or an omelet. The front—floor-to-ceiling

sliding glass—stood open to the street. TVs affixed to the walls showed a baseball game. He stepped inside and let his eyes grow accustomed to the light. Patrons were perched on barstools. Greg wasn't one of them. Ferko turned back to the sidewalk, but he found only the efficient processions walking east and west. No loiterers or malingerers.

"Table?"

The hostess wore a red tank top and black pants. Her black hair (and a few errant strands of gray) fell past her shoulders. She wore eyeliner, a half-dozen earrings, and had a tattoo—a braided vine—around her wrist. She held a Bloody Mary in a tall glass, revealing the fine tone of her triceps.

"Actually, I'm meeting some folks." He craned his neck toward the booths in back.

"Oh," she said, "describe them."

"Well, there's a guy, with longish hair. He's about my age. They both are, actually. The guy and this woman."

"Oh," she said, "what does she look like?"

He was about to break away, excuse himself and take matters into his own hands. There couldn't have been that many tables in the back. He would look for Greg himself. The drink had a straw and a stalk of celery and flecks of black pepper floating on its surface like the freckles on the woman's nose. Then she raised her eyebrows and put the straw to her lips and sucked the juice into her mouth.

He stopped.

"Jen?"

"Ha! You haven't changed a bit."

"Gullible?"

"I didn't say that." She kissed him on the cheek and squeezed his wrist, then led him to a corner of the bar where there was an empty stool next to hers.

The bartender appeared, and Ferko ordered a Bloody Mary, too. He was hungry, he told her, and her drink looked nutritious. It was a weird thing to say, he feared, but Jen pulled her celery stalk out, dripping tomato juice and vodka, and presented it to him. He took it and, without missing a beat, chomped.

The bartender delivered his drink, and he touched the celery that curled from the red juice and the floating ice. He raised his eyebrows.

"You owe me a french fry," she said.

Time had evened things out, leveled the playing field and all that. She was still attractive—out of his league, really. But she was a trader, a taker of orders. Someone smarter had written a program, an algorithm, that dictated her actions day after day. Commodities? Mined in Russia or Angola, some such country that denuded its land, sacrificed its resources for the efficiency of the market? She placed bets; her bets set prices. It was perverse, almost immoral.

He dunked her celery stalk in his drink and ate the rest of it. "What do you trade," he asked, "when you're not trading celery for french fries?"

"Aluminum." She sipped her drink, and bugged her eyes. "Isn't that ridiculous?"

"I guess."

"I'd rather trade celery for fries, or volcanoes for operas." She raised her glass. "Cheers."

"Aluminum wasn't what you aspired to in high school?"

"I said, *cheers.*"

"I can look it up." He touched her glass with the base of his.

"Where? In the *yearbook*? We were children. *Drink!*"

He did so. It was strong, with pepper and vodka. He had no meetings the rest of the afternoon. Some guys had the attitude that Friday afternoons were optional. Ferko didn't think he'd be missed.

"I would be a singer," she said, "but I can't sing. I would play piano or guitar, but I have these short, stubby fingers." She held them up, all ten, splayed in the air between them. They *were* short and stubby, the nails clipped straight.

"What would you sing? If you *could* sing, that is."

"It doesn't matter. It's the hours. Nine at night until two in the morning. Hey, that's what I worked today—nine to two. Where's Fletcher?"

Ferko looked around, out to the street, where the traffic—both pedestrian and automotive—blurred. He checked his watch (2:13) and shrugged.

"I'm better at night," she said.

"You seem okay now."

"And I'm not touring. Too tedious. The only place I travel to is New Jersey. I could work in a mall."

"Playing piano?"

"Mannequin."

"Well, I'm pretty sure they're manufactured. Cheaply in China, I'd wager."

"They're a commodity," she said.

"You could trade them."

"Don't be patronizing. No one shops at Nordstrom or Macy's because of their mannequins. But a live one," she said, "would be a draw. Everyone would gather round to see if she blinks."

"Mannequins don't have short, stubby fingers."

"Shut *up*! I've known you for what, like, four minutes?"

"Not counting thirteen years of Edgefield schools."

"Did we know each other?"

"You told me once to walk briskly across the room."

"What! And *why*?"

"We were in English class in eighth grade, with Mr. Beiler—"

"Who was so gay."

"Not really the point of the story."

"But he *was*," she said.

"I accept that."

"Anyhoo." She waved Ferko on.

"He called you and some of your smart, popular friends to the front of the class. To demonstrate adverbs."

"Which end in *l-y*. Usually," she said, drawing out the *l-y*.

"They *do*. So you turned to me. I didn't think you even knew who I was."

"I knew who you *were*."

You said, 'Gil, walk across the room.' And I did. And when I got to the other side, you said, 'Now, walk *briskly* across the room.' And I did that, too, and everyone laughed at how I walked briskly across the room.

I closed my fists and pumped my arms." Ferko closed his fists and pumped his arms to demonstrate, and now *she* laughed.

He said, "And that was the only time we spoke, I think, until just now, when you told me you aspire to be a mannequin."

Ferko awaited the return volley. There was something desperate to her. She wanted to be liked. Maybe that was what happened to the popular kids. They peaked early. He'd grown used to the rhythm of their conversation, the bounce back and forth. But now there was no response, and he saw why. She'd struck a pose, back arched, arm extended, like a mannequin. She didn't move. She didn't blink.

"Wow," he said. "You're good at that."

She stayed frozen, longer than he thought necessary. The point was a good one, but it had been made. He was left with nothing to do but laugh nervously, sip his drink, and glance at the TV, where the Cubs were playing the Phillies. Still she froze, and he decided to stare at her instead. It was what she wanted. She was looking off toward the street, her expression confident, knowing, like a real mannequin, or a fake one—*manufactured.* He was getting confused himself. She was in command. He tried to remember if she'd been in the drama club.

Popular girls didn't act in plays. He couldn't picture her onstage. Only on the floor of the gym, in her white cheerleader uniform, and on the track that ran around the football field. Now her expression remained cool and distant. Her head wavered, maybe. Her arms. It could have been his eyes playing tricks. The seconds stretched. She was good at keeping still.

A phone rang. She pressed her lips together, then reached for her bag. "I wouldn't take this if I were being paid." She glanced at the phone. "Fletcher. Hey!" she said into it. "Of course. How come? You're an asshole. Okay." She handed the phone to Ferko.

"Greg?"

"Gaylord. How's it going? Did you recognize her?"

"No. Where are you?"

"Triage. You won't believe this. Roy Grove's car blew up. He's dead."

"Dead?"

Jen studied a menu she'd found on the bar.

"As in not breathing, dead."

"He was just here."

"And now he's not. I'm reading it on the Internet."

"His car blew up?"

"In downtown Tampa. Police are investigating."

"Damn."

"I'm flying down tomorrow. To give my condolences to the family and try to figure out who owns his stock. Any idea?"

"The estate of Roy Grove?"

"I'm serious."

"Check with that attorney, Horowitz."

"Too obvious. Too soon."

"It might be too soon for deal salvaging."

"Well, I'm going. I guess the poor dead dude won't be buying us lunch."

Ferko closed Jen's phone.

"Or a detective," she said.

"What?" He handed her the phone.

"A detective. What I want to be when I grow up. Mannequin, detective. In that order."

"I need to make a call."

"Your client's dead," she said.

"Greg's client."

"Whatever."

He walked toward the street.

"I'll be here," she called after him.

He fluttered his fingers. Then he called Prauer.

There was a premium, in deal making, placed on news. News was information, and information was power.

"Bill," Ferko said, when Prauer picked up, "it's—"

"Gil," Prauer interrupted. The background hummed, and Ferko pictured Prauer, headset on, behind the wheel on some wide highway, accelerating, changing lanes, weaving through traffic, an endless quest to the front of the pack.

"Roy Grove—"

"—is dead."

"That's why I'm calling," Ferko said.

"Retail was a bad idea. I'm thankful we didn't waste the time. We drive on."

"We're done?"

"It's Friday afternoon. The sun is out. Grove's dead. We're alive."

Through the window, he saw Jen at the bar, stock-still. The mannequin act, he thought. Then she brought her straw to her lips.

"There were no other Groves at that meeting," Prauer said, "because Roy was the only one who wanted to sell. Maybe they killed him. Maybe they didn't. Who knows? It'll take months, years to sort through. It doesn't matter. We're out."

"Okay."

"Have a good weekend."

"You too."

They hung up.

A cab stopped to settle a fare next to a double-parked truck. The cars and cabs and trucks behind them queued up along Fiftieth and unleashed their horns. He left them to it. And the people on the sidewalk, with phones pressed to their ears (and now hands cupped to ward off the complaining horns). He threaded his way through them, and back inside, where the horns faded, replaced by a song he remembered from a certain summer years ago, when he and Mary Beth had rented a house at the shore in Manasquan with friends. There was a bar called The Room that sold steamed shrimp, ten bucks a pound, and beer in twenty-four-ounce bottles that sat in tubs of ice until some thirsty soul plucked one out and slapped a five on the bar and twisted off the cap and left it in the ice. And later, at night, when the sun had set, they turned up the music, brought in a DJ who played songs about parties and sex and this one, pure and simple, about dancing. There was no partner other than the music. He remembered dancing with Mary Beth, but he remembered dancing with the rest as well, in a big, loose circle. Friends and friends of friends, and probably a few strangers who'd happened in. They'd conquered the bar. Now some had moved on, to San Francisco and Chicago, to London and Hong Kong. Some had had children, and could be found, Ferko supposed, if one wished to find them. Ferko and Mary Beth had merely vanished; visited by tragedy, then gone.

Ferko moved his hands, his phone in his fist, in a serpentine, the way he had the summer he'd danced at The Room to this very song. His gait matched the beat.

Jen watched him coolly as he approached. He was hungry. He wanted his drink.

"A detective," he said, wrapping his fingers around his glass.

"A mannequin."

"But not a trader."

"No," she said. "Definitely not."

CHAPTER FIVE

Of course, what Jennifer Yoder really wished to be was an actor. Then she could have been a detective or a mannequin or an astronaut or a mother of six. Whatever the part called for. In New York you were defined by what you did. An actor would have been okay. Or a rock musician. There were plenty around.

She'd gotten a return call from the woman who'd posted the audition flyer in Chelsea. Her name was Queenie. That was it. No last name, which made Jen suspicious that Queenie was a poseur. But Jen looked up Queenie online and was surprised to find that she was legit. She wrote and directed short plays and videos. The plays were performed in Chelsea spaces and galleries, and the videos were screened in these same

galleries and others, in cities as far away as Los Angeles.
Queenie said she was collecting names, getting funding, and would be holding auditions soon, though
she couldn't say when. Maybe this summer but more
likely fall. It was open-ended, squishy, and the lack of
structure confirmed for Jen that her aspirations, if that
wasn't too strong a word, were in the formative stages.

Jen watched one of Queenie's videos—called *Cul-de-
Sac*—online. A woman wakes alone in the center of a
circle of grass. She wears a mid-twentieth-century dress,
hemmed below her knee. Royal blue. The colors—the
blue of the dress, the green of the grass—are too bright,
preternatural. The woman's hair is red, shoulder-length,
styled with a wave. Her makeup is bold. The woman sits
up, then stands. The streetscape is suburban. Kids walk
to school. A man walks a dog. A late-model car—yellow, so bright it seems to glow—coasts past. The houses
that encircle the cul-de-sac are large, the way new houses
are now, but with bright siding—turquoise, lime, and
vermilion—garish colors, like the grass in the middle
of the cul-de-sac, where the woman is now standing. A
soundtrack plays, woodwinds and strings. The camera
begins a slow arc, clockwise, around the woman, along
the curb of the circle. The sky is blue, cloudless. The
woman's face is filled with wonder. It's as though she'd

been plunked there by a time machine, or had fallen through a wormhole. Perhaps she's dreaming. Then she begins to turn slowly, counterclockwise, opposite the direction the camera is turning, faster now, or maybe speed is an illusion. Her expression loses its wonder, flattens to indifference. The strings go cacophonous. The camera's pace quickens. Fear, now, on the face of the woman in the center of the cul-de-sac, who's whirling like a child playing the game where she makes herself so dizzy she'll fall. And the camera, too, continues to accelerate; the outsize houses behind the woman blur, multihued, flickering lights, until the woman collapses in the grass and closes her eyes and the music stops and a white car drives past.

Like the woman in the video, like the character Gail in *Tri*, Jen too often felt out of place. She swigged her second Bloody Mary—she'd dispensed with the straw—and crushed an ice cube in her teeth. "Do you mind if I call you Ferko?" she asked.

He shrugged, and shoveled a forkful of omelet into his mouth. Had she ever known him?

"It's more fun to say," she said.

He shrugged again. "It beats Gaylord."

"Tell Greg to fuck off."

"Next time I speak with him." Ferko's lips formed a smile. "You're not what I thought you'd be."

"Compliment taken."

"At all," he said.

She decided not to tell him about wanting to act, about Queenie and the flyer and the auditions. Instead she said, "I was in a band once."

"A band," Ferko said, without inflection, as though the band in question might have been a marching band, in matching polyester uniforms with gold stripes.

"A punk band," she said. "The Mannequins."

"You're kidding."

"You've heard of them?"

"Absolutely not. What did you play?"

"I didn't."

"You sang?"

"I posed." She lifted her chin and arched her back, one arm forward, elbow crooked just so, two fingers out, as though reaching for a cigarette to bum. It was the best she could do in a restaurant booth. Sometimes on stage, when she'd strike such a pose, Ross, the lead guitarist, would wedge a cigarette between her fingers. When the song was over, he'd pluck it from her and smoke again. She was a prop. She bought skimpy outfits, dressed like Barbie. Now she blinked, dropped her arm. "You can Google it."

"Okay."

"Mannequin with a *q*, not a *k*."

"You're really out there."

"You owe me a fry."

He framed his plate with his open palms, and she grabbed a few fries and dipped them in ketchup.

Her aspirations might have been formative, but she was convinced that it meant something, that it was fate that had snarled traffic on Fifth Avenue and led her westbound to the approximate spot where Felix had fallen to his death and where now a flyer advertising auditions had been stapled to a utility pole by an artist named Queenie. Jen pictured herself in that moment of discovery like a character in one of Queenie's videos. Of course, Queenie might never call again, might never get funding, might move on to a different project, might lose Jen's number. Or maybe Queenie *would* call, but Jen would be too sick or too fucked up that day to make it. Maybe Jen wasn't what Queenie was looking for. Maybe Jen wasn't good enough for Queenie.

The conversation lulled for the first time. Ferko awaited the next serve, the volley thumped across the net. But there was none. Jen blinked and held her half-empty glass. Every interaction he had now was colored by what people knew and didn't know about him. It was true at work—with allies and adversaries—and at home, with Mary Beth. It had been nearly two years. He needed to find a different way forward.

"There's something you should know," he said before he had a chance to change his mind. It was abrupt, awkward, but there was nothing he could do now but clean it up and complete the thought: "There's something I want you to know."

She looked at him and waited.

"We lost a child. My wife and I."

Jen blinked, a subtle flinch.

"She was a girl," Ferko said. "I never talk about it."

His voice was stronger than he might have thought possible. This was what experience earned you. He'd negotiated with billionaires. He'd pretended enough times he was bigger than he was. He'd puffed his chest out, and grown men had stood down. It had surprised him at first. It surprised him still. The afternoon had been building to this, first at the bar with the Bloody Marys, where the notion of revelation had assembled, unseen, but perceived, yes, on some subconscious level, and then grew, its presence felt in his gut—no, in his *heart*—when he'd ordered lunch and a second Bloody Mary. It was still nebulous, the outlines indistinct. But then they formed, like in a Polaroid. The grays took on shapes, then colors, and materialized as an image discernible only in the last few minutes.

"A hit-and-run," he said. "She was a baby in a stroller."

And there it was. That part of it. The beginning. An ending, too, but that wasn't how Ferko thought of it. In that instant everything had changed, even as he was sitting on a plane, flying home from Chicago, oblivious to the event. Often, since then, he'd imagined himself aloft, buckled, gazing out the window, despite the sameness of the fields below, the clouds like rocks you leap, in a stream, one to the other. Commodities, all of it—the land and the clouds, the earth and its atmosphere. Such was the view from ten thousand feet. There were people, invisible in the fields and the rights-of-way that separated the fields, and in the towns, in huddled shelters. There was death and dying, birth and sex, commerce and crime, indifferent strangers. There was the hum of voices, of media, of engines, the persistent gain in volume. But the sky, from inside a plane, with the drone of engines, the flips of pages, the taps of keys, the occasional murmur, was peaceful, soothing.

There were witnesses, though no one got the plates of the blue car. They didn't get the make, either. Someone said it was an Audi. Another said it was an Acura. Mary Beth said nothing, though she, too, was a witness. She didn't have a scratch, but she couldn't remember, either. *Emotional trauma*, the policeman had told Ferko when she was out of earshot. She was in a fragile state. Of course she was. So was he. You probably didn't need a PhD or MD to make such a diagnosis, if it was a diagnosis. *Emotional trauma.* Two words. Adjective and noun. But he didn't need the vehicle's make. He didn't need the plates. He needed to know why she was on the street, beside the curb, on Lyttondale Avenue—a busy road with a double yellow line— when there was a perfectly good sidewalk up the curb, just beyond the ribbon of grass that buffered it from the traffic.

Two years later there still wasn't an answer. And Mary Beth was gone, beyond repair. But Jen was here, tattooed and pierced. And looking bored.

"That sucks," she said.

"Sorry." It had been a mistake, after all.

She clenched her jaw. "I need a smoke."

He watched her and waited.

"Let's get our bill." She raised her arm to flag down the server.

Ferko wasn't done. He scooped up a few more fries and dragged them through what was left of his ketchup. He should have felt exposed, vulnerable. Instead, he felt only numb. His child was dead, and he cleaned his plate. What sort of father did such a thing?

The waiter brought the bill.

He reached for his wallet. "I'll get it."

She folded her arms. The waiter took his card. She swung her legs from beneath the booth and stood. "I've got to score."

"Score?" he asked, but she was gone, flouncing toward the bar, where two guys sat on stools. Each produced a pack of cigarettes. She selected one from a red box while the other guy shook his gold box, and she took one from him, too. The waiter returned with Ferko's card and a pen and a little slip of paper for the tip and total. He signed and collected her bag from the booth. Ferko's was at his office; he *had* planned to return. Now, with Roy Grove dead, with Prauer crushing speed limits upstate, with Greg Fletcher chasing Grove's heirs before another banker got the bright idea, with Ferko two Bloody Marys closer to joining Mary Beth for an early night, the idea of going back to the office seemed futile. There was nothing in his bag he needed anyway.

Jen was laughing with the guys at the bar, a full-out, throw-your-head-back laugh. He offered her the bag. They laughed. Ferko couldn't imagine anything so funny. He wondered if it was him, the fool from high school, the butt of the joke. The laughter waned to snickers, then gasps.

"Let's go smoke," Jen managed.

The guys looked at Ferko, as though registering his presence for the first time. They waited.

He was still holding Jen's bag, which he now shouldered and said, "Let's go." He led the way. He couldn't be sure, without looking back, who, if anyone, was following. Doing so risked ridicule. He walked through the open doors and found a nook on the sidewalk, beside a column, out of the flow of foot traffic. When he turned Jen was there. Only Jen. And the two cigarettes she'd pinched off the guys. She retrieved a lighter, a real one—the kind you refill instead of toss—with a silver lid she shut when the cigarette tip flared.

She pointed the other one at him.

"I don't smoke."

"Neither do I." She took a drag and tucked the second cigarette behind her ear.

"Nice lighter."

She rubbed her thumb across its smooth surface, as if it were the belly of a Buddha. "It's my boyfriend's. I carry it with me." She regarded it, then squinted at

Ferko. It was bright on the sidewalk. "He's not really my boyfriend. He's a friend who's a boy."

Ferko nodded. "Those are funny words. *Boyfriend. Girlfriend.*"

"Stupid words," she said.

The traffic passed, wheels and feet.

"We were at one time," she said, "in the conventional sense."

He looked at her.

"Boyfriend and girlfriend."

"What happened?"

She paused as though she'd never considered the question. "We got tired."

"You get tired, you go to sleep."

"Tired with a capital *T*." She took a drag, held the smoke, then exhaled, chin raised toward the sky.

They fell silent. Jen smoked and watched the traffic. Then she said, "I'm sorry. I freaked in there. I'm sorry about your baby."

"Catherine."

"Nice name." She thrust her jaw forward and bared her bottom teeth. She stubbed the cigarette against the brick column and let it fall to the pavement.

She took her bag from him, unzipped a pocket, and retrieved a ring of keys as big as a bracelet, the sort a jailer in a black-and-white movie might carry. She searched the ring until she found the smallest key, then dropped her bag to the sidewalk. There was a bike behind her, a blue Schwinn, a cruiser, with handlebars like a gull's wings, cabled to a pipe with a rusted valve that might once have held a spigot. She went to work on the lock.

"Is that yours?"

"Sssshhh! I'm stealing it."

"You could steal a better bike." He squeezed the front tire, which seemed to him an intimate gesture. He was surprised to find it firm. "It's a one-speed."

The cable came undone. She removed the key, dropped the ring and the cable into her bag, and zippered it. "There aren't a lot of hills in Manhattan." She straddled the bike. She leaned forward and kissed him on the lips. It was a simple kiss but it was real and percussive and it surprised him.

"Are you going back to work?" she asked.

"I guess so." He looked at the sky, the blue sliver beyond the buildings. He shrugged. He'd assumed he wouldn't. Now that she was leaving, what was left? "It seems a shame."

"Don't be so sad."

"Sorry."

"And don't apologize."

His impulse was to say it again, but he held the apology.

"Aren't you going to give me your card?" she asked.

He thought it was a joke. He waited for the punch line.

She put a foot on one pedal, rolled it back until the brake caught. "Isn't that what you bankers are supposed to do, just in case I have a piece of business to throw your way?"

"An aluminum company for sale?"

"Fletcher gave me his."

She wasn't flirting; it went beyond flirting into something selfless. It was disconcerting; he felt pathetic. It was a nice rhyme—*flirting* and *disconcerting*. He imagined the Mannequins, four or five guys with spiked hair, clad in black leather, rhyming *flirting* with *disconcerting* in faux British accents, while their prop, the dark-haired fan with the piercings and the ink, struck a pose that went beyond flirting. He could Google it. He had something to do back at the office. He found a card in his wallet and handed it to her.

"Swell," she said, a word that was nearly impossible to use without irony. She beamed at the card and pocketed it. Then she stood on the pedals and she was off.

She disappeared around the corner. His phone rang. *Jen,* he thought, though he didn't know how she'd managed to call so quickly, what with the pedals and the handlebars, her balance and the traffic and the buttons on the phone. He checked the number. Two-oh-one. He thought it odd she'd have a New Jersey area code. For an instant muddle ruled. Then he recognized Mary Beth's cell. It had been some time since she'd called him from it.

"Hey," he said.

"Hi." Her voice cracked, and his heart sank. She'd been fragile, even before the bad stuff happened.

"Is everything okay?"

"I'm outside, walking."

"Me too. It's a nice day."

"It is."

He was standing on the sidewalk. He'd asked her to do this very thing, to go outside on a nice day. He'd asked her to call him. And here she was doing both at once. He didn't know what it meant. "I'll be home early tonight," he said.

"Okay." She didn't sound convinced.

"We could go out."

"Out?"

"Out."

"Don't push it."

"Okay." He heard voices in the background, the shouts of children. "A picnic," he said. "I can get sandwiches at Nora's."

"Really, don't. I'm out. I'll be home soon."

"You're fine?"

"I'm just tired." A scream. In the background. A bona fide shriek.

"Where are you?" He didn't mean to sound suspicious, but still.

"The School on the Ridge. Everyone's hanging out. The ice cream man is parked at the curb like a crack dealer."

"You should get yourself a treat."

"The line's too long."

He was standing on the sidewalk. People pushed past. He followed them, west toward Sixth Avenue. Through the earpiece, the shouts and shrieks of kids grew louder. On his end, a car horn blared. He didn't know what it meant that she was outside and calling. He didn't know what it meant that he'd told Jen Yoder, someone he barely knew, about Catherine. He didn't know what it meant, and now he didn't know what to say. It occurred to him that if he were there, physically, with Mary Beth, he'd merely have walked beside her.

He didn't need to speak. His presence, distant as it was, borne by the electrical currents that sifted through the air, was enough.

CHAPTER SIX

She sat on a bench, a woman in her midthirties, at the edge of the elementary school playground, where there were lots of women her age, give or take a few years—dozens, in fact, not counting the nannies, who kept to themselves. But these other women, the mothers—distracted by the responsibility of finding *their* children in the blur of children, by the persistent requests for snacks and playdates, by the injuries that seemed, for certain children, as inevitable as the kisses their mothers imparted on their elbows, by the news from school, the bits of neighborhood gossip, by the cries of the younger siblings, the ones who wanted in (or out of) their strollers—didn't pay any mind to the woman on the bench. She'd always been one of those people others didn't approach—an

introvert, shy, and though such shyness was often a burden (like at a party), she was grateful for it now.

When she was young, in summer, when other kids
would hang out at the pool, Mary Beth had wished for
rain. She liked to stay indoors and watch the puddles
form in the backyard, where the drainage was poor.
People who weren't shy didn't understand why someone
would rather stare out the sliding glass door of the family room and watch the rain fall than spend a hot, sunny
day at the pool with her friends. But other kids learned
how to ride their bikes at age five, and write their lessons
on the fronts of their papers, so that the hole punches
were in the left margins, not the right. After school, they
played on the playground, while Mary Beth was made
to take speech therapy, hours of it, so that her *R*s didn't
sound like *W*s (though Mary Beth thought her speech
therapist made her *R*s sound like *L*s).

People knew better than to talk with the woman
on the bench.

When she'd been in law school, in Montclair, her
apartment was a mile from campus. It was a safe neighborhood, as neighborhoods go, but her classes were at
night. There was a bus she could have taken, but it was
quicker to walk. And she did, most nights, along the
sidewalks illuminated by streetlamps. Sometimes there

were others out, walking in pairs. But there were solitary figures, too, a few jogging, some with a dog on a leash, but most, like her, just walking, from point A to point B. And she noticed how many of these solitary figures were talking on phones. Mary Beth kept a phone in her pocket, and she used it sometimes to call her parents, who lived in Richmond, Virginia, almost four hundred miles away, or her friends from college, some of whom lived in New York and northern New Jersey. But Mary Beth couldn't help but wonder who these solitary figures were talking to every night, and she began to suspect they were talking to no one at all. Extroverted or not, it was a trick. Open your phone and talk to it and deter the assaults from the other solitary figures. And Mary Beth found she could talk to her phone. She employed a vocabulary for these conversations—one-way as they were—that she believed sounded authentic.

"What?" she'd ask her phone.

"Right."

Then she'd throw her head back and laugh. "That's exactly what I told her," she'd say.

In April, trees blossomed. In May, they leafed. The lower boughs blocked the streetlamps, and the sidewalks became shadowed, darker. There were more people out, though she didn't feel any safer. By fall she had a new boyfriend, one with a car in the city, who'd pick her up after class and drive her home and spend the night. She liked this guy. He made her better than her prior self, the one who'd pretended to have someone to call after class.

She called him now. (He was her husband.) She dialed his cell, and he answered, "Hey." She imagined his mouth open, his face in the air.

"Hi." Her voice gave a little.

"Is everything okay?"

She never knew how to answer this question. After a moment she said, "I'm outside, walking."

"Me too. It's a nice day."

"It is." She watched the contrails from a long-vanished jet drift like clouds.

After another pause, he said, "I'll be home early tonight."

"Okay."

"We could go out."

"Out?"

"Out."

"Don't push it."

"Okay." A horn sounded through the earpiece. Three successive taps. "A picnic," he said. "I can get sandwiches at Nora's."

"Really, don't. I'm out. I'll be home soon."

"You're fine?"

"I'm just tired." A child screamed behind her.

"Where are you?"

"The School on the Ridge. Everyone's hanging out. The ice cream man is parked at the curb like a crack dealer." She tried on a smile. She thought he'd appreciate the joke. Instead he was earnest:

"You should get yourself a treat."

"The line's too long."

She heard his breathing. Probably walking in Midtown. He worked in private equity. He bought and sold companies. She didn't know which ones. Then a transaction would hit the press, and he'd copy the headline and e-mail it to her under the subject *My Deal.* He kept secrets well.

"Do you need to go?" she asked him.

"No."

It was the last day of school, as Mary Beth understood from the snippets she'd heard—camps, playdates, vacations, fall. She recognized some of these faces and she guessed that some of these faces recognized hers. She held the phone to her ear. "Why don't they go to the pool?" she asked, but he didn't answer.

Summer's arrival made her sad. It wasn't a routine, exactly, walking up Amos Avenue to the School on the Ridge for the three o'clock dismissal, but it was something she did, more and more, as the weather grew warm. She'd happened by one day in February, with snow still in the school yard, and only a dozen or so students running around, and she'd stood behind the bench where she now sat and watched the children play a game, where the one who was *it* had to close her eyes and listen to the sounds of the other children as they scampered around the climbing bars. (Their feet couldn't touch the ground.) The girl who was *it* tried to tag the ones who weren't. The game was like Marco Polo, without the call-and-response, substituting the climbing equipment for the swimming pool. And, as in Marco Polo, whichever child was *it* eventually peeked, because the laws that govern children's play state that a child shall peek if the rules of the game call for that child to keep her eyes shut. Mary Beth went home that day and made a cup of hot tea and found the website for the School on the Ridge. There was a picture of the school, a list of the staff, and a welcome from the principal.

She clicked on *Events* and up popped a calendar for the remainder of the school year. There were monthly PTA meetings, a school-wide talent show in March, and performances in April from each grade. She decided on the kindergarten concert, and, on a sunny, chilly day in April, she walked up Amos Avenue in the early afternoon. She arrived at the all-purpose room, where the lunch tables had been folded and pushed to the side and the metal chairs had been arranged in rows. She chose a chair on the aisle. The children filed in, class after class, and sat on the floor between the stage and the chairs. Parents waited with cameras. They waited with fidgety preschoolers on their laps.

Then the curtains parted. The kindergartners stood on risers on the stage. A twitter rose from the audience. Then applause. The kindergartners giggled. Flashbulbs flashed.

These are kindergartners, she told herself. She snapped a picture of the entire ensemble. Then she zoomed in, as far as her lens would zoom, on the group in the middle. Then she swung the lens to stage right. Then to stage left.

A woman stepped to the foot of the stage. She introduced herself as Mrs. Laird, the music teacher. "Welcome to the kindergarten concert." Mary Beth took a picture of Mrs. Laird, with her students behind her. "The children have been working very hard on these songs welcoming the arrival of spring. We hope you enjoy them."

She walked to the piano on the floor in front of the stage. She sat on the bench and began to play. They sang songs about birds in blossoming trees, about daffodils and tulips. They sang songs about rain, about splashing through puddles with boots pulled to knees. They sang songs about dandelions, yellow and white, and blowing the seeds on a current of air. They sang songs about turning cartwheels on the new-mown grass and hitting a baseball over the fence. They sang the timeless spring themes of renewal and hope and joy upon which young children have a special claim. It was cute, of course. Some children stood straight and faced forward and sang with their arms at their sides, while others stood less straight and swayed, and others, still, bounced between the shoulders of their neighbors and didn't sing at all.

No matter. The parents sat in wonder, shutters clicking, videos running, tiny images of their tiny children on tiny screens, and the children in the audience, the ones in the upper grades on the floor in front of the metal chairs, grew bored and were shushed by their teachers, separated from their friends, and separated again.

And Mary Beth began to cry, though she never cried anymore, boosted as she was with eighty-milligram doses. Yet here she was, with a tear in her eye, though not on her cheek. She dabbed it with a tissue. The camera sat on her lap. Then the lens closed.

There was one little girl in a green turtleneck. She wore glasses with black rims. Her hair was cut to chin length, the way Mary Beth wore her hair. The shirt had long sleeves, and the girl had slipped her arms up into her sleeves and out of them so that her arms were inside the shirt and the sleeves swung empty in front of her, not even in time to the music. She didn't sing. She turned from right to left. Then she spun all the way around to show her friends how clever she was, that she didn't have any arms, and those around her, those who wished to be distracted, laughed, while others kept singing with shoulders and arms straight.

If the parents had noticed Mary Beth, if they didn't know the mother of the girl with no arms, they might have thought Mary Beth was that mother, that she was crying because her little girl was ruining the performance. Maybe the girl with no arms was notorious as a troublemaker. Maybe she'd had a difficult birth. Maybe she'd been fed formula instead of breast milk. Maybe she hadn't been held enough as a baby. Maybe she'd been dropped by her brother. Mary Beth envisioned a strict music teacher admonishing the girl for such behavior. If she'd acted this way during rehearsals, steps could have been taken to rectify the situation before the concert. But Mrs. Laird played song after song. And the other children sang. The girl with no arms was not Mary Beth's problem. She pulled herself together and clutched her tissue.

There were two elementary schools in town—the School in the Glen and the School on the Ridge, a bit too clever when you considered the town itself was called Glen Wood Ridge. At least the schools' names (and that of the town) were based on physical and tangible features like geography and elevation and not on the arbitrary naming rights exercised by an influential member of the town council or, worse, a developer. Mary Beth knew about developers. They were her clients when she'd been in practice, a world she left when the baby was born.

Mary Beth and Gil had bought their house on Woodberry Road three years ago, when Mary Beth was six months pregnant. Woodberry was a new street, one that had replaced the last stand of trees separating the older sections of Glen Wood Ridge (the part in the Glen) from the newer sections (the part on the Ridge). *Woodberry* conveyed neither wood nor berry but a meandering horseshoe with amazingly precise symmetry observed once you found the satellite image on the

Internet. There were four house models arranged in a pattern designed not to look like a pattern. Mary Beth and Gil chose the "Belvedere," a Cape Cod with fiber-cement siding and dormers on the second floor and a porch with an actual swing. Mary Beth had imagined herself in the Glen, with its small commercial district and its preponderance of wood-framed Victorians and stone Tudors on the narrow streets that intersected Glen Road at funky angles, acute and obtuse, in the parlance of ninth-grade geometry.

But the houses on Woodberry Road were new, with one other selling point: residents could choose to send their children to either the School in the Glen or the School on the Ridge.

And the Glen was where Mary Beth was drawn, at first by herself, then with Gil, then with the baby in the jogging stroller. Mary Beth walked down Amos Avenue, then around the Glen, then back up the hill to Woodberry Road. This was her route. When the baby was twelve weeks, Mary Beth began to jog it, four days a week. The baby hit her milestones—the way babies do—more or less on time. She babbled at ten weeks. She rolled over from front to back at five months and from back to front two weeks later. She could sit on a rug without falling at six months, could clap at seven months and wave at eight months. At nine months she began to crawl. She pulled herself to her feet at ten months, and she said her first word—*Hi*—at eleven months. She said it a hundred times a day. She said it when she meant hello and when she meant goodbye. It came with a wave and friendly smile. She greeted Mary Beth. She greeted Gil. She greeted any stranger on the street. She greeted her reflection in the mirror.

Milestones were important, Mary Beth had come to learn after the baby was born, because everything was quantified, from the Apgar score at birth (the baby scored nine out of nine!) to test scores in school. But Mary Beth's favorite milestone was one she'd never read about. Her jogging route took her diagonally across the ball fields at the School in the Glen. One day, when the baby was between eight and nine months, she sang a single note—*Aaaaahhhh*—that broke into staccato as the stroller's sixteen-inch tires bounced over the ruts and mounds of the imperfect earth. Mary Beth began to laugh, so much that she had to stop running and catch her breath, and the baby stopped singing and then *she* began to laugh. Then Mary Beth started up again, and again the baby sang her single, staccato note. And this staccato song became a regular part of the jogging route.

And then, before the baby turned one, the mile-stones ceased because the baby died.

Mary Beth jogged her regular route—across the ball fields at the School in the Glen. Sometimes she had to prompt the baby to sing, but the baby always sang. On this particular morning she sang without prompt, and Mary Beth raced across the fields to the baby's delight. At the far end was Lyttondale Avenue, which intersected, a half block farther, with Amos Avenue, at one of the Glen's funky intersections—acute or obtuse, depending on your direction. For Mary Beth it was obtuse, and it required her to cross Lyttondale to begin the ascent up Amos Avenue to Woodberry Road.

There was a sidewalk on Lyttondale—there were sidewalks on all the streets in Glen Wood Ridge—but Mary Beth wasn't on it. She was on the street, running against traffic, one tire in the gutter near the sloped curb, looking for an opportunity to cross. She glanced behind her, over her right shoulder, and waited for a truck across Lyttondale to pass. The truck slowed, and she thought for a moment he might stop and wave her over. A lot of drivers were good about yielding to pedestrians. It helped to have a stroller. But the driver of the truck hesitated, then continued on. Once he was by, she nosed the front wheel out. But she'd been preoccupied by the truck, frustrated by its hesitation, its slowing and not yielding, and she hadn't noticed the car going up Amos Avenue that was now turning right onto Lyttondale. The blue hood blurred. There was chrome around the headlights. A thud, a jolt she felt in her arms. One moment she was holding the stroller's handlebar and the next she wasn't. The black bumper grabbed the front tire and dragged the stroller sideways. Then tipped it. The car stopped. The bumper released the stroller. The car waited, and Mary Beth watched, breathless, her arms in front, fingers curled to the approximate, loose circumference of the handlebar. The police report would say the car dragged the stroller thirty feet. It felt like three hundred, like it would take forever for Mary Beth to close the distance, even in her spandex and running shoes, even with her adrenaline pumping. Then the blue car steered around the stroller and sped off. And still Mary Beth couldn't move. The stroller's green awning looked like a discarded umbrella lying in the street. It was a sunny day. She couldn't see her baby. She couldn't hear her baby cry.

"You're still at the school?" Gil said.

She sat on the bench at the School on the Ridge, children running circles around her. A game of tag.

It had been some minutes since either Mary Beth or Gil had spoken. He was walking; she was sitting. "It's crazy here," she said. "I'm going to get past this line of kids." She almost called out, *Excuse me!* for the sake of authenticity, but she didn't wish to call attention to herself.

"So, I'll see you tonight," she said instead.

"Early. I'll see you then."

She closed her phone. Once she would have said, *I love you.* Three words. She would have made a point to say them.

It was past three thirty now. There was no sign of anyone leaving. She stood and looked for the girl with no arms. She did this from time to time, when she came to the school at dismissal. She put her flat hand over her eyes like a visor and scanned the crowd. She looked behind the bench, where children were scrambling up and down the hill to the side of the school. Little girls who wore glasses were few. She could find none now. She hadn't seen the girl with no arms since the kindergarten concert. Maybe she took a bus home after school. Maybe her mother picked her up and whisked her away to an appointment for vision therapy or psychotherapy or occupational therapy. Maybe she was at home being punished for a poor report card in the final marking period. Maybe she watched TV after school because she had no friends. Maybe all the TV she watched accounted for her poor vision and inappropriate behavior.

"Who are you looking for?"

Mary Beth looked down, where a girl in pigtails stood squinting up at her. She was one child, by herself, no one Mary Beth knew or thought she knew. She clutched her phone in her fingers. "Catherine," she said.

"Oh." The girl squinted harder. "Who's Catherine?"

Mary Beth realized her face was contorted. She could feel it now, as the girl regarded her. She often wished she could get outside of herself so that she could see what she was really like. She let her muscles go. She tried on a smile. "*My* Catherine."

"I don't know Catherine."

Mary Beth held her smile. "What's your name?" she asked.

"I'm not supposed to talk to strangers." The girl turned and ran across the field.

CHAPTER SEVEN

Ferko was on Sixth Avenue, on the wide sidewalk between Forty-Eighth and Forty-Ninth. He could see his office building now, the white façade and the blue-flecked windows. He was planning on shutting his computer down. Prauer was gone. Grove was dead. Ferko had nothing, really, to do. He would go home and investigate Mary Beth's burst of energy. He hoped it was something sustainable, something that his presence wouldn't quell. Maybe this weekend would shed light on things in a way that all the therapy they'd attended, both separately and together, in fits and starts, hadn't.

From his seat on the plane, in his descent into Newark, he'd looked for landmarks—I-287 or the Parkway—but found only farms and fields, industrial parks and towns, residential developments buffered from other developments and highways by thin stands of trees. A pastiche, random and indiscernible. And if you were in this landscape, you could have looked up into the sky and watched the plane descend. Unless you heard the brakes squeal and your attention was drawn to the street, where the blue car dragged the green stroller, paused, and then left.

Now there was a break in traffic, and he crossed Sixth Avenue. His phone rang, a number he didn't recognize. He answered anyway.

"Ferko?" There was interference, other voices competing with the caller.

"Yeah?" he said.

"Shit."

"Who is this?"

"Jen."

"Jen? Where are you?"

"Fuck."

"What happened?"

"I got hit by a car."

"Jesus. Are you okay?"

"I'm scraped, but my bike's fucked. Can you come here?"

"Of course. Where's *here*?"

"Where's *here*? Fifth and Thirty-Eighth."

"Where're the police?"

"No police."

"What about the driver?"

"Here, looking like a moron. He's Chinese. Doesn't speak English, or pretends not to. His daughter is drawing flowers on the sidewalk with chalk. He offered me three hundred dollars. I'm asking for five. He's got it. I saw his wallet."

"Are you sure you're okay? If he walks—"

"No police," she said. "No doctors. I know what I'm doing."

Ferko was standing on the curb, just north of his building, when Lisa Becker and George Cosler emerged from the revolving door. They turned and walked south. Coffee? Cocktails?

"Can you come?" Jen asked.

"I'm on my way," Ferko said, and he recrossed Sixth Avenue.

He found Jen ten blocks later, sitting cross-legged on the sidewalk with the bike before her, like an abstract sculpture. Her elbow was bleeding. She held a piece of paper against it. Her shoulder was scraped. She could have written a sign on cardboard, shaken a cup, and collected money.

She saw him and stood. "I asked for five and he gave me seven. I really don't think he understood what I was saying. I could have done better. I should have acted crazy. Oh, well. I'm rich."

"You don't look rich." Her pants were torn at the ankle. The bike's front tire was flat, the wheel bent. The chain was off the front sprocket and lay on the sidewalk like a dead snake.

"Well, I am."

"Let's see this." He touched a corner of the paper she held to her arm. It was printer paper, folded in quarters. She turned from him, but pulled the paper away to reveal the cut, which wasn't deep, but big—about four inches up, across her elbow, and three inches wide. He thought he saw the United States, turned on its side, in the outline.

"Not bad," she said. They admired it. "I'll have to put my mannequin aspirations on hold."

"Wear long sleeves."

"The fall lines don't come out until July." She looked at him. "Get a cab, will you? Something big enough for a bike?"

"You're keeping it?"

"Yeah, I'm keeping it."

"You've got seven hundred dollars. Get a new bike. One with gears."

She shooed him with her fingers. "Get the cab. No one's gonna pick up a bleeding woman with a broken bike."

And so he did, a full-size van that fit the bike on the floor when Ferko wedged the bent wheel over the backseat. He got grease on his fingers, and he rode to Jen's place with the backs of his wrists on his thighs, fingers in the air, like a surgeon after scrubbing.

She lived in the East Village, on Twelfth Street. The cab cost nine dollars, but the driver didn't have change for Jen's hundred-dollar bill. Ferko paid.

He retrieved the bike from the back. Her building was a walk-up, and he carried the broken bicycle to the fourth floor. She keyed the door, which had three locks. She used only one.

"Set the bike in the corner," she instructed.

"This chain is a mess. Do you want me to put anything under it? Newspaper?"

"Ha, ha. You're funny."

He knew that he wasn't. But Jen was. Both ha-ha funny and strange. *Enigmatic* was the word. It made him uncomfortable. What was he doing in her apartment, anyway?

He kicked some books and papers out of the way and leaned the bike against the wall, behind where the door had swung open. He propped the bent wheel against the frame. The floor was wood, parquet, the tiles loose beneath the molding, where the wall met the floor.

The apartment was a studio, a single room that was smaller than his bedroom, a kitchen with a half wall, and a closet you walked through to get to the bathroom. In the center of the main area was a rug, a nearly square section of red shag. Ferko followed Jen into the kitchen, where roaches scrambled on the counters and ducked for cover. She ran the faucet and turned her elbow under the water.

"Do you have bandages and disinfectant?" he asked.

"Are you kidding?" she said. The water ran. "Do you remember my dad, Dr. Yoder?"

"Vaguely." Ferko squinted. An image came to him of a short man with straight, black hair. "Did he have a beard?"

"He still does. He was an ER doc at Valley. He sends me a first-aid kit every year. I've never had a need. I finally get to use one. He'll be thrilled."

"I thought he was a rabbi."

"Ha! That's a good one. I'll tell him you said that."

In fact, Ferko wasn't sure if he'd ever contemplated anything about Dr. Yoder. But now that he had the image in his head, rabbi seemed right. That or Hasid. Something bookish. Not an ER doctor.

Jen splashed water, pumped soap from the dispenser onto a dish towel, and went to work on the wound. "Can you grab one of those kits? They're on top of the cabinet in the bathroom."

He poked his head inside the closet, a walk-in with no door. Her clothes hung haphazardly on wire hangers from two wood poles supported by brackets, above which a single white shelf held cardboard boxes, a dozen or so, stacked to the ceiling. Clothes lay on the floor, flung there after use or having fallen from hangers. Two nested laundry baskets leaned against the wall in the corner.

The bathroom was tiled—blue and green. It reminded Ferko of a fish tank, though one with a darker hue. It didn't help that she'd duct-taped a green plastic trash bag over the window. He turned on the faucet to wash the bicycle grease from his hands. There was no soap at the sink, but he found a sliver on the edge of the bathtub. He dried his hands with a peach-colored towel. Then he found the kits, five or so, uniform in size, on the cabinet above the toilet. He selected the top one and took it to her.

She was sitting on the sofa when he returned, a clean paper towel on her arm. "What do you need?"

he asked, and opened the kit on the cushion next to her.

"Cotton balls." She stood and went through the closet into the bathroom.

A drawer opened and shut, and she returned with several cotton balls smushed in her fist. She rolled them onto the open lid of the first-aid kit like dice.

"Have a seat," she said.

When he didn't, she said, "There's beer in the fridge." She looked up at him, hovering. "I'll take one if you're going,"

Ferko put his hands in his pockets. "Medicinal purposes," he said.

She grimaced.

The refrigerator was half-size, like you'd find in a college dorm room. There was a Styrofoam box of takeout and four bottles of beer. He grabbed two. The roaches were back on the counter, paying Ferko no mind. The bottles were twist-offs. He didn't see a trash can. He was afraid of what he might find under the sink, so he left the caps on the counter with the roaches.

Jen had slathered the wound with a generous layer of disinfecting ointment, which looked like jam on a piece of toast. Then she fit a piece of gauze over it. "I'll hold, you tape." Ferko set the beers on the glass coffee table, next to some rock 'n' roll zines. He stripped out sections of tape, cut them, and affixed the gauze to her freckled skin.

"Good as new," she said. She picked up a bottle, leaned back on the couch, and drank.

Ferko still stood, but there was nowhere else to sit except the futon, which was unmade, so he straightened his pants and sat next to her on the couch.

He sipped his beer. He sipped it again. After a minute he said, "I should go."

"No, don't." That was all. No explanation as to why he shouldn't. It was up to Ferko, apparently, to figure it out or interpret whichever way he saw fit.

"I feel like I'm intruding," he said.

"Intruding on what? You saved my life. I owe you."

He considered telling her about Mary Beth, about the phone call she'd made earlier, how rare such a thing was. He'd told her he'd be home early, and he pictured her in that moment, in their bedroom with the door shut and the curtains drawn, spent from her walk past the School on the Ridge, from the phone conversation with Ferko when they were both walking and mostly silent. The clock on Jen's nightstand said it was 4:45, still early.

"You're right." Ferko leaned back on the couch to match Jen's posture. "You owe me."

Jen was on her phone, sending texts, checking the screen every now and then. They drank their beers, draining the last drops in unison and placing the empties next to one another on the coffee table. Jen stood and slipped the phone in her pocket. "Let's go."

"Go? Where?"

"An errand."

Ferko stood. He checked his phone.

"You don't need to go back to the office," she said. "Your client died."

"He wasn't my client."

"Whatever."

"He was Greg Fletcher's client."

She touched the gauze over her wound, poked along the edges. "Let's go."

"I should go home."

She retrieved a long-sleeved shirt from a hanger in the closet, slipped it over the tank top, straightened it in the mirror with the buttons unbuttoned. She balanced a pair of sunglasses on her head. Then she turned toward him as though presenting herself.

He watched her watch him. He shrugged. "Let's go."

She led him out of the building, then east on Twelfth Street. They walked one block. Another. It was a residential neighborhood, with old buildings and rehabbed buildings. An empty park. An art project. There were restaurants and florists. There were kids on skateboards, white and black and Hispanic. Ferko knew about the East Village. He'd lived in New York long enough to remember. It had been a slum. Now it was this. They turned south on Avenue C. Another block. And another. They walked in silence, Jen's desperate chattiness replaced by a grim determination he'd not noticed until now. Graffiti blossomed. Made-up words he could put no meaning to. Jamaicans sat on the steps of buildings, drinking from dark bottles. Music poured from the open windows, a cacophonous mash of horns and drums and guitars. There was a haze, a burning substance he couldn't identify. Men played dice and girls skipped rope, while others, Ferko and Jen included, walked into it or through it, Ferko wasn't sure which.

"Are we scoring drugs?" he asked.

"Shut up."

"We're scoring drugs?"

"Shut the fuck up, Ferko." She stopped and faced him. "I'm the buyer and you're the tourist."

He was this far. And so he did. He shut the fuck up. Another half block, and she turned up a stone path to a gray building that reminded Ferko of a fifties-era vision of a robot's head. A looming head, to be sure, but a head nonetheless. There was a black man in front of an iron gate. He had a shaved head, wore a white tank top and blue pants with white stripes. As Jen and Ferko approached, the man extended his arms, which had been folded across his chest.

"Jen-Jen," the man said, to which Jen answered, "Ben-Ben." They hugged. The man had huge arms, covered in tattoos of dragons, knights, and castles. Ben-Ben was one hundred percent medieval, apparently. He was probably six foot three. He looked like a good friend to have. Ferko stepped closer, expecting an introduction. But instead Ben-Ben fixed a scowl on Ferko, and Jen said, "He's with me."

Ben-Ben stepped aside to let them through the gate. Ferko considered telling Jen he'd wait here, outside, but he didn't know how long she'd be, nor was he sure whether such an arrangement would be cool with Ben-Ben. They walked up the stairs, past a kid—nine or ten, Ferko guessed—bouncing a tennis ball and catching it with a baseball glove.

Through the doorway was a dark alcove, and Jen stopped there. Ferko could hardly see. The door opened behind them, bringing a stab of afternoon light. After a minute, his eyes adjusted. They were in a queue, arranged between two velvet ropes like in an old movie theater. A man was stationed at the head of the queue in the black-and-white-tiled lobby, next to a card table upon which sat a cardboard box, like the cookie boxes the Girl Scouts paraded up and down Amos Avenue each spring in Glen Wood Ridge. In fact, the box said GIRL SCOUTS OF AMERICA. Two badasses stood behind the table dealing Thin Mints. Ferko nearly laughed, but then the heavy door opened again, daylight flashed, and the door banged shut. It was jarring, each time it opened and closed, though it seemed to bother only Ferko.

There were three guys in line ahead of Jen. The transactions were quick and wordless. When it was their turn, Jen moved forward and Ferko followed. She held out a bill from the roll the Chinese man had given her. In exchange, she received four small bags with white powder, each stamped with an image of a black cat. She stuffed them in her pockets, and they turned to leave.

Outside, on the sidewalk heading north, she said, "I'd rather do that in the daylight." She dropped her sunglasses back over her eyes. "My friend Amy says nighttime purchases are more authentic. She's romantic."

They crossed the street.

"That was heroin," Ferko said.

"Yeah, sorry."

"I'm glad we didn't get busted."

"Pfft! Me too."

"Jen-Jen," he said, and he chucked her arm with his open palm. He did so lightly; he barely touched her. Still, she said, "Hey! I was just run over by a car."

He raised his hands as if to say sorry. In fact, though, he felt giddy. It had been fun, a cultural experience. He'd been a tourist. Once upon a time Ferko had used drugs—pot and cocaine, mainly. In college, he'd dropped acid. For one two week period, when he'd managed to buy a quarter pound of pot from a friend of a friend who lived in Texas, Ferko had even sold drugs, though he hadn't liked the attention, even if the attention came with cash. Once, in graduate school, he'd bought pot from a couple of white dudes from Queens who came to the apartment Ferko shared with another student, Tom DePellier, a friend, though not yet a close friend. Inside the apartment, the dealers unbuttoned their jackets to reveal pistols strapped across their chests in holsters. It was an obvious don't-fuck-with-me gesture, and Tom and Ferko didn't. They bought the drugs and the thugs left. For two MBA students, the encounter was a lesson in capitalism, in the purchase of unregulated commodities, in contingency planning and security measures. Plus, it was a pretty good story, one that endured long after the pot had been smoked, long after they'd graduated, gotten married, and stopped taking drugs altogether. It was the sort of bonding experience that can last a lifetime.

Ferko hadn't made a new friend in years. After a certain age, the supply of new friends faded with the demand, and old friends drifted away. He wasn't sure what sort of friend Jen was, but, through the course of the afternoon—through lunch, her getting hit by a car, and the procuring of heroin from a gang of Jamaicans—she'd come to feel like a real one. Maybe this was merely a day in the life of Jen Yoder, but he was grateful she'd shared it with him.

Back at her apartment, they cracked the last two beers. He was determined to see it through that far. It still wasn't six o'clock.

Jen went to the bathroom, and Ferko checked his e-mail. There was nothing of consequence, though Lisa had sent a news story with an update on the Roy Grove car bombing. It looked as though she was back in the office. Then he called Mary Beth, first on her cell and then at home. He had worked out that he would tell her he'd been delayed, that he wouldn't, in fact, be home early but he wouldn't be home late, either. Definitely before dark. But he got her voice mail each time, and he knew she was shuttered in their room. He was determined now not to rush. So he truncated the message: "Hey, honey," he said on the home voice mail, "things have come up and I won't be home as early as I thought. It's a little before six now. I hope you're well. Bye."

"Nice shading." Jen had changed out of the ripped pants into a pair of black jeans. "'Things have come up.' Who could argue with that?"

"I'm not here to be judged by you."

"Who's judging? I'm genuinely impressed. Just don't think you're getting any action from me. We're hanging out."

He was grateful for the clarification. Hanging out was fine. Hanging out was better. He took a swig of his beer.

Jen sat on the couch. She set one of the clear Baggies on the glass coffee table.

"What's up with the black cat?" he asked.

"The power of branding."

"You're kidding." He examined the image—a collection of black shapes, which, collectively, formed a cat, curled and ready to pounce. "How long have you been doing this?"

"Six years." She tapped the contents of the Baggie onto the coffee table and began cutting it into lines.

"Off and on," she added. "And I know what you're thinking: that I'm an addict. I guess I am. That I'm a junkie. If this is junk, I guess that's true, too." She retrieved a section of straw from the breast pocket of her shirt. "I can get off this stuff. I've done it before. When the time's right, I'll do it again."

"Okay," Ferko said.

"Okay, it's not nothing," she said. "It's a pretty good something. But it's not like air or water or food."

"I get it."

"If I pass out, call 911."

"You're serious?"

"I'd do it for you." She snorted a line. Then another. She leaned back on the couch. Her face got sad for a moment, but only a moment. Then it flushed pink. He watched her for a full minute from where he was standing at the edge of the coffee table, between the couch and the futon. She didn't move, but she hadn't passed out either.

"And?" he asked.

"And?" she said. It was an invitation. She'd cut two lines, he understood, for him.

"I'm only having one."

He sat next to her. He took the straw, and before he could change his mind, he leaned his face to the glass and started on the line nearest him. He snorted an inch of it, paused, switched nostrils, and snorted the rest.

The warmth came first to the space behind his eyes, then to the bridge of his nose. It was warm and cool at once, an amazing numbness that spread down his spine and out through the muscles of his chest and shoulders and down his arms. It spread through his heart and stomach and intestines, and all those vital organs he once could name but had since forgotten. They didn't matter. Nothing mattered. Only the blood that brought the warmth and cool into his hips and buttocks, into his testicles and penis and down his legs, through his knees and ankles to the soles of his feet. It was bliss. He sat there for a long time soaking it in. And it refused to stop, refused to get old, to get weak. His lungs filled with oxygen, and the blood grabbed the oxygen and coursed with the beating of his heart, wave after wave, beat after beat. He kept feeling good, again and again.

"You should see yourself," he heard her say.

"I can't get up."

"The first time's the best. I envy you. I wish I could go back, make it my first time every time. It will never get better than it is for you right now."

He accepted this. He couldn't imagine how it could get better. He couldn't imagine how anything better would feel. He wondered what might happen next, but it didn't really matter. He tried to close his eyes but he couldn't. The sun, low in the sky, shone through the windows, while his blood, so much of it, so much more of it than he'd ever sensed before, flooded every radiant organ and tissue of his body.

CHAPTER EIGHT

Mary Beth watched the girl run across the field at the School on the Ridge, away from the playground, toward the woods that led down to County Park, with its duck pond and bicycle trails. At the field's edge, she slowed to a walk. She was a young girl, perhaps one of the kindergartners who'd performed the songs of spring. Mary Beth waited for an adult—a parent or friend—to see the girl and chase her down, but no one other than Mary Beth appeared to notice. Then the girl looked back (was it at Mary Beth?).

Mary Beth approached the two nearest women, who'd been talking to each other since she'd arrived. "Excuse me," she said, and the mothers turned. But as they did, the girl slipped into the woods and was gone.

Mary Beth flattened her mouth. "There was a girl here," she said, "with pigtails. Light brown pigtails. Just a minute ago. Did you see her?"

The women wore blank faces.

"She ran that way." Mary Beth pointed to the place in the woods where the girl had disappeared.

The women followed Mary Beth's arm through the empty field. They shook their heads.

"What's the girl's name?" asked one.

"That's just it. I don't know."

"I didn't see her."

"I didn't, either."

Mary Beth began walking in the direction the girl had run. She walked faster. Then she ran, all the time concentrating on the seam in the trees where the girl had entered the woods. When Mary Beth reached it, she saw there was no trail, that the woods were thick. Vines with leaves shaped like arrows choked the trunks and limbs of the smaller trees.

She moved some brush only to find more brush. There was poison ivy, she supposed, growing on the ground. She wore open-toed sandals, poor for hiking and worse for bushwhacking.

"Little girl," she called, at first too softly, then louder: "Little girl!" She walked along the edge of the woods, peering in. She glanced back toward the playground, but no one was coming. Twenty feet off she saw the worn dirt of a trailhead. She entered, and inside the brush was thinner and she could see for some distance on either side.

"Hello," she called. The dirt path was marked by tire treads. There was mud in the low spots from recent rain. She walked farther, where the path sloped to a swale, and a wash that held standing water and mud. Kids had piled dirt and packed it to make a bicycle jump. She stepped over it, and walked up a rise. The path narrowed, then steepened. She stood on the lip before the descent and called out again, "Hello."

"Hi." The girl stood on a fallen tree at the bottom, a hundred feet below, off the narrow path another fifty feet.

"What are you doing?" Mary Beth asked.

"Playing."

"Why down there?"

"Why not?"

"Where's your mom?" Mary Beth asked, but the girl didn't answer. Instead, she skipped across the fallen tree. She jumped like a gymnast on a balance beam. "Is she at the school?"

"I told you, I'm not supposed to talk to strangers."

"I'm just trying to help."

"I don't need your help."

"Where do you live?"

"In this tree." The girl stopped jumping. She stood, toes pointed out.

"What street do you live on?"

"Tree Lane." The girl giggled.

Mary Beth folded her arms. "I'm sorry your house fell over."

"It didn't *fall.* This is how we built it."

"Who's *we*?" Mary Beth tried.

"Did you find Catherine?"

Mary Beth could almost close her eyes and pretend: here was one of Catherine's friends.

"We built this house," the girl said. "Me and Catherine."

"Oh, *really*?"

"Did you find her?" the girl asked. "Maybe she's down here."

"It's not nice to tease."

"I know *that*." The girl glared at Mary Beth. Then she jumped off the tree and squatted next to it. "Yeah, she's right here," the girl said, "under this tree. She's smushed under this tree."

"Okay, stop it!"

"We were building this house, and Catherine got under it. Come out, Catherine. Someone's here to see you."

"I said, stop it!" There were birds on the tree branches and squirrels in the brush. Cars whined from a highway and a train horn sang. There were animals and machines, Mary Beth and the girl.

"Come up," Mary Beth said.

"Come down."

So she did. She started down the steep slope, faster than she should have. The dirt was loose. Rocks tumbled. She reached for exposed roots but missed. The girl screamed and started up, off the path, through the green ground cover. Gravity and momentum carried Mary Beth. She nearly toppled, head over heels. Her sandals slid, and she fell on her butt, and grabbed a thin tree, which bent but didn't break. The girl was three-quarters up the hill now. Mary Beth could have caught her, maybe, by the time they reached the field. But how would that look? CHILDLESS WOMAN, TEASED BY KINDERGARTNER, TACKLES CHILD.

She let go. She was near the bottom. She rose to her feet and stepped off the trail, through the brush, using the small trees growing from the incline to steady herself. She watched for prickles but they found her.

They tore the skin on her wrist. Then her ankle and toes. Then the tops of her feet. After a time she made it to the tree where the girl had stood. Its main shaft was two feet wide. Mary Beth stood on it, then peered under it. There was nothing, of course, but dead leaves and branches. She glanced up the hill. She sat on the tree and poked at her cuts. Then she threaded her way through the brush and the prickles to the trail, which she took down, toward County Park, where there was a paved path that followed a stream to the duck pond and the playground with its preschoolers. Her knee hurt, and she limped. She was filthy and bleeding. But she wasn't tired. In fact, she felt rather alive. She walked the long way home. There were hours of daylight. When she got home she soaked in the tub. She cleaned out her cuts. It was nearly dusk and she wasn't tired. She didn't know what to do next.

CHAPTER NINE

They spent hours on her couch. Ferko had his cushion, and Jen had hers. They slept and woke. They didn't eat, and they barely talked. After a time, Jen got up and went to the kitchen and splashed water on her face. "It's night," she said.

"What time is it?"

"Nine fifteen."

"I forgot I wear a watch," Ferko said.

"Let's go to a party."

"No way."

"Well, I'm going."

He used the bathroom. When he came out, he said, "We look high, don't we?"

"People will know. Your pupils are pins." She curled her finger to make a tiny hole and peered through it.

"Where's this party?" he asked.

"On the way to the PATH. I'll get you there by midnight. You'll be home by one."

But it took time to get out of Jen's apartment. They ate falafel sandwiches on the way to the party. They arrived at ten forty-five and stayed until one thirty. Then they went to a club nearby, where bands played, one after another, hour after hour, until there were no more bands, and a DJ played MP3s until dawn. Ferko paced himself, beer and water—lots of water—while Jen switched to Diet Coke and hits off joints. She had friends, so many of them. There were musicians and artists and carpenters and writers. There were actors and computer geeks and ne'er-do-wells. There were kids in their twenties and old punks in their fifties, multipierced, with hair that fell in their eyes. Irony and cool were the same. The women wore black, except those who wore metallic dresses. The men wore black, except Ferko, whose khakis and blue button-down were the uniform of business casual. He didn't feel conspicuous, though. Might he not have been ironic?

He sent a text to Mary Beth at two thirty: *mb— late. home tmw xo g*

They arrived at the PATH station in the morning, just as the sun was coming up. Jen bought a ticket, too. "Since I'm here," she said, "at the gateway to New Jersey. Let's go shopping. You owe me."

"I thought you owed me."

"I did. But now you owe me."

"I'm going home."

"Take me to Paramus first."

She was relentless. But he wasn't tired.

"Or don't," she said. "Take me to my dad's. I'll get his car."

"Paramus. For an hour."

"Yippee." She put her palms together and tapped her fingers, mock applause.

They were in the mall by ten, the only customers, it seemed, in one of the anchors. Music played from the speakers in the high ceiling. He followed her to formal wear. She sized up a mannequin in a black dress, hemmed at the knees. She found the dress on the rack and took it and a blue scarf to the dressing room.

Ferko waited in the center, near the escalator, wondering if there was something he should buy for Mary Beth. A wallet. A belt. It was all stuff. Random junk.

Jen emerged in the dress, barefoot, with the scarf draped to cover the bandage on her arm. He went to her. She found a pair of black shoes on a sale rack.

They were high-heeled, open-toed, and she slipped them on her feet. They were a little big; her toes got lost in the thin straps. Still, she looked hot, despite having partied all night, despite having been hit by a car the prior afternoon.

She handed him her bag, which had grown thick with, he guessed, her jeans and shirt and sandals. "What am I supposed to do with this?" he asked, but she was straightening her shoulders and fixing her hair.

"I'm going out there," she said.

"Out where?"

She pointed her chin toward the front of formal wear. "Keep an eye on me. I want reviews and reactions."

"A mannequin?"

She walked ahead, turned her ankle on a heel.

"This is stupid," he said.

"You owe me." She righted herself.

"What for?"

She didn't have an answer. She walked ahead, more carefully now, and, truth be told, Ferko didn't mind. He steered away from her, past the dressing rooms and up the next aisle. He checked his phone. No reply from Mary Beth. It infuriated him. When he saw her, he'd tell her about his night. All of it except the heroin. And the mannequin part, which was a little weird and hard to explain. But he'd tell her about Jen Yoder and Greg Fletcher, about the lunch and about the parties. He actually had a lot to tell her. And if she didn't care, if she was indifferent, that would be one more disappointment in a series of disappointments.

He was back in the center again, near the down escalator, waiting and watching as Jen stepped up on the pedestal with the mannequin, which was wearing the same black dress and posed with legs apart, right hand on right hip, chin down, white lips curled in a pouty expression, evoking an attitude that said, *The night is mine.* Jen struck the same pose, though opposite (left hand on left hip), so that the two looked like bookends. She was shorter than the mannequin, didn't have the same Barbie features in neck length and leg height. Jen had freckles, too, on her arms and nose. But she kept as still as the mannequin. Amazingly so. From Ferko's vantage point thirty feet away, she wasn't breathing.

He glanced around the store. No shoppers in sight. Two salesladies were talking behind the counter in handbags. Another was walking the floor. Ferko pointed his phone and took a surreptitious picture. Then he walked by Jen and took another. She didn't blink. He went to the opposite side of the escalator and touched the silk scarves, while watching the pedestal. Then he moved on to the leather belts. He went through them—black, brown, blue, red, yellow. The world was filled with crap. You could clothe an entire town with the inventory of this store alone, one of four anchors in one mall, not counting the dozens of boutiques in the hallways. He thought about Grove Department Stores. Would an acquisition and investment improve demand and profits? Wasn't there a fundamental problem with the whole retail model in this country? Didn't it start with too much supply?

Then a shopper appeared—two, actually—a mother and daughter in almost-matching shorts and T-shirts. They meandered by the escalator, looking lost, and their meandering took them directly by Jen. She didn't blink. Nor did they. The mother and daughter wandered past as though nothing in the world were out of the ordinary. Maybe the mother had noticed something awry and had cautioned the daughter, *It's impolite to stare*, but Ferko didn't think so. Jen really wasn't moving. But they didn't stop and look at the black dresses on the rack, either. Wasn't that part of Jen's hypothesis? That live mannequins would boost sales?

More shoppers happened by, and these, too, didn't pay any mind to Jen or her pose or her black dress. She became part of the store's wallpaper. She was a pillar, a mirror, merchandise on the racks, one more ingredient in American retail's assault on the senses.

She'd been up there for twelve minutes. (Ferko was timing her.) He'd seen her twitch a couple of times—nearly a hiccup—but recover to hold her pose. But now the two salesladies from the handbag counter were on their way, squinting, it appeared, at Jen. They were in their fifties, dressed to the nines in blue and gray pantsuits. Ferko imagined that they spent their entire paychecks buying merchandise with their employee discount.

He circled toward them, to a sale rack within earshot, where random items had been placed according to size and marked at forty percent off.

The women stopped five feet from Jen and studied her.

"Is she real?" the one in the blue suit asked.

"I don't remember her."

"That's not what I asked."

But the other woman didn't answer, and there was a pause when no one said a thing. For her part, Jen stepped it up a notch, if such a thing were possible. She looked like the real deal—as in *fake.*

Then the woman in the blue suit stepped forward and touched Jen's wrist and recoiled. "She *is* real."

Jen didn't move.

"She's got hair on her arm," the woman said. "See?"

The woman in the gray suit stepped forward with one foot, but kept the other back.

"Right here." The woman in the blue suit pointed.

"Do you *mind*?" Jen turned her head to face the women, who jumped back. She held the rest of her pose.

"What are you doing?" the woman in the blue suit asked.

"I'm working," Jen said. "What are you doing?"

Ferko kept his head down and examined an orange blouse with an ugly green swirl.

"You're working? Does Mr. Davies know about this?"

"Mr. Davies hired me."

"Hmmm," the woman in the blue suit said. "He should have warned us."

"We should tell the other girls," the woman in the gray suit said. They stared at Jen, who looked off again, toward the far wall, to resume her pose. After a minute the women wandered off to, Ferko assumed, find someone.

When they were gone, Jen frowned and kicked off the heels. She put them back where she'd found them. "That sucks."

"You did well."

"I need my sandals." Ferko handed her the bag.

"Let's go," she said as she slipped them on. He followed her around the perimeter of the store, to the other side, toward the door where they'd entered.

"That was the hardest thing I've ever done. I need a nap."

"What about the dress?"

"Look at me." She stopped. "I'm sweating."

Her forehead glistened. Perspiration collected in the cleft where her throat met her collarbone.

Ferko scanned for store security.

"Be cool," she said. They were nearing the glass doors, the white cement, and the sea of asphalt. "I'll meet you at the car." She veered off, through racks of jackets and swimsuits. He watched her for a moment, sighed, and continued on.

At the door a hand grabbed his elbow. "Excuse me, sir." The hand belonged to a man in his sixties. He wore a white beard and round glasses with metal frames, a brown suit with a name badge: Reynolds.

He gave Ferko the once-over. Ferko thought he must look awful—messy hair and stubble peeking through his chin, a wrinkled shirt and khakis he'd been wearing for twenty-six hours straight—not quite homeless but possibly criminal. Reynolds checked the polished floor by Ferko's feet.

"Where's the bag?" he asked.

"What bag?"

"You had a bag, a black leather bag."

Ferko played dumb, eyes big.

"No bag," Reynolds said, though it could have been a question. His eyes scanned the immediate area. "Where's the woman with the dark hair?"

"Sir, I'm just a customer with a wallet, keys, and phone." Ferko showed Reynolds these things, then remembered, too late, the photos of Jen he'd shot on his phone. But Reynolds was looking past Ferko now, out the glass doors, into the bleak landscape of the parking lot.

Reynolds sighed. "Sorry for the misunderstanding," he said. "Thank you for your time."

It was quarter to eleven when Ferko returned to the car. Jen wasn't around. He unlocked the door, and his phone rang.

"What happened?" she asked.

"I got stopped." He got in and closed the door.

"I saw that. You didn't have anything."

"Well, that's what happened." He started the car. "Where are you?"

"In the trees beyond the parking lot. I'm watching you now. They may be watching you, too."

"Okay," he said.

"I owe you," she said.

"Damn right."

"There's a driveway at two o'clock, do you see it?"

"Two o'clock? Are we in a spy movie?"

"Ferko, do you see the driveway?"

"I see it."

"Exit the parking lot there. I'll meet you. My dad's expecting us."

"*Us?*"

"I told him you were giving me a ride home. He's thrilled."

"Thrilled?" Ferko asked, but she'd ended the call. He couldn't imagine that Dr. Yoder would even know who he was, let alone be thrilled to see him. He waited. The engine idled. Then he called home, but Mary Beth didn't answer. The trees beyond the parking lot were evergreens. He backed out of his space and wended his way toward the driveway at two o'clock.

CHAPTER TEN

That morning she'd dreamed about a forest. She'd left something there, among the trees, though she didn't remember what, and when she went, in her dream, she couldn't find the place, the right trees, to search. There were lots of trees in the woods, but none were the right trees. And so she searched, got lost in the woods, which were expansive in her dream—not the narrow stand of trees that buffered one development from the next—and she kept circling back to a footbridge over a stream and a waterfall. And each time she circled back, she became more anxious, because time was short and you couldn't stop time, just as you couldn't stop the stream from running over the rocks in the fall below the footbridge.

Gil wasn't home, hadn't been home, and she was relieved. She'd read his message in the middle of the night. He was chasing a deal.

She rose, drew the sheets and blankets up, and stood in the quiet house. She couldn't shake the pull of her dream. She made coffee and ate cereal. The woods were shaded and cool, a secret, covered place. She wondered what was there, what she was looking for. She couldn't shake it, and so she dressed, this time appropriately, in long pants and closed shoes, and she set out on Woodberry Road. There were children about, chasing one another through front lawns with squirt guns. An older gentleman walked his three dogs. Somewhere behind her, a gas lawn mower ran. It was ten minutes to ten when she turned up Amos Avenue.

There was a clamor at the School on the Ridge, a baseball game on the ball field. Dads shouted positions from the bench. The teams wore red and blue uniforms, each with pinstripes. Kids played catch behind the backstop. Others swung bats. Parents fanned the foul lines, on blankets and folding chairs.

But the woods beyond the ball field were empty. She sat on the fallen tree, where the girl with the pigtails had stood. It was a warm day, though cool in the woods. Occasional cheers rose from the baseball game. But mostly the leaves rustled and the insects whirred. She loved the security offered by the cloak of the trees. She was invisible, a piece of the landscape. If anyone wandered down the path they wouldn't notice her, sitting on the tree, if she kept very still. It wasn't the place from her dream. Maybe there was no such place. Mary Beth sat for some time wondering what sort of place this was. She decided she would stay until it revealed itself.

When she was a girl, Mary Beth's house had backed to woods. She was a middle child, a cautious girl, but she valued time alone and she could find it in abundance in the woods behind her house. The ground sloped away from the kitchen to the edge of the woods and kept sloping, and she could go into the woods in summer, when the leaves were green and thick, thirty or forty feet, no more, close enough to be within shouting distance if her mom or her sisters called for her, but far enough to lose sight of the house completely and pretend she was alone in the middle of an ancient forest. The slope ended. Pools of water and animals—insects, birds, and frogs—gathered. Mary Beth loved the dragonflies best. They were proxies for fairies, and fairies were her friends. They lived in the earth and came out only at night. But these fairies made an exception for their one human friend, and Mary Beth was grateful. She watched them flit about in the dappled sunlight. They entertained her. When the frogs sang, the water shimmered with bubbles blown from beneath the surface.

Now her phone rang, and she was no longer invisible. She was a woman sitting on a fallen tree in the woods near the school field. "Gil," she said.

"Hi, where are you?"

"Where are you, Mr. Stay-Out-All-Night?"

"On my way home."

She waited for him to tell her more, but he didn't. "I'm just out," she said.

"Where?"

"Walking."

She braced herself for the question, in one of its two principal forms: *Are you okay?* or *Is everything all right?* She never felt she had his permission to not be okay. She was fragile, she knew, like a young tree growing from the floor of the forest. But she could get better. If she sat on this tree long enough, perhaps she would.

But he didn't ask the question. Instead, he said, "That's great. I have a lot to tell you. I met up with these folks from high school. It was kind of crazy."

She waited for him to tell her how crazy.

"When will you be home?" he asked.

"I don't know. A couple hours?"

"That's a long walk."

"I guess."

"I'm glad you're getting out. I'll see you then."

"Bye."

He could be sweet. And he definitely was patient. She turned off her phone. The woods were silent. She waited on the log for something or someone. She wasn't sure which.

Ferko drove them to Edgefield, to her dad's house, a ranch with white siding and black shutters. Jen, still wearing the dress from the mall, let them in with a key on her ring. "Hello," she called when the door gave way.

"Hello." Dr. Yoder emerged in a pair of green shorts, a white shirt buttoned to the collar and black socks pulled to his shins. His head was bald, smooth, and freckled. His beard was white. He wore glasses that made his eyes look small and set way back in his head. He stood there for a moment, it seemed, sizing Ferko up—friend or foe.

Jen kissed his temple. "Dad, this is Ferko."

"Gil," Ferko said and extended his hand, which the doctor made no effort to take.

"Ferko," he said, "the man who thinks I'm a rabbi. If it were only true." Dr. Yoder stuck out his hand in Ferko's general direction. He was blind, Ferko realized. He wondered why Jen hadn't warned him.

He stepped forward and shook the doctor's hand. "Come in," Dr. Yoder said.

"I'll be down in a few minutes," Jen said, and hung her bag on the newel post and bounded up the stairs.

"Have a seat." Dr. Yoder gestured with his open hand toward the living room. "Can I get you anything? A glass of water?"

Ferko was thirsty, but he didn't wish to trouble his host. He imagined the old man feeling his way along the walls toward the kitchen, up into the cabinets for a glass, ice from the freezer, and water from the fridge.

"It's hot," Dr. Yoder said. "I'm getting one myself." He doddered off toward the kitchen.

"Sure." Ferko followed him.

"Jen comes here to nap. I don't think she gets any sleep in the city." Dr. Yoder took two glasses from the cabinet and filled them, nearly to the brim and without spilling a drop, from the dispenser on the door of the freezer. "Where do you live now, Ferko, in Sodom or Gomorrah?"

"Glen Wood Ridge."

"Edgefield's rich cousin," Dr. Yoder said. He brushed past Ferko on his way to the living room. "Nice town."

Dr. Yoder sat in a wing chair, and Ferko sat on the sofa facing the fireplace. He set his glass on the coffee table. Ice clinked against the sides.

"She tells me you saved her life yesterday."

"Hardly."

"She wasn't wearing a helmet, was she?"

Ferko hoped it was a rhetorical question.

"What, she's going to mess up her hair?" Dr. Yoder asked the center of the room. He sipped his water, then set it beside him on the end table. "I tell her, you ride that bike all over the city, in and out of traffic, all those frustrated drivers beating lights to get across town. It's a wonder it didn't happen sooner."

He paused, and Ferko nodded in agreement— pointlessly, he realized.

"She takes some chances, that one." Dr. Yoder's tone softened. "She always has. But she's a sweetie. And smart—book smart and street-smart, even if she's not common-sense smart."

Ferko thought that summed Jen up pretty well, and it also explained why she hadn't gotten stopped that morning. What did it say about Ferko, though, stopped for merely swimming in her wake?

They sat in silence. They sipped their water. Then
Ferko stood to read the spines of the paperback books
on the mantel above the fireplace. There were four
books, each a thin volume in a different dark color—
navy, maroon, forest green, and black—wedged between two bricks that served as bookends. Each spine
bore the name YODER and some variation of the same
title.

"The *Ghosts of* books," Dr. Yoder said. "Is that
what you've found up there, Ferko? First editions, all
of them, though not worth the paper they're printed
on. Still, I'm proud of them."

"You wrote them?" Ferko pulled one down. *Ghosts
of Brooklyn.* Inside was a map of Brooklyn with circled
numbers. Each of these, he learned upon turning the
page to the table of contents, corresponded to a chapter in the book.

"They occupied me when I was younger. A lot of
research and a lot of writing. I love ghost stories."

"Where did you grow up?" Ferko asked, his finger
marking the first chapter, titled "The Orange Street
Ghost."

"Washington Heights. Is that the volume you have
there?"

"*Brooklyn.*"

"A contractual obligation. Start with *Washington Heights*, the top of Manhattan."

Ferko replaced *Brooklyn* on the mantel and chose *Ghosts of Washington Heights*, the book with the black cover.

"In the first half of the twentieth century," Dr. Yoder said, "Washington Heights was remote and insular, the perfect place for ghosts to thrive. I explain it in the introduction to that book, my first one. Ghosts are like animals that live in the forests. Encroachment from new development destroys their habitat. Ghosts of Edgefield or ghosts of Bergen? I imagine there are, but their presence is too diffuse to be felt. There's too much here that's new."

Ferko had his own apparition, even though his house was only three years old. "You know a lot about ghosts," he said.

"I'm not a scholar. But I'm not a kook, either. Unfortunately, the latter outnumber the former by a wide margin."

"Have you ever seen one?"

"Seeing is not the right question. I'm blind now, but long before I became blind I knew what it was like to feel a presence without seeing it." He stood and turned toward the stairs. "Peruse *Washington Heights*. The house in the

first chapter is on the street where I grew up. It's a book-
store now. They still sell the book." He trundled forward.
"Let me see what's become of our Jen. She's supposed to
take me to the pharmacy." He mounted the stairs.

Ferko turned to the first chapter—"The Preacher's House (185th Street)." The narrative described a
house built in 1925 by a Methodist preacher, a Reverend Hurlingham. Now the house had a ghost—the
spirit of a boy in its basement, a shallow space, five feet
deep, once accessible only by a ladder that hung from
a trapdoor in a closet. Legend had it that the preacher
sent his children to the basement when they were un-
ruly or when he was in a sour mood. The basement
had no lights, no windows. You closed the trapdoor
leading to the closet, and the basement contained the
sort of blackness that had a tangible quality.

Reverend Hurlingham and his wife, Libby, had
eight children—six boys and two girls—before Libby
died of an unexplained illness at the age of thirty-seven.
A few years later, so the story went, the youngest boy,
Sebastian, who was five and particularly prone to fits,
bit his father's arm. It was the sort of infraction that,
in many households of the time (and, indeed, in many
households today, Dr. Yoder noted), would have result-
ed in whacks with a stick or a belt or an open hand. But

the preacher had a better punishment in the basement of the house on 185th Street.

It was late, past bedtime, which further fueled the preacher's impatience and rage, and so he caught Sebastian by the collar and dragged him toward the closet, picked the boy up, and dropped him, crying, down the hole. The preacher shut the hinged hatch, which stifled Sebastian's screams, and placed a heavy trunk over it, and the other children, Sebastian's brothers and sisters—each older from two years to twelve—watched from a safe distance, peering around corners, because they had each spent time shut in the black basement and did not wish to incur their father's wrath.

"Ferko."

He looked up from the book to find Jen's head in the stairwell. She tromped down the steps in sweats and a T-shirt. She must have kept clothes at her dad's for her frequent visits (and naps) on the weekends.

"I can't believe he gave you required reading."

"He found the books himself." Dr. Yoder was at the top of the stairs now, taking them one after another. "Ferko is naturally curious about ghosts."

He wasn't sure if Dr. Yoder was being sarcastic, though it was true enough. Perhaps it showed. "Can I borrow this book?" Ferko asked.

"You can have it." Dr. Yoder's legs were visible now, more and more of him with each step. "I have a box of them in the basement."

"We're going to the pharmacy," Jen said.

"I've got to go," Ferko said.

"We'll meet you out front, Dad."

She walked him to his car. "I fell asleep."

"I wondered." Her face looked misshapen, her eyes puffy.

"Isn't my dad sweet?" she said, perking up.

Ferko waved the book, an affirmative answer.

She leaned against his car. "We had fun, right?"

They had, but he wasn't saying.

"We should do it again," she said.

"Will I ever be the same?"

"Don't be dramatic."

Dr. Yoder stood on the steps, locking the front door.

"Thanks for the book," Ferko called.

"Nice to see you, Ferko. Stop by anytime."

"Isn't that cute?" Jen asked him. "Nice to *see* you?"

"I heard that," Dr. Yoder said.

First, Mary Beth grew hungry. Then she grew tired. Then a shaft of sunlight found its way through the leaves on the trees and fell directly on her arm. She moved out of its way. And all this time, while one baseball game ended and another began, no one came up or down the path or through the woods at all that she could discern. No strangers and no one she knew. No dragonflies flitted by. Or fairies, either. She stood and stretched her legs. She even hopped off the tree, careful not to get her pants caught by the prickles. Then she climbed up again and sat, and the girl was standing in front of her.

Mary Beth nearly fell to the ground.

"Why are you here?" the girl said. Her hair was still in pigtails, the same fuzzy braids as the day before.

Mary Beth recovered. "I'm waiting for you."

"It's my house, not yours." The girl looked at the fallen tree.

"Of course," Mary Beth said. She shifted backward on the tree to give the girl room to hop on. When the girl didn't, Mary Beth stood to get off.

"You're invited to stay." The girl put her hand on the tree to claim her space. "For tea."

"Okay." Mary Beth sat again. The tree shaft here was narrower, and Mary Beth straddled it like the back of a horse. The girl sat cross-legged and faced her.

She made an elaborate show of preparing the tea—filling the kettle with water and putting it on the flame—and while they waited for the water to boil

Mary Beth thought of things she might say (she had a lot of questions), though she didn't wish to ask them in a way that would upset the girl and destroy the camaraderie they were now developing. Mary Beth had just come up with a question she thought innocent enough and nonthreatening—what plans did the girl have for the summer?—when the girl began to whistle, a single, unsteady note, like a boiling teakettle.

"Oh," Mary Beth said.

"The tea is ready."

The girl placed teacups on saucers and poured the tea, slowly and carefully, into two cups. She passed one to Mary Beth, who took it with two hands, one on the saucer and the other with her thumb and index finger on the delicate handle of the cup. She brought the cup to her lips and made sounds with her tongue on the roof of her mouth, a proxy for sipping.

Then the girl held out her hands again, both this time, as though proffering a large platter. "Cakes?" she asked.

"Why, thank you." Mary Beth made a show of choosing one. "They all look delicious."

"You can have more than one."

Mary Beth raised her hand above the platter. "Hmmmm. I'll start with this one. No!" She moved her hand. "This one." She picked up a cake and nibbled it. "Mmm."

They sat for a time, enjoying the tea and cakes, each other's company, and the ambiance offered by the shaded woods.

A cheer rose from the ball fields above. The girl looked up the hill. "Is Catherine playing baseball?" she asked.

"No."

The girl sipped her tea and waited.

"If Catherine was playing baseball, wouldn't I be up there, cheering, with the other parents?"

"I guess so."

Mary Beth wished to cut through the ruse, through the games and the tea and cakes. But this was a child. Still, she said, "Catherine died."

"That's sad." The girl didn't blink. She just looked unhappy.

"I'm Mary Beth."

"I know."

"How do you know?"

"I followed you here."

"From where?"

The girl paused to consider her answer. Mary Beth felt as if she were floating in some sort of liquid—a thick, warm syrup—from which she might never escape.

"From your house," the girl said.

"Do you live on Woodberry Road?"

The girl smiled. "I live *here*, silly." She touched the bark of the fallen tree.

It was a *game*, Mary Beth reminded herself. It was real and make-believe all at once. She wasn't sure of the rules. She wasn't sure if she'd get another opportunity to play. She sipped her tea.

"I used to live there," the girl said.

"Where?"

"Where you live. Before you lived there."

"How old are you?" Mary Beth asked.

"Six. My name's Amanda." She presented the platter of cakes.

"Amanda." Mary Beth selected one and nibbled it. "It's nice to meet you."

"It's not polite to talk with your mouth full."

"Mmm. You're right." Mary Beth pantomimed swallowing. "It's nice to meet you, Amanda."

A breeze came through and swept the bangs from the girl's forehead.

"My house," Mary Beth said, "was only recently built. I don't think you lived there." It was too logical an argument for such a fanciful game. Mary Beth wished she could take it back.

But it didn't faze Amanda. "Is that where Catherine lived?" she asked.

Mary Beth nodded.

"What color was her room?"

"Purple."

Amanda frowned, as though disappointed by the choice. "Light purple or dark purple?"

Mary Beth paused. It wasn't a baby's room anymore. She remembered the crib and the mobile and the morning sunlight shining through the window. "More light than dark. More blue than red."

Amanda considered this.

"Did you know that that's how you make purple? You mix red paint with blue paint?"

"I knew that," Amanda said.

"What do you get," Mary Beth said, "when you mix red paint with yellow paint?"

Amanda squinted a moment at the bark on the fallen tree between where the two sat. Then she said, "Blue."

"Orange."

"Are you done with your tea?" Amanda reached out to take Mary Beth's cup and saucer.

"I can bring paints and paper." Mary Beth touched knuckles with the girl in the pretend exchange.

"I have another party I need to get ready for." Amanda stood.

"Next time."

Mary Beth swung her leg off into the brush, and the girl hopped down on the other side. "Bye," she said, and she ran off in the direction opposite the trail. Perhaps there was a different trail that way. But it didn't matter. Amanda leaped like a deer, pigtails flying. She skipped and then ran and soon her image blended with the rest of the landscape and disappeared completely.

CHAPTER ELEVEN

Ferko called up the stairs when he arrived home. He called again. No response. Then he took them two at a time and found the bedroom empty, the bed made. Not its normal state. He touched the bedspread, ran his fingers over its raised pattern—green leaves—as though reading Braille. She'd taken great care to smooth it. He stood and absorbed the room's silence until he heard more than silence—the thrum wrought by the weight of the roof and the floors on the walls and the foundation. He sensed something behind him—not motion, exactly, but not stillness, either; a presence—and he knew it was the girl, though he wasn't sure how he knew. Remnants from his high coursed through his body. His senses had been dulled and heightened—both, inexplicably, at once.

He turned and the girl was standing in the hallway just outside the bedroom. She wore her pigtails and a striped shirt and blue shorts and sneakers, and Ferko wondered if her presence now was somehow linked to Mary Beth's absence. Not the big absence, which was linked, of course, to Catherine's accident. But the small absence, today's absence—could that be connected to the girl's presence here, now? And the made bed? He wished to ask her. He formed a question in his head: *There's a woman who lives here with me—us?—do you happen to know—* But the girl vanished before he could ask or even get it right in his head. He cursed his indecision. He should have just blurted it, which he did now, to the empty space: "Do you know where Mary Beth is?" He walked out of the bedroom and into the hallway. "Where's Mary Beth?" he asked, but his senses, keen only a moment earlier, now told him nothing. The girl was gone. He retrieved his phone and asked the question—*where's mary beth?*—directly to the subject via text. The reply was instantaneous: *home soon.*

He sighed. He had Dr. Yoder's book in his hand. *Ghosts of Washington Heights.* He shook it in the air to show the girl, if the girl cared, that he was armed with information. He went downstairs and onto the front porch to wait for Mary Beth. He opened the book and found his place. Sebastian Hurlingham, the reverend's son, had been forced down the hatch to the basement, and his siblings did not step forward to rescue the boy. Instead, they retired to their bedrooms, while the floors and the walls and the doors muffled the boy's cries, and soon weariness and dread and futility and possible injury muted him completely.

The house was silent. The family slept.

Richard Hurlingham, the eldest at seventeen, would recount years later how he wished he'd done something as Sebastian cried out in that first hour. Richard woke early the next morning and saw that Sebastian's bed was empty and made. His brothers were sleeping in the other bunks. He ran down the stairs to the pantry off the kitchen and the hatch to the cellar, his father at his heels. Richard pushed the trunk off the trapdoor and lifted the latch. What little light there was in the pantry barely reached the basement's dirt floor. Son and father peered down into the stillness. Neither said a word. They waited. Then the preacher cleared his throat. "Sebastian," he intoned. There was no response. "Get the lamp lit," he told Richard.

The preacher climbed down the ladder. His feet had found the floor by the time Richard returned with the kerosene lamp. The preacher took it and ducked his head, while Richard lay on the floor of the pantry and put his head through the hole in the floor. "There," he said.

His father turned around. Sebastian lay facedown on the floor, the crown of his head against the concrete wall of the foundation.

They lifted the body through the hatch. It was cold and stiff and bruised, the face harrowed. They reported an accident, the preacher and the eldest. And when the other children woke to find Sebastian gone, they, too, learned a lesson about language and the nature of "accidents." And with the reportage of the accident, over the years, each family member became complicit, some immediately and some later, and each would come to shoulder its burden.

Mary Beth was on the front walk. She might have just appeared, the way the girl had at the top of the stairs. She waved, and he said, "Hey," to which she answered, "Hello," like a stranger. She wore jeans and a T-shirt and a pair of running shoes. She came up the stairs and onto the porch and stood in front of him. He scooched to make room, but she stood there, hand on her hip.

"What happened to you last night?" she asked.

He patted the bench seat next to him, but her face was a mask of indifference, lost in thought. Her eyes refused to meet his.

"I'm thirsty," she said, and pushed open the front door and disappeared.

He considered following her inside, but he'd done that too often, trailed after her in her silence. She'd left the house today. And yesterday, too. He hoped it meant something. He hoped she'd come back outside. She'd left the door open, which was promising. He heard her in the kitchen. The rattle of ice from the ice maker. Then she was in the entry, a hand on the door, and back on the porch. She pulled the door shut behind her. Was there a buoyancy about her that he remembered from before? She had a plastic bottle, the kind that fit in a cage on a bike frame. They had two bikes with four flat tires in the garage, leaning against each other like wasted lovers. She squeezed water into her mouth, then sat next to him on the bench. He pushed off with his foot to start them swinging but she kept her feet on the floor to stop them.

Ferko sighed. "What have you been up to?" he asked.

"You first."

"Okay." He paused to get the story straight himself. It would require some essential edits. And in the next breath he told her—*a* story, one version of the actual events: Greg Fletcher, from Edgefield Elementary School, representing Grove Department Stores, and his invitation to have lunch with Jen Yoder, another Edgefield classmate. The Grove car bomb, Jen's accident, the $700, the parties, the lack of sleep. He left out the illegal parts (the drugs and the shoplifting) and the hard-to-explain (the mannequin act) and the fact that Greg had blown the whole thing off, figuring Mary Beth would be more okay if another guy was there, and, of course, this morning one was. Dr. Yoder, both old *and* blind. And she received the story without apparent distress. Ferko should have been relieved, but it angered him. Did she even care what he did? Were they that ruined?

"And the book?" she asked.

He showed her the black cover, the block letters: *Ghosts of Washington Heights.* "Jen's dad wrote it."

"Ghosts," she said.

He pictured the Hurlingham boy, Sebastian, by the hatch that opened to the basement. He pictured the girl at the top of the stairs.

"And you?" he asked. "What have you been up to?"

"Walking."

"Apparently."

"Just around." She rocked the bench with her feet, but kept them on the floor so that the swing couldn't swing. "It's what you asked me to do."

It was what everyone had asked her to do, starting with the doctors and the counselors.

She stood.

"That's it?" he asked.

"That's it." She swigged water from the tip of the bottle. "Lunchtime." She opened the front door again and left it open. It was an invitation for him to join her. Or an indication that she'd return. Or neither.

He hadn't eaten since the falafel sandwich the night before, and this realization brought a pang of hunger. He kicked his feet and picked them up and the swing started up. Maybe she'd fix him something, too. Or not. It would be fine either way.

He opened his book and found his place. The boy, Sebastian, was dead. Within a week his spirit appeared, sitting on a wood crate in the pantry off the kitchen, too skinny and sickly—ghostly, with a lack of color— but recognizable as Sebastian. Dr. Yoder had a theory regarding the manifestation of spirits:

Collective burden, defined as the aggregate, internalized guilt and complicity of a group of people, is the wellspring from which spirits arise. The entire Hurlingham family was complicit either directly (as was the case with Reverend Hurlingham, who dropped the boy through the trapdoor and locked him in the basement, and, possibly, Richard, who, at seventeen, was arguably old enough to intervene) or indirectly (as was the case with the seven-year-old twins, who understood Sebastian's death was no accident but never suggested otherwise). And, in each case, the complicity was internalized.

Dr. Yoder then suggested that other ghost stories he'd uncovered shared similar traits. He admitted the support for his theory was anecdotal.

Ferko closed the book. Mary Beth was in the kitchen. A lawn mower started down the block.

According to the story, the Hurlingham family later moved to Queens, yet the subsequent owners reported that the spirit remained in the house on 185th Street. Why had the ghost attached itself to the house rather than to the family, whose collective burden produced the spirit in the first place? Ferko thought about the girl upstairs. The house was only three years old. He and Mary Beth had bought it new. He remembered what Dr. Yoder had said about ghosts in Bergen

County. There were too many new buildings. But the Hurlingham house was built in 1925, was less than twenty years old when Sebastian died. Ferko had a lot of questions for Dr. Yoder, who'd probably get a kick out of answering them.

Ferko remembered the drugs, the washed-out feeling from the first few hours. He'd never experienced anything as perfect. He wondered if he'd ever be the same. He wondered where a friendship with Jen could take him.

He pushed off the porch floor. The swing swung. He closed his eyes. He knew bliss. A breeze blew. *Collective burden.* He pictured the girl, her pigtails. Sometimes she came to him in his dreams. They lived in a large stone house, Ferko and the girl, situated in a forest of trees.

He shifted his body and the book fell to the floor. *Collective burden.* Catherine had been a baby. The girl with the pigtails was a child. He opened his eyes, half expecting to find her there, but he only ever saw her in the hallway near their bedroom. He closed his eyes again and pictured her waiting for him at the top of the stairs.

PART II
JULY 2007

CHAPTER TWELVE

Mary Beth was more blue than usual. The Fourth had come and gone. It was a climax and a cliff, an event that marked, at once, summer's apex and the beginning of its end (the remainder of July and all of August consisting of a dull wait in haze and heat, while the evening daylight waned and the stores in the air-conditioned malls swapped summer lines for fall and all things back-to-school). She was falling.

And Gil was more distant than ever. It bothered her, though she knew, in her silence, in her determination to get out of the house and up Amos Avenue in the heat, she was complicit. At the School on the Ridge, on the treeless, childless field, she sweated. But it was cool in the woods beyond, on the fallen tree at the bottom of the ravine, where Mary Beth stayed, sometimes for hours, while the sweat dried on her skin. She packed water, a snack, sometimes lunch. She peed beyond the tangles of prickles, squatting with her shorts wrapped around her shins. Once, sitting on the fallen tree, she spied a doe and her fawn. Mary Beth froze as the deer foraged and drew ever closer until, at last, no more than ten feet away, she was discovered, and the animals fled with such quickness and grace they sucked the air from her lungs.

Was she becoming wild herself? She contemplated how long she could stay on the fallen tree until hunger or thirst drove her from it. What would she do when the weather turned cold? Sometimes, when she became lost in the quiet minutes, she imagined herself a shy animal—quiet and furtive and vulnerable—whose only defense was to stay still and blend in. But no one came by the fallen tree but the girl in the pigtails. Amanda. She had three outfits, which she'd mix and match in no pattern Mary Beth could discern. She tried to figure it out. She was looking for clues about the girl, and because she was looking for clues, Mary Beth developed a routine, like Gil, with his 7:40 train. She left the house a half hour later, starting up Amos Avenue before the heat of the day wholly arrived.

The routine became paramount, the thing least intangible in a string of intangibles, for there was nothing else—except the occasional scratch from the prickles and the hunger and thirst that sometimes drove her from the woods—to show for her days. Plus the hours that slipped by. But hours had elapsed for nearly two years, more than fifteen thousand by her rough calculation, since Catherine had died. These new hours, though, were different. Mary Beth was onto something, though she wasn't sure yet what it was.

She grew frustrated with the girl's inconsistencies, her secrets, her *enigma*, which, it seemed, outstripped Mary Beth's by a wide margin. She still knew next to nothing about the girl. There was a name—Amanda—but little else. And Mary Beth wanted to know things about Amanda. She wanted to know lots of things, though, three weeks since their first encounter on the field after school, Mary Beth would have settled for morsels. She had supposed she knew about children. She had once been one, after all. She had once been a mother, too, though she'd become conditioned to avoid this notion, freighted by the rush of guilt that grew ever more furious with the dry eyes that accompanied her regret. She'd always been a thinker. The medicine dulled the thin edges of her emotions.

On this morning, July 9, it was hot, nearly noon by the time Amanda appeared. Perspiration beaded the dimpled skin between her nose and upper lip. She settled onto her end of the fallen tree. She straddled it and let her shoes fall to the ground.

"Let's play the street game," Mary Beth suggested.

Amanda cocked her head, pressed her toes into the earth.

"You know what street I live on," Mary Beth said.

"No, I don't."

"You know where I live."

Amanda nodded. Her eyes met Mary Beth's with an air of suspicion, or indifference; the girl was hard to read.

"I live on Woodberry Road," Mary Beth said.

The girl crinkled her nose. "That's a funny name."

Mary Beth pondered this. "It is," she admitted. "The people who built the houses probably named the street after what was there before the houses."

A sliver of the sun's rays threaded through the leaves and limbs on the trees and found Amanda's forearms, folded on her lap. But only for an instant.

"Wood-berry," Mary Beth said. "Wood and berries." She left a pause and placed her palm on her stomach, a pantomime gesture. "Maybe blackberries. Mmmmmm."

"There were no blackberries." Impatience occupied the girl's voice. "There were woods, though."

Mary Beth waited for more. They'd had this conversation before. There was no more. Still, Mary Beth waited, and at some point in that interval, as the seconds elapsed, the girl's face shifted.

"I think you should go now," Amanda said.

"But we just got here."

"I just got here. You've been here for a long time."

Mary Beth pursed her lips. She neither admitted nor challenged. She was losing again, Amanda's game. If the girl followed Mary Beth here every day, what did Amanda do and where did she hide while Mary Beth sat on the fallen tree alone? "Who are you?" she demanded, finally.

The girl flinched, then recovered. "Amanda."

"I know your name."

Amanda stayed, eyes fixed, unblinking. Mary Beth assumed the girl could outwait her. It was summer, and Amanda was a child. Mary Beth remembered the endless July days when she was a girl. She remembered the woods behind her house, the spring where the frogs sang. How many hours had Mary Beth spent in those woods, no one bothering to look or even call for her? But the physical laws of time didn't seem to apply to Amanda.

Seconds passed. Mary Beth could have counted them now as she watched the girl and the girl watched Mary Beth, one to sixty, twelve to twelve, a full minute, and then another, endless loops that cycled back to begin anew, while time for the girl never budged, even while the sun made its slow arc across the sky, even as days ended and new days arrived, hotter or colder, wetter or drier, and no one—no matter how long Amanda sat here with Mary Beth—ever looked for the girl. Even Gil would eventually call. Amanda could play all the games she wanted, and Mary Beth couldn't. She was impatient, disappointed with herself, with the limitations imposed by her physical presence, by her height and weight, age and maturity, mortality and fragility. The earth spun on its axis, and gravity grounded her. She sensed that the girl could fly if she chose to, that she could disappear and reappear, and pass through objects—huge objects, trees with girths like pillars in grand cathedrals—all while Mary Beth grew old, day after day, and some cruel god counted the rotations, the laps around the sun. She had only so many—days and months and years. A tree grew until it fell.

She reached out, fingers splayed, and touched the girl's shirt, at the seam, where the tunic met the sleeve. There was bone beneath, the slight shoulder of a six-year-old girl. She was real, after all. Or perhaps that was another bit of her magic.

"Who are you?" Mary Beth asked again.

"I said, 'You should go now.'"

Amanda's tone was solemn, prescient, a little spooky. Mary Beth wondered whether she should be frightened, whether the girl's next act would be to point a finger at Mary Beth and turn her into stone. But the girl merely waited, and Mary Beth's inclination was to turn her shoulder, fold her arms in a childish manner, and pout. *I was here first*, she might have said, as though she and the girl were peers, having one of their daily fights over some small transgression that meant the world at the time but, with the perspective of years, would prove meaningless, even humorous, if the two remained friends. Instead, she said nothing and studied the girl's face, which she half expected to turn sour and spill tears. But the face stayed blank, and Mary Beth waited with the girl for what would happen next.

The air moved about them. A dog barked from the park below.

"Why do you keep her caterpillar?" Amanda asked after a time.

"What caterpillar?"

"The blue one with the red rings."

Mary Beth became dizzy for an instant, a combination of the day's heat and a surge of blood pumped by
her heart. She pulled the hair off her neck and held it on
top of her head. The rings were for teething. Sometimes
Mary Beth sat on the floor next to the toy chest, opened
the lid and retrieved the stuffed caterpillar, squeezed the
soft sections and held them to her nose and breathed.
Once, she put the rings in her mouth and scraped them
against the hard enamel of her teeth. She put her tongue
to them and tasted them. Now she imagined Amanda,
peering around the doorjamb from the hallway into the
room, where Mary Beth sat with Catherine's things.

"It was her favorite toy," Mary Beth said, "the thing
that could make her most happy." A memory came to
her: Catherine, in her stroller, fussing from fatigue or
hunger or teething, one of a dozen unexplained com-
plaints, each concluding in the same place—tears—and
Mary Beth offering the stuffed caterpillar, Catherine
grabbing it in her greedy fingers and shoving it into her
hungry mouth. Mary Beth had forgotten what need was.

Amanda's face had changed—an expression somewhere between disappointment and indifference.

Mary Beth asked, "Do you have any brothers or
sisters?"

Amanda shook her head no.

Mary Beth asked, "What's *your* favorite toy?"

Amanda scrunched her eyes and glanced sideways, an expression that conveyed either process or evasion. When her eyes met Mary Beth's again, the girl shrugged.

"You have a vivid imagination, Amanda. You play with what's here. This tree is your home."

Amanda lowered her head and traced her finger along the sections of bark where moss furred. Silence again. Mary Beth was at a loss. She and Gil sometimes sat across from each other at the dinner table, flatware scraping plates, the modern tools of sustenance, the ancient laws of gravity.

There was nothing to say.

Now she believed she'd have made a bad mother, after all. It wasn't the first time this thought had occurred to her. It had once brought tears.

But then Amanda said, "I don't really have a home."

The girl would talk, maybe, if Mary Beth let her.

"It's gone."

No more quizzes or interrogations. She let go of the hair piled on top of her head. Amanda watched her, and Mary Beth waited. All those afternoons spent on therapists' couches, while the professionals practiced expressions evoking kindness and empathy and asked their open-ended questions. It all came down to waiting.

A breeze blew hair into her eyes, and she tucked it behind her ear.

"We had a gray house," Amanda said, "made from big rocks, like a castle. We had chickens in the yard. They pecked in the grass and lived in cages. Sometimes kids came up our drive on their bikes. We didn't know them. I stood in the yard with the chickens, while the kids sat on their bikes. They wanted to see the chickens."

Mary Beth didn't get the point, but she resisted the urge to ask.

"They were older kids." Amanda looked past Mary Beth, as if seeing the kids on bikes coming up her drive. Mary Beth imagined a gravel drive, a wooded lot. She had no idea if this was the right image, but it was the one she had. And then some sticks snapped up the hill, at the ridge, and a kid on a mountain bike coasted down the trail, riding his brakes so that they shrieked like a jazz horn. It was a steep hill. Mary Beth was surprised he could manage it. He stood on his pedals and leaned his entire body back for balance. He wore a T-shirt with a logo she didn't recognize. He wore plaid shorts and tennis shoes without socks. He wore a helmet painted orange and blue. When he reached the bottom, he pedaled down the path, toward County Park, as though he hadn't seen them.

She looked at Amanda, and made her eyes big.

"He wasn't one of them," Amanda said.

"I was going to ask." Mary Beth tried on a smile but Amanda was serious.

Mary Beth glanced over her shoulder toward the top of the hill to make sure no more bicyclists— imagined or real—had been summoned by Amanda's thoughts. They were alone again.

"Who were they, then," Mary Beth asked, "these kids who wanted to see your chickens?"

"Kids from around here."

"But your house isn't here."

"It was my grandma's house."

"It's not here."

"Not anymore."

Mary Beth had retreated into interrogation mode. She needed to be more careful. She waited, but Amanda waited, too. Mary Beth counted in her head, one to ten, then she asked, "Where's your mom?"

"Dead." Amanda nearly interrupted her, as though she'd anticipated the question. "They're all dead."

"The kids who came to look at the chickens?"

"I don't know about them."

"And the chickens?"

"Chickens don't live that long."

Mary Beth wasn't sure what she was doing. "I'm sorry," she said.

"What are you sorry about?"

It was a question, but Mary Beth heard it as an accusation. She had a lot to be sorry about. Maybe that was the point, or maybe it wasn't. "I'm sorry that they're all dead," she said finally.

Amanda watched her. Then her eyes softened and lost focus. Mary Beth remembered the frogs that sang from the puddles in the woods behind her childhood home. All she had to do was sit with them and they sang. When she wasn't there they'd sing anyway.

"Why here?" she said.

Amanda blinked.

"Why don't you come see me at my house?"

"I like it here."

Mary Beth took a moment. The green leaves at the tops of the trees were sun-dappled. Bugs flew in shafts of light. "Me too."

A bird was singing—*doo-eee, doo-eee.* Then a breath. *Doo-eee, doo-eee, doo-eee.* The song had been playing, verse after verse, for a while, she realized. She only now noticed.

"I don't know what happened to me," Amanda said.

Mary Beth watched the girl.

"In case you're wondering."

"I was," Mary Beth said, though she wasn't sure what, exactly, Amanda thought Mary Beth might have been wondering.

"It doesn't hurt," Amanda said.

The bird sang. Then again.

"It's sad, I guess, but it doesn't feel sad. It doesn't feel *anything*." Amanda shrugged. "It's okay."

"Amanda, I don't understand what you're—"

"What happens to people in the woods?"

"I'm sorry?"

"Bad things."

"Amanda, you're scaring me."

"I'm a ghost. Boo!"

"A ghost." Mary Beth braced herself.

"What'd you think?" Amanda stuck out her tongue, though not actually at Mary Beth.

"I don't know what I think."

"I'm talking about dying, silly."

The bird had stopped singing. There was a time to talk and a time to listen. "Okay," she said.

"What happens to people in the woods?"

Mary Beth was thinking violent acts, abductions and rapes and stranglings and mutilations, Amber Alerts and senseless gang initiations, the savage stuff of cable and Internet news, of media drawn to the sensational. She was thinking about strangers and loved ones, homeless men and runaway teens, the lone guy on the mountain bike riding the sheltered trails, the floodplains between developments and towns, the rare remote corners of suburbia. She was thinking about people. Instead, she said, "A bear?"

"There was no bear. I'd see a bear. Or hear one or smell one!" Amanda wore an expression of disbelief, as though she'd just discovered that the adult across from her was the most ridiculous adult she'd ever encountered in her brief life and afterlife.

Mary Beth shrugged, a go-figure gesture.

"I was there," Amanda said, "and then I wasn't." She paused. "In the woods." She looked directly at Mary Beth, who nodded.

"I get it," she said.

"It didn't hurt."

"Maybe a tree fell on you." Mary Beth looked up, where the branches reached the sky. "Or a big limb."

The air was fixed, the green leaves still like a photo. All these hours they'd sat together in the woods and nothing had happened.

"Was there a storm?" Mary Beth asked.

"No."

Trucks flipped on highways. Lightning struck beaches.

"Were you alone?"

"I don't think so." Amanda squinched her eyes. "No, I think I was."

She was unreliable, of course, a child. It happened long ago. Who was to say she was real, actually here?

"It doesn't matter," she said.

"What doesn't matter?"

"That I'm dead."

This was life: you're here. And this was death: you're not. And then you're here again, haunting some stranger. And none of it matters. Mary Beth waited. The bird was gone.

"How do you know?" Mary Beth asked.

"Know what?" Amanda wrinkled her nose.

"That you're dead. You're sitting here with me," she said, "and I'm alive."

She expected Amanda to demonstrate—to disappear and reappear, change shapes or stir the air. Some ghostly trick. Instead, she sat on her end of the fallen tree, looking bored.

"Where does the dad go?" she asked, after a time.

"Which dad?"

"The dad who lives with you. *Catherine's* dad."

"Gil. His name is Gil."

"Where does he go?"

"He goes to work. He takes a train into the city."

"Oh."

"Come see us at the house," Mary Beth said.

"I do."

"Let us see you."

"I do that, too."

"I've never—"

"The dad does."

"Really!" Mary Beth thought about Gil. What did she actually know about his days? Sometimes, after work, he lay with her in their dark bedroom. It was a way to express his grief, perhaps. To lie with her in solidarity. Sometimes they spoke, inconsequential words, while the pauses and the sighs and the expressions on their faces, if they could be discerned in the dim light, said the opposite. Their circumstances were extreme, perhaps unique. But as a couple, engaged in the inconsequential-word dance, they weren't unique. You didn't need to lose a child to lose a marriage. Still, they *had* lost a child. Or it was *she* who had, in the active, culpable sense of the verb, when she'd nosed the front wheel of the jogging stroller onto Lyttondale Avenue and caught the jaws of the painted bumper, the teeth of the fast car's grille. Gil had lost a child, too. It just wasn't his fault. But now, she realized in a dizzying revelation, they'd found one, each of them, separately and together. Amanda.

"Show yourself to me," Mary Beth said. "Show yourself to *us*." It was a statement, a demand, something a mother might say to her daughter. She hadn't said *please*, though pleading was in her tone. She wasn't used to giving orders. And she knew that Amanda, on the receiving end of such orders, could simply vanish. There was no balance between them. Mary Beth needed Amanda more than Amanda needed Mary Beth. Or so it seemed. She made as stern a face as she could muster, in hopes that Amanda would notice.

"I live here." Amanda tapped her fingertip to the tree bark beneath where her ankles were crossed. They were back to square one. Nothing had happened. Worse, they were back to zero, as, in the next moment, Amanda was gone, vanished, though not like in a B movie or a TV show, where the air goes wavy like water. Rather, Mary Beth blinked, one moment in a near-infinite continuum of endless moments, and when she opened her eyes, the space Amanda had occupied on her end of the fallen tree was empty.

Mary Beth considered calling out. Instead, she sighed. She thought of Gil, his presence in their bedroom, his head next to hers, backs turned to one another, close enough to feel the heat from each other's body. Silence was better. She reached into her bag and retrieved her water bottle, some crackers with peanut butter, and she ate and drank and concentrated on being a quiet presence. When the crackers were gone and she was still alone, she heaved herself off the fallen tree to climb the hill to the field at the edge of the School on the Ridge, to Amos Avenue, and the long downhill home.

CHAPTER THIRTEEN

The sun waned while the humidity waxed, and the air, which had crept all day across inland swamps and seas of asphalt, stalled and smothered Manhattan. Jen's window unit rattled in its casing and waged a losing battle. There was something about changing the filter, instructions, a note that the management company had sent her months ago. It was probably somewhere among the stacks of paper on her dining table. Now summer was half over. She dragged a floor fan in front of the air conditioner to give the dribble of cool air a boost. She sat in front of both—the air conditioner and the fan—and pulled the hair off the back of her neck and held it in a fist.

Unease had been building, along with the heat, all week. She felt it in the pit of her stomach—a seed taking root, with shoots growing up and out, tendrils threading through her ribs, grazing and then clutching her heart, and now spilling up through her shoulders and down her arms. It was dread that she felt. She tried to identify its source. She made a list in her head, each possibility: work, friends, drugs, money.

Was she lonely? She definitely was. Did she want to use? She *hoped* not to, which wasn't, of course, the same as not *wanting* to, and, as she constructed this distinction in her head, the urge shaped by her habit became that much greater. It was a combination of loneliness and urgency, she decided, that was turning the little propeller in her stomach, the one that brought her disquiet. Then another thought came unbidden, surfaced suddenly from the dark recesses inside her: she was wasting her life. And, with that thought, the tendrils growing inside her blossomed. She'd found the source of her bother.

The apartment walls were close, radiating the cumulative heat of the day. Escape was required—a public place with real air conditioning, a central unit forcing cool air through wide vents. She'd need to cop or find a friend who had.

Friend. The word brought a new round of unease. She had many friends. She'd once had more. Here was a truth of getting older: friends decreased in number and stature. They dived deeper into the drug world and drowned, or they quit and got out of the pool. The rest, like Jen, treaded water in the deep end. She wished to tread closer to the side, which meant using less. It was Wednesday. She'd hoped to wait until Saturday.

She opened her phone. There were no messages. She checked her contacts—Amy, Jane, Nick, Larry, Gordon, Ferko. Jen clicked this last name, and sent him a text: *what's up?*

He'd become, over the past few weeks, an enthusiastic user, and demonstrated a willingness to leave work early to accommodate her schedule. He insisted that work was slow, though Jen had her doubts. She knew people in M&A. It was never slow. *Look at the deal flow*, Ferko had told her last week, when she'd questioned him, and she might have checked it—the deal flow—if she knew how or cared enough to do so. Aluminum prices were near record levels. That was the only indicator she needed that the world was busy.

She awaited his reply. The fan was working, sort of, blowing a bit of cool air from the weak vent into the room. She felt it on her arms and legs and the place on her neck where her hair usually fell. Her urge was becoming chronic. She contemplated a backup. Amy was always up for something. Jen's phone said it was 4:25.

She'd give Ferko until 4:27 before moving on. But then her phone rang. Ferko.

"Hey!" she said.

"What's up?"

"That's what I asked you."

"I'm playing softball."

Jen had no response. She wasn't sure if she'd heard him right. Finally, with nothing else to say, she asked, "*What*?"

"Softball. I'm playing. My boss's team."

"You don't play softball."

"How would *you* know?"

"*Do* you?"

"I'm putting you on speaker. I'm tying my shoes."

"Your *spikes*?"

"Sneakers. And you're right. I don't play. But tonight I am. I've been asked to." The quality of the sound had changed. His voice went thin. There was noise in the background.

"I suspect I'm being set up," he said. "That's what people do here. If they're not working with you, they're working against you."

"Sounds like fun." Jen calculated in her mind how long it would take to play a game of softball, when he'd be free. "You're playing now?" she asked.

"Five thirty." A shuffling in the background, then the noise disappeared. The quality of sound had changed back. He was on the handset again. "Tomorrow?" he asked.

"Maybe." It was important that she not reveal the crisis that had prompted her text. Her stomach—the dread that blossomed there—had settled for now. She could bear tonight on her own. It was better that way. If she were to continue to tread water, to do so closer to the side of the pool, she'd need to toughen and find a way to use less. "I'll call you tomorrow," she said. "Hit a homer."

CHAPTER FOURTEEN

Ferko did a hurdle stretch in foul territory while the rest of Prauer's softball team, the Large Caps, paired up and played catch, one guy standing on the third-base line and another in the outfield. Ferko wore jeans and tennis shoes and a too-large white T-shirt with the Large Caps logo. George Cosler had recruited Ferko and procured the shirt from a box of extras in his office, then customized it—name and number—with sections of blue electrical tape.

"Zero?" Ferko asked when he saw the number Cosler had given him.

Cosler shrugged his big shoulders. "It's available."

"You don't want me," Ferko said.

"I don't want you," Cosler confirmed, then paused, perhaps for effect. "But I *need* you."

When Ferko didn't respond, Cosler said, "Vacations. Everyone's out. Or else they're unavailable."

Ferko had his doubts. "What about Lisa?"

"It's a men's league." He dropped the shirt on Ferko's desk. "Besides, I told Bill we had you. He likes the idea."

The Large Caps, as in a certain class of equity investment, were composed of a bunch of bankers and restructuring advisers who'd played baseball in high school and college. Cosler was one. Ferko was not. There was a win streak at stake. In fact, the Caps had never lost a game. Five years. The hardware was perched on the credenza above where Helen, the receptionist, sat in the Riverfront lobby. Cosler had a Word file on his computer with a single letter—W—in three-hundred-point font, bold. The morning after each win he printed the file on a single sheet of paper, trimmed it with scissors, and taped it to the next space across the top of the wall. Like the wallpaper border in a nursery. Or the fans at Yankee Stadium who counted strikeouts with Ks.

Ferko had played baseball as a kid in Edgefield, some intramural softball in college. Now, prostrate in his hurdle stretch, he delayed the inevitable—seeing what was left of his candy arm. His teammates had started their warm-ups close enough to each other, but then had moved back some distance. Then they'd moved back again, and now the softballs were zipping across great expanses, glove to glove, with machinelike accuracy and efficiency. Prauer was throwing with Pete Johnston, who, according to Cosler, had played beyond high school and college—professionally, up to AA in the Phillies' farm system. They were hucking it pretty good. And Cosler, paired up with Alan Friedman, a partner at Forten Banneker, Prauer's house firm. Then there were the interns—four on the field now—Prauer hired each summer based, it seemed, on the athleticism demonstrated on their resumes.

Ferko's legs were stretched. His throwing arm—not so much. It was too late now, given the intimidating distances his teammates were throwing. Plus, he was the ninth man, with no one to pair up with.

He stood, relieved to find a familiar face on the opposing team, firing bullets from shortstop to first base. Long hair. Tan face and arms. Greg Fletcher. Ferko jogged out to say hello.

"*Gaylord*?" Greg fired the ball to the first baseman.

"You still got it," Ferko said, meaning Greg's arm.

Greg caught the return throw and, in one smooth motion, flipped the ball with his glove to Ferko, who caught it in his bare hands. (He'd left his glove—Cosler's backup glove, actually—on the grass flattened by the hurdle stretches.) Now Ferko wrapped his fingers around a softball, weighing its heft, noting its size, for the first time in, perhaps, fifteen years.

Greg pointed at first base, an invitation for Ferko to show Greg what he had. It wasn't a long throw, as softball throws go, but Ferko wasn't going to try it now. The Large Caps had brought it in, had collected around the bench beyond the third-base line. They were watching Ferko with Greg Fletcher—Cosler and Prauer and Lisa Becker, too, who'd shown up in her jogging clothes, carrying a water bottle, which she now dragged across her forehead before twisting the cap and tipping the contents into her mouth. Ferko flipped the ball to Greg, who caught it in his throwing hand and, in one smooth motion, launched it back to first.

"I didn't peg you for fast-pitch," Greg said, and it took Ferko a moment to register what he meant. Sure enough, the pitcher for Greg's team had taken the mound for warm-ups and was windmilling darts from the rubber over the plate, where the catcher squatted in full gear. Ferko had known on some deeper level what a game with the Large Caps would entail. Now it became apparent. This wasn't intramural softball, where the pitches were lobbed like horseshoes, or even fourth-grade baseball in the Bergen County rec league, where half the kids played because their fathers wanted them to. This wasn't for fun. The speed of the pitches would dictate the speed the runners ran the bases and the speed of the game. The catcher would back up first base, the center fielder second base, the left fielder third base. Et cetera. Runners would take leads and steal bases. There were cutoff men to hit, situational defenses. He'd suspected, of course, that his recruitment by Cosler had been for derision. Now he was sure of it. He was the ninth man. He'd been picked last. It was Edgefield Elementary all over again. But he'd learned how to survive, to blend in, to limit his mistakes to those that wouldn't cost Prauer the game. At least, Ferko hoped that was the case. Now the Caps donned batting helmets, swung bats. So he jogged back to the bench, where Prauer was waiting.

"Who's that?" he asked.

"Greg Fletcher. EastWest Partners. We met him at the Grove meeting."

"Ahhh, Grove," Prauer said wistfully, though it was unclear whether he was thinking about poor dead Roy or the retail assets Prauer had once hoped to acquire. It was long ago, the meeting with Grove. Prauer had moved on, while the rest of New York, it seemed, had not. It made no sense, but the news of Grove's death had produced a pall and an interminable heat wave that spread up the coast from the Deep South, where Grove's stores languished. And, as the heat crept in, a somnolent indecisiveness descended. Deals got stalled. The malaise was bigger than Grove's absence, bigger than the July heat, bigger than the snorting of dope with Jen Yoder in various downtown hovels, which was occurring now at regular intervals, if not, yet, with increased frequency. Daimler had announced it was selling Chrysler to private equity. The deal had been struck. Financing was committed. But now there were rumors that the lenders wouldn't lend, that the parties couldn't close, that Chrysler as a stand-alone was unfinanceable at any price. There were rungs on the ladder. No one climbed now. Everyone held fast and hoped not to fall. Ferko had been running a long time. Now there was no place to run to, except around a softball diamond. Prauer pointed at Greg. "Guy's got a hell of an arm."

"You're batting last," Cosler said.

"Cool," Ferko said, hoping to sound like a good sport, a team player, someone who'd contribute as best he could.

"Batter up!" the umpire called.

Alan Friedman stood five foot seven and was built like a bowling ball. He took two high pitches before lining a single over the second baseman's head. Ferko stood with

Lisa, between the bench and the backstop, and clapped. She sat in the dry grass and Ferko sat next to her.

"Shouldn't you be with the team?" she asked.

"I'm batting ninth."

"So I hear!"

One of the interns, a guy from Dartmouth, hit a hard-liner up the middle, above and to the left of Greg, who jumped, higher than seemed humanly possible, and snared it, then threw to first, beating Alan Friedman back to the base for a double play.

"Whoa!" Lisa said. Her presence as spectator heightened Ferko's suspicion that his role here was jester.

"Greg was all-state in three sports."

"They have that in junior high?"

"High school. I Googled him." He stood and dusted off his jeans.

"You got this, Ferko."

He grimaced.

"The winning streak means more to Prauer than his money," she said. "George isn't going to risk something like that."

If she'd meant to reassure Ferko, she'd failed. The third batter, Pete Johnston, the former minor leaguer, hit a long ball to left-center, which the center fielder tracked down for out three.

"You got this," she repeated, and Ferko gave her a thumbs-up, proving, once again, who was a good sport. He went to find his glove—Cosler's backup glove—and his defensive position.

Right field.

Alan Friedman, the Caps' pitcher, was still in his twenties. Here was the reason he'd made partner at his firm: he could windmill the ball over the plate in the blink of an eye. Cosler said that Friedman had been clocked at eighty miles an hour, and now, watching him pitch, Ferko had no reason to doubt Cosler's claim. Cosler played third and Prauer played first. Ferko, in right, stood behind Prauer, who waved Ferko toward the gap, and Ferko obliged a few steps, before Prauer waved him over more. The first two batters struck out on six pitches. Prauer called time, and jogged out to right and physically escorted Ferko to the spot where he should stand. Then the third batter chopped an easy hopper to Friedman, who tossed to Prauer. One, two, three, and Ferko never actually had to move.

It was still zero-zero a half inning later, when Greg Fletcher led off the bottom of the second. He adjusted the strap on each batting glove, rested the bat on his shoulder, and surveyed the field. Then he stepped to the plate, took the bat off his shoulder, and waggled it high in the air. Alan windmilled a high hard one, outside— what would have been ball one—that Greg went after anyway. He stepped across the plate and tomahawked the pitch, deliberately, the way one directs a tennis ball with a racket, over Prauer's glove and in front of Ferko. Then Greg ran, a hard sprint that seemed unnecessary until he reached first base, ignored the coach, and went to second. The Caps yelled to Ferko to throw the ball, and he did, into the outfield grass, where it bounced and then rolled into the infield, while Greg rounded second and made it to third with a stand-up triple. He clapped his hands and yelled across the diamond to his team on the first-base line. "Right field's got no arm!"

They moved Ferko off the line, toward the gap, where Prauer had placed him in the first inning. But everyone on Greg's team was hitting to Ferko now. Some struck out. Some hit it to the intern from the University of Virginia, who played second base. But some hit it through the infield or over the infield to Ferko and took advantage with an extra base or two. There was nothing he could do—no matter how well he prepared himself mentally with each pitch—to field the ball cleanly and get it into the infield. One speedster made it all the way home when he directed a soft-liner that bounced through Ferko's legs. They moved Ferko back toward the foul line, and slid Pete Johnston from center into the right-center gap.

By the sixth inning the Large Caps were losing eight to six, the win streak in jeopardy, when Ferko's final turn at bat came with two outs and a runner on second. Through all the defensive miscues he still hadn't made contact—oh-for-three, all strikeouts. He hadn't spoken with Lisa since the first inning, but between innings they'd made eye contact: he'd grimaced at her and she'd grimaced back. Prauer was the only one who'd actually talked to Ferko. In the early innings he'd barked things that, in a certain light, could have been construed as encouraging, like, "Let's get it done." But by the middle innings Prauer's entreaties hadn't been positive in any light: "Where's your head at?" By the later innings, he'd slapped his mitt against his thigh and muttered something Ferko didn't wish to decipher.

Now Ferko stood at the end of the bench with Prauer and Cosler (who maybe felt responsible for re-cruiting Ferko and putting the win streak at risk), while Prauer explained that Ferko wasn't, in fact, going to bat, that he needed to leave the game, that an emergency had come up, that his wife wasn't well. Ferko wondered what Prauer knew about Mary Beth and her chronic condition, before he realized that it was all a lie, a story designed to skip Ferko's sure out in favor of the top of the order and Alan Friedman, who hadn't yet made an out, who already had his helmet and batting gloves on and was making his way toward home plate.

"Take your helmet off and skedaddle. I'll see you in the office tomorrow." Prauer stepped close. He smelled of sweat and desperation, a stew that produced, within Ferko, a wave of nausea and unease. He felt embarrassed for Prauer. But only for a moment. Because Cosler was at Prauer's elbow, the interns were on the bench with various Riverfront advisers and associates, and Lisa Becker was somewhere in the grass behind him, and Ferko realized that the embarrassment actually flowed the other way. He gave Prauer a curt nod and shed his helmet and placed it on the bench, while Prauer called time and went to the ump, who removed his mask. They talked the way managers and umpires have talked since the dawn of baseball, with gestures and shrugs, with smiles and scowls, an unknown language of fact and fiction and spin, of secret deals, perhaps, of bribes. Ferko had watched such discussions all his life, from the stands at Yankee Stadium and on TV.

Cosler had edged closer. So had the bench. Lisa, too, behind the backstop. And, despite Prauer's demand that he skedaddle, Ferko followed. They'd all seen Prauer negotiate. They'd seen him cajole and persuade. His success came partly from his belief that he was smarter than his counterpart. It didn't matter if he was or wasn't. What mattered was his belief, conveyed through a winning combination of deference and arrogance, of accolades and insults. Ultimately, attitude amounted to little without leverage, and Prauer's came from his money, his ability to pick up his ball and go home. Here the ump had the rule book, and Prauer had, what? Ferko had to find out.

Alan Friedman was taking practice cuts outside the batter's box. Prauer gestured with his hand toward the Caps' bench. "He can't stay."

"Do you have a pinch hitter?"

Prauer half turned and Lisa sidled with him, so that she remained out of sight. Prauer placed his hands on his hips, then turned back to the ump. "No."

"Then he hits."

"He can't."

"Have more faith."

"Ha! I told you he needs to leave."

Now Greg Fletcher was jogging in from shortstop, and his teammates followed, tentatively, with half steps. And the Caps, too, moved en masse toward home plate. They carried bats and mitts and balls. Only Ferko remained behind, near the bench.

And Prauer, desperate and near defeat in his own game of embarrassment, asked, "What if he got a call from his wife and it was an emergency? You'd make him stay and finish the game?"

"Hey," Greg called, "you can't just *skip* him for your leadoff hitter."

"What if—" Prauer said.

"He'd be out," the ump said. "You'd lose."

"We can play with eight."

"You can."

"Great!" Prauer said.

"But the game's over. Your ninth hitter didn't bat. He's the last out."

"He's got to go." Prauer pointed at Ferko, still standing beside the bench.

"The game is just him," the ump said. "A few pitches and we're done. Batter up!"

And with that Greg Fletcher took two steps toward the Caps' bench and pointed at Ferko. "Come on, Gaylord." Greg punched his fist into his glove. "Let's end this."

And Ferko did. On three pitches.

CHAPTER FIFTEEN

She was using more, even after deciding to use less. It was Thursday, 5:00 PM, and she sat with Ferko in her favorite booth (the second one, so she could see who came in the door, straight or high) in Café Ivy. Ferko was still buttoned down from work, though it was a hundred degrees outside. Ivy's fans spun from the painted ceiling at an impressive clip, conducting cool air from the two vents in the high duct to the bar, booths, and tables below. They'd met outside, where Jen chained her new bike (forty bucks from a med student who'd gotten a residency in, of all places, Oklahoma) to a lamppost. The bike had gears—twenty-four speeds—and she was sure it would be stolen. She'd written it off, in fact, like dropping forty bucks on the sidewalk, which she'd probably done anyway on more than one occasion.

They ordered sodas, then adjourned to the unisex bathroom, up a flight of ten stairs, each stair gaining, it seemed, a single degree of both temperature and humidity, so that the windowless room at the top, past the sink, where the wood door swung shut and locked with a hook and eye, lacked almost all oxygen. "Let's make this quick," she said, and pulled from her bag a compact and a Baggie and cut lines with a pen cap. There was enough room only for a toilet and two standing adults. She snorted two lines with a fiver. Then she cut two more lines for him, which he snorted in rapid succession. Then they descended the stairs into the cool of the café and the drinks on the table in tall glasses with ice and rainbow straws, and they waited for something to happen.

She sipped her soda and he sipped his.

After a time, he said, "I thought of something else."

"What else did you think about?"

"The guy who hit my daughter with his car."

She knew, of course, what he was thinking about. Once a week, since their crazy night out, they'd gotten together and gotten high, sans the live modeling or shoplifting. Instead, they talked. Then they went out, sometimes to a club to see a band she knew and sometimes to a party thrown by someone else she knew, or someone who knew someone she knew. And it was then, in the late evening hours, in her element—in a rock 'n' roll club or at a party in the basement of some warehouse—when she realized she had to use less. Or even stop. What would that feel like?

Now, it was just starting: the feeling of normal, of warmth, mingling with the cool on her skin. The hairs on her arms stood erect. Outside, through Ivy's window, there was actual sunlight on the bricks across Houston Street. Yes, it was optimism that swelled in her chest, dampened only by the shapeless sense of disappointment that it wouldn't be enough. That it was never enough.

"I thought you said you didn't know it was a guy," she said, unable to resist the non sequitur.

"I'm using *guy* the way I use *Coke.*" He lifted his glass.

"That is a Coke," she pointed out.

"But suppose it wasn't. Suppose they had Pepsi here. I'd still call this a Coke, even though it wouldn't be as good as a Coke."

She resisted the urge to talk.

"Or take it a step further," he said. "It could be Sprite or Mountain Dew or Dr Pepper. It doesn't matter. *Coke* means soft drink and *guy* means person—"

"Okay," she interrupted him.

"In this case, *driver*."

"Okay, but why do you do that? Call sodas Cokes? You're from New Jersey. You're not supposed to do that."

He shrugged. "My mom did. She was from Connecticut. I try to take all my life lessons from her, not my dad or my brother."

"I always wanted a sibling."

"I always wanted a sister."

"You got one," Jen said, meaning her.

But Ferko didn't acknowledge or register the gesture. Instead, he shook his head. "I just remembered my dream last night."

"The *guy*," she reminded him, "the *driver*."

"First this." He licked his lips. "It's a recurring dream. I have this huge stone house. It goes on, like, forever. I'm always discovering new rooms. Sometimes the roof leaks when it rains. But the real problem is the basement. Sometimes the back door is missing. Sometimes it doesn't lock. Sometimes I forget to lock it. And I feel exposed, because anyone can just come in, and, since the house is so big, anyone could hide for a long time and never be discovered. I live in the house with a girl. She's not Catherine. At least I don't think she is. She's older, but still a girl. She's a daughter, or like a daughter. Mary Beth isn't there. Never. It's just me and this girl. My daughter. My dream daughter. And a lot of the time I'm anxious with the leaking roof and the basement door that won't shut, but last night we were looking out a second-floor window, and it was like we were in a tree house in a forest. It was summer, and the leaves on the trees were thick and green."

The door swung open and shut. Two guys she didn't know. Jen trespassed in basements in her recurring dream. Ferko guarded against trespassers in his. Greg Fletcher destroyed evidence in his. "Why are you telling me this?" she asked.

"Because it was beautiful. I felt good when I woke up this morning. And I feel good now."

She shrugged. "I don't dream."

"You dream. You just can't remember them."

"I don't think I do."

"Yes, you do."

"No. I don't." She clenched her jaw like she meant business. "You were going to tell me something about the driver of the car."

His eyes followed a patron ascending the stairs to pee or to use. "He was probably scared."

She waited for more.

"I forgot to say that last time, I think, in my whole speech about how it didn't matter whether the driver stopped or not, because the baby was dead."

"Catherine," Jen said.

"The baby," Ferko said. "It's easier to say."

"'The baby' makes it sound like a thing."

"A baby is not a thing."

"It is in this context."

"Shut *up*," he said.

"I can't." She let out a tight, inexplicable laugh, one that wouldn't have escaped only five minutes before. It came from her throat, mouth, and nose, pushed by air expelled from her lungs—quick, fleeting, benign.

"We're talking," he admitted.

She ran her finger along the edge of the wood table and found the notch she'd carved late at night years ago with the pocketknife her boyfriend had carried, just in case. His name was Steve, which he'd carved on the wall of a booth two back, probably with the same knife Jen had used. His name was still there, but he never came around anymore, and hadn't for years.

"Do you think about him?" she asked, meaning the driver.

"I'm thinking about him now."

"What would you ask him? Assuming you wouldn't punch him in the jaw."

Ferko raised his face, tipped his chin toward the stairs that led to the bathroom, where the air was stale and hot. Only his pupils—narrowed to pencil points—reminded her of the maelstrom in his blood. She felt hers surge, a fresh wave of fineness, and she was thankful now that, no matter what he said, things would be okay.

"I'd like to know where he was going." Ferko worried his face. "Wait," he said, "that sounds wrong." He lowered his eyes to the table, where Jen was still working her finger into the notch she'd cut.

"I don't wish to presume," he said, "to judge the driver's errand."

She joined her hands around the base of her glass, like a scarf around a neck, his eyes fixed on the gouge she'd abandoned.

"I only want facts," he continued, "and only to confirm my theory, the way I think about this." He looked at her with his crazy eyes. "I guess I'd like to know where he was going." He shrugged, an indifference that belied his wish. "I'd like to know about that last traffic light, the one before that intersection. There's a light at Glen and Amos, and I wonder whether he rushed to beat it or stopped when he could have run it. One or the other. You see, it's not good or bad. I'd just like to know."

"I get it," she said.

"Because it's fate," he said. "That's my theory. Almost by default."

"Fate," she repeated, remembering the day last month when she'd detoured west on her old bike to Felix's building, stood on the sidewalk on Twenty-Fifth, the approximate spot where Felix had died, and spotted the flyer for play auditions just as Greg Fletcher called, pitching lunch with Ferko. Queenie still hadn't called about an audition. Perhaps she never would. Jen had the phone number in her bag, zipped in the pocket with the postage stamps.

"Like if I knew what the errand was," Ferko was saying. "Maybe he was going to the dry cleaner, and he usually went on Tuesday, but instead he went on Wednesday and that was the morning, and that was the morning that Mary—" He stopped himself. "You get it," he said.

"Yeah, but he might not have been from town, right? He might have just been passing through."

He gazed past her, as though weighing this development against the version he held. Glasses clinked in the booth behind her.

"Maybe," he said. "But it doesn't matter. It doesn't change the theory. The beauty of fate is there's no way to prove or disprove it. It just is. Like those guys you read about who've booked tickets on doomed flights only to miss the plane because of something silly, like a flat tire on the way to the airport."

"Or the opposite. They miss their flight and get stuck on the doomed flight."

"That never happens," he said.

She laughed, and he laughed with her.

She said, "I'm not sure that helps your argument."

"It helps," he said, squelching his laugh.

"Do you ever wonder," she asked, "what he'd like to ask *you?*"

And with that question, Ferko's laugh recommenced, high in his throat and exiting his mouth from the side, like the sniggering of a cartoon dog.

She almost followed his lead but caught herself. "I'm serious."

"I'm sure you are."

"Then stop it."

But it had picked up again. She gave it some time to die down.

"I've never thought about it," he said, when it did.

"Well, think about it."

Felix DeGrass had a brother, Solomon, a theater professor at Princeton. Jen had thought about what she'd want to ask Solomon.

"How about, 'Do you forgive me?'" Jen said. "That would be good to know."

"This is what the driver's supposed to ask me?" Ferko's expression was incredulous, bordering on grotesque. "He'd have to show himself and risk jail. People don't do that. It would be stupid."

"I don't think it would be stupid."

"What does it matter, anyway? I'm aggrieved, not him."

"You don't know that."

"I don't care."

She'd been following Solomon DeGrass for years. Not physically, but electronically, from a safe distance, from whatever downtown space in which she happened to dwell, or from her terminal at the trading desk, after the London Metal Exchange closed. It was an easy thing to do; he had an unusual name. He'd graduated from Harvard with a degree in biology in 1996, from Florida State with a master's in theater in 2002 and a PhD in 2004. Now he taught adjunct at Princeton. His CV was the first hit when you searched his name. In spring, he'd taught two courses, one in the 100s, called Contemporary Playwrights, and another, an upper-class course called The 1950s: Ahead of the Revolution. Now it was summer, and it wasn't clear what he was doing or where he was doing it. Given his interests, though, how far could his field research take him from Manhattan?

He was nearby. He had to be. She'd always assumed so, anyway, within a day's trip of the city by car or train. The proximity was comforting, an ever-present and necessary opportunity. It didn't matter that she never made plans to see him, because the opportunity remained, static, like the bricks on the buildings now bathed in the sun across Houston. But something had shifted the day she met Ferko for lunch and he told her the unexpected story of his baby getting hit by a car. And how the driver left. It was inexplicable, to leave like that. Whenever Ferko talked about it, he described it as if the collision wasn't even the driver's fault, though speed was a factor. Even the clear crime—the leaving—was mentioned as an *oh-by-the-way*. But from Jen's perspective, sitting across the lunch table in the Friday afternoon buzz and relative sobriety of one and a half Bloody Marys, listening to the almost-whispered retelling, it seemed a cold, cruel gesture, for the driver to leave.

Ferko didn't care, but what about Solomon? Did he forgive her?

She'd left by the stairs, from the roof to the lobby, fourteen flights, if she remembered correctly. It must have taken several minutes, back and forth and back and forth in the stairwell, and when she got to the lobby she was dizzy and disoriented, panting and drunk, nauseated. She left by the door on Eighth Avenue and turned south, only to realize that Felix had fallen onto the sidewalk on Twenty-Fifth, north. It was barely 6:00 AM, but there were people out already, sober people, Sunday morning people, walking on the sidewalk north, toward the intersection with Twenty-Fifth. She imagined pieces of him there. His beautiful face broken. She ran south, around the corner at Twenty-Fourth, and threw up on the curb. Then she walked and kept walking. Between Sixth and Seventh she heard a siren.

Five and a half hours she'd known him. At the club the night before she'd wandered off from her friends—two guys, both gay—and bumped into him, literally, at the bar. He was a playwright celebrating his first staged reading earlier that night in a warehouse south of Times Square. He was almost her age. He wished to direct. And she told him about her time at Columbia, how she was involved in the theater program there and regretted getting away from it. Now she traded com-modities. How boring, right?

He turned toward the bar, the direction she was facing, and placed his forearms across its polished edge, an elaborate gesture of non-judgment. He pointed to her empty glass, where there was only ice and a spent wedge of lime. "Gin or vodka?"

"Vodka."

He ordered for her, Scotch for himself. Then he bent an elbow and ran his finger through his errant strands of misbehaving locks and tucked them behind his ear.

His play was about a dead girl and her ghost. "My dad writes about ghosts," she said, and he told her his ghost stories and she told him her dad's. They talked ghosts until after her friends found her and said goodbye (they didn't get an introduction) and after his friends found him and said goodbye (they didn't get an intro-duction, either). And Jen and Felix shared his last glass of Scotch and cabbed down Ninth Avenue to his place, where there was a roof deck and, it being already four thirty and summer and a clear night and all, wouldn't it be nice to see the sunrise? When was the last time she'd seen the sunrise? She told him she couldn't recall, although it had been only a year earlier, at a beach house on Long Island, but she didn't wish him to associate her with unimaginative pursuits like a beach house, the post-college version of a frat house, especially coming on the heels of her revelation that she was a metals trader. They took the elevator up and stopped at his apartment. She waited in the hall while he grabbed a bottle of Scotch, two glasses, and an ice tray from the freezer. Then they took the elevator to the top floor, found the stairwell, and took it to the roof.

The rooftop was gravel. There was a flagstone path that led to a patio of sorts, with iron tables and chairs. The flagstones were painted with abstract designs. The condensers whirred. The fans exhaled the building's stale air. He filled the glasses with ice, then with Scotch. They stood on the northwest corner, beside the parapets, two feet high, metal flashings mounted across the walls of the building. He sat on one wall and she sat on another. The city traffic moved below. The lights on Eighth Avenue flashed yellow. Trucks made deliveries. The moon was gone. Stars and planets paled in the night's haze. Then a gray light emerged behind them. They turned to face it, reflections of the tips and spires, the blinking antennas and towers of the buildings in Midtown. He stood and stumbled. He needed to take a leak, he said, and disappeared behind the mechanical systems. She needed to, too, but decided to hold it. She was standing when he appeared again. It was brighter now, the light revealing the other rooftops. He said he didn't want the night to end. He said something about his play, about the ghost in his play, a girl who had died years ago. Then he whooped and kicked his heels in the air. She said she needed to go to sleep. He said not yet. They went back and forth like this. Then he did something unexpected, the way she remembered it. Or maybe it was the way she constructed it in her mind, with her memory fuzzy from alcohol and fatigue. Or maybe she dreamed it. He leaped onto the parapet and balanced there. She might have turned away. She needed a place to lie down. Sometime later he was gone. Maybe to pee again. Maybe to bed. She went to the parapet, across the painted flagstones and the gravel on the roof deck. She peered over the edge. Something told her to. Like a command. Perhaps it was a command that told the playwright to jump onto the wall. She peered over the edge and found him, crumpled clothes and body on the dawn pavement. Fall, jump, or push. There were three possibilities. No more.

"He was frightened," she agreed with Ferko. "The driver."

"He didn't need to be."

She pushed her lips together, weighing this.

"Okay," Ferko said, "of course he was frightened. But he didn't need to turn tail and run. Mary Beth would be better if that hadn't happened."

The bells on Ivy's front door jingled, and Tina and Dave came in. Tina had dyed her hair deep red. Dave had added a splash of purple to his black. They'd copped. Jen could tell by the way Tina tapped her finger against her front pocket, where Baggies bunched like tissues.

"Look at *you*," she said, meaning Jen's eyes. She wrapped an arm around Jen's neck and squeezed, then placed her purse next to Jen's. "Can we join you?" Tina looked at Ferko, ceding to him the right to reject.

But Ferko responded only with his mild face. Jen guessed he didn't mind. Jen guessed he didn't mind anything.

"Tina and Dave, do you know Ferko?"

"Ferko," Tina said, "the name everyone loves to say."

Dave stood behind her, hands in his front pockets, rocking on his toes and heels. "We'll catch up and find you," he said, meaning it was time to use in the tiny stall upstairs.

"Where were we?" Ferko asked when they reached the stairs. "Let's put this to rest before your friends come back and start talking about skateboards."

"They don't ride skateboards."

"Where do they work?"

"They don't do that, either."

"I *love* your friends."

"You were talking about Mrs. Ferko." Jen considered warning him against betrayal, but there wasn't time. She was on the cusp of some meaningful connection she'd been waiting years to make, a connection that Tina and Dave's eager presence would likely impede.

"The point was closure," Ferko said. "The guy's leaving somehow prevented that for her. Maybe. But I wasn't there. She was."

"*She* meaning the Mrs."

"But the leaving part," Ferko said, "the running. That wasn't necessary. Nor was it fate. It was a decision. I understand the motivating factors. Still, it was a decision, and that's what made it wrong."

He was getting somewhere, Jen could see. He was putting two and two together. But Jen's problem was vexing. When she'd finally sorted it in her mind, after she'd associated Ferko's hit-and-run with her night

with Felix DeGrass, she came to recognize that everything since—the bike accident, the copping and using, and all the subsequent copping and using—had
occurred for a reason. Not fate, like Ferko suggested,
which connoted an accident, a fatal accident (wasn't
fatal a derivation of *fate*?), an unpreventable fatal accident. No, she thought, fate had no room for reason,
for purpose, for a higher purpose. Maybe she believed
in God after all. Because they *were* connected—Felix
DeGrass, the baby Catherine, Solomon DeGrass, and
Ferko himself. She recognized it, or thought she did.
Now she just needed to figure out what it was telling
her to do.

"I guess I'd ask him," Ferko said, "whether he re-
grets that decision." There was something like emotion
on his face, and Jen wondered if it was on hers, too.
But then Ferko's vanished. Dave and Tina appeared at
their sides. Ferko scooted to make room for them.

"Let's talk skateboards," he said.

CHAPTER SIXTEEN

Mary Beth got out of bed, as usual, after Gil had left to catch his train. She packed a bag with water and snacks. She left the house at the usual time, but, instead of turning right on Amos Avenue and walking up toward the School on the Ridge, she turned left, down Amos Avenue to the Glen, the way she once had with Catherine in the stroller. Despite Mary Beth's entreaties, Amanda hadn't revealed herself in the house, and Mary Beth didn't yet know how to confront Gil about the ghost.

But she had a theory, which took her down Amos, to Glen Street, past Lyttondale and the School in the Glen, past the coffee shop and hair salon, the store that sold toys and children's books, past the pub and

restaurant to the town's public library, a freestanding structure built with stone left in the Glen when
the ice retreated tens of thousands of years ago. The
library stood next to the municipal building, which
stood next to the train station, all built with the same
stone.

She arrived just as it was opening, just as the librarian turned the key in the front door and pushed it to let
Mary Beth in. She was the first visitor, and she greeted
the librarian, and, not knowing what else to do, followed her to her desk in the center of the main reading
room. Computers lined the wall to the left, and the
popular library, arranged alphabetically by author, was
shelved to the right.

"I'm wondering if you could help me."

"That's what I'm here for." The librarian wore a
cheery smile. It seemed suddenly important that Mary
Beth not act desperate, that her research was for casual
interest only. Glen Wood Ridge was not a place of desperation. Lives were lived here—normal, productive
lives. She wished to adapt.

"I'm looking for maps of the town, something his-
torical, maybe going back fifty years."

"Of Glen Wood Ridge."

"Yes."

The librarian stood, holding her smile. Mary Beth supposed that a library was a wonderful place to work. "Let's see what we can find."

Mary Beth followed the librarian past the line of computers, past the sections for biography and world history and US history and New Jersey history to a section comprising two shelves: Local Interests.

"Here." The librarian hooked her finger to the top of a thin volume, pages folded and stapled, not bound, with a beige cover: *Glen Wood Ridge: A History*, by Emmanuel Wright. "This was commissioned by the town council to commemorate the fiftieth anniversary of the town's founding." She opened the book to its title page. "See." She tapped her painted nail to the copyright—1968. "The town was founded in 1918."

Mary Beth knew this, of course. The metal signs stationed at various points on the town's perimeter said so, and it was the thing the real estate agent had shared when he'd driven them out here the first time, giving Mary Beth hope for the old house she'd wanted. But she'd wound up with a new one, and only now had learned that, despite being new, it inexplicably had a ghost. Things happened for a reason, she thought, with such clarity it startled her.

"It has a map?" she asked.

"Two." The librarian flipped the pages until she got to the center, where longer pages were folded into each other. "They're a bit brittle. I don't want to rip them. They need a flat surface to lie on." She handed the book to Mary Beth and tipped her head toward the nearest table in the main reading room, at the end of the row of books in which they now stood.

More patrons had entered the library. Senior citizens booted up computers and browsed new releases. A young mother queued in line at the checkout, preschoolers hopping around her like bunnies. *Catherine's friends*, Mary Beth thought.

It felt good to be in a public place, in air conditioning, where normal people went about their business. It wasn't her house, and it wasn't the woods beyond the field at the School on the Ridge. Perhaps Amanda was lurking behind the study carrels or among the shelves, wondering why they weren't on the fallen tree, talking.

The book was a homegrown affair. The author was a resident, born in Glen Wood Ridge in 1922. Mary Beth wondered if he was dead now. The two maps were uncredited, mimeographed from originals drawn by the same hand with what looked like a black felt-tip marker. Labels, such as names of streets, municipal buildings, the rail line, and schools were written in all capital letters. The town boundary was drawn in dots and dashes. The flourishes were charming, with open spaces depicted with out-of-scale grass blades and rows of crops, such as corn, complete with tassels and thieving birds. Trees were drawn with half circles and S-shaped lines. The 1918 version showed the houses in the Glen, and a farm, PORTER'S FARM, on the land that now encompassed the newer developments on the Ridge. By 1968, Porter's Farm was gone, replaced with the Ridge's familiar streets, including Porter Lane, which bisected the old farm, ranch houses drawn with precise uniformity, the School on the Ridge and its ball fields behind it, and the edge where the woods met the ball fields, where the path led down into the ravine and Amanda's tree. COUNTY PARK, the newer map said. And up Amos Avenue, between the Glen and Porter's Farm on the earlier map and the Glen and the Ridge on the later map—in a space that had only since been replaced by a parenthetical curve called Woodberry Road, containing thirty-some houses, including a four-bedroom Cape with dormers and a front porch situated in the center of the block and sold to the Ferkos in 2004—was a long driveway and a structure in the woods: MILLERS' PLACE.

Mary Beth glanced up, hoping Amanda would be there, but all she found were the same senior citizens at the same computers and no line to check out books. She left the maps spread on the table and returned to the Local Interests section, where she located the town's master plans, updated every five years. She knew how to read these documents. She'd reviewed the most recent version when she and Gil had bought their house. Now she pulled one from 1975 and the most recent one, from 2005. In the 1975 master plan the property on the map labeled Millers' Place was identified solely as *Existing Residence on 18 Acres*. The 2005 plan showed Woodbury Road. She went back and pulled each version of the master plan off the shelf, then stacked them next to her on the long table. She paged through these chronologically. By 1990, *Existing Residence on 18 Acres* had been replaced by *Private Acreage to Be Purchased by County for County Park*. By 1995, the land's use had changed to *Residential Housing, R/5*.

Mary Beth retrieved a pen and some scrap paper from her bag, and made notes:

1918–1985 (approx): Miller House
1990: to be bought by County for park
1995: Woodberry development on the board

She remembered reading old newspaper articles on microfiche. Now newspapers had digitized their archives, hadn't they? The library hummed. Voices murmured and pages rustled. Fingers tapped keys and clicked mouses. She found an open computer next to a man scrolling through text, and she found the website for the *Bergen Crier.* She typed "Glen Wood Ridge" "Amanda Miller" and came up with no hits. Then Mary Beth removed the quotes around Amanda's name, and the hits appeared, pages and pages—honor rolls, a woman with an award-winning garden, book reviews, feature profiles, business news, race results, births and obituaries, home sales, but none in which the names Amanda and Miller were connected in any meaningful way.

Mary Beth narrowed her search to the five years between 1985 to 1990, when the use of the Miller property changed, according to the master plan, but again there was nothing useful, though there was significantly *less* unuseful content than before. So Mary Beth went back further and limited the search to the period from 1980 to 1985. The first headline astonished her: GIRL, 6, HITS TREE ON BIKE, DIES. *July 18, 1983. Amanda Russo, who lived with her grandmother, Dorothy Miller, on Amos Avenue in Glen Wood Ridge, died Monday after the bicycle* . . . That was the extent of the abstract, but it was enough. Mary Beth's pulse quickened. Her breath came in audible rasps. She knew what she needed to do—click on the link and pay the newspaper's fee, but she was unable to do so. Not yet. She wished to savor the moment of discovery. She thought of all the libraries around the world, the universe of data loosely connected by wires and codes, by signals that traveled through air. She imagined government and university archives, where scholars burrowed into warehouses of books, galaxies of paper, of words, pictures, and records. She imagined the smallest branch of the smallest system, with a few books on a few shelves and a terminal or two, possibly none. She imagined the sweep, and how the greatest discovery today would take place here, now, while the residents of Glen Wood Ridge checked out and returned and renewed books, while children were read to, while magazines were browsed, and while a ghost spied from behind a shelf.

In a matter of weeks she'd been catapulted from a place like death into the blue sky by some unseen and untapped energy. She didn't know where she'd land, whether she'd land on her feet or her head. *It's okay*, Amanda had said. *It doesn't hurt.* And Mary Beth conveyed the words to Catherine, the way mothers have conveyed words to their children for thousands of years. *Okay. Didn't hurt.* And what else?

She clicked open the article.

Girl, 6, Hits Tree on Bike, Dies
July 18, 1983
By Vern Merriman
Staff Writer, *The Bergen Crier*

Amanda Russo, who lived with her grandmother, Dorothy Miller, on Amos Avenue in Glen Wood Ridge, died Monday after the bicycle she was riding collided with a tree in the woods adjacent to County Park.

The accident occurred at the bottom of a steep ravine. Town police believe that the girl, 6, may have lost control of her bicycle at the top of the ravine or ridden down it purposely and lost control in the process.

The dirt trails connecting the School on the Ridge to County Park and other parts of the town are popular with children on bicycles, according to Barry Saunders of the Glen Wood Ridge Police Department.

"The hills are steep, and there's loose dirt and rocks, roots and other obstacles. The thing we want to tell kids and their parents is to slow down and wear helmets," Saunders said.

Mrs. Miller, who has lived in Glen Wood Ridge since before the town's incorporation, said her granddaughter came to live with her last year.

"She didn't have permission to ride down there," Mrs. Miller told the *Crier*. "She could only ride her bike in the front yard and driveway."

Mrs. Miller, who raises chickens in her yard, said one of the birds was found a quarter mile down the trail from where her granddaughter died. The chicken has been returned unharmed to Miller.

"We get kids all the time up here curious about our chickens," she said. "I don't know what one's got to do with the other. But I wonder."

Mary Beth read it twice. The article at once made perfect sense and no sense. Amanda had mentioned chickens. She'd mentioned boys on bikes. Mary Beth searched for more stories but there were no more. An accident, based on the one article she'd found. But what about the chicken? Was that a clue? Mary Beth could have gone next door to the police department. She calculated back. It was twenty-four years ago, almost to the day. Amanda would be thirty now, only five years younger than Mary Beth. Were there any officers who would remember the case? No one Mary Beth had met after Catherine's accident would have qualified. They were all younger than she was, as though the Glen Wood Ridge force was reserved for entry level only, a place to get your toes wet before moving on to larger towns with more challenging crimes. Nor did she want to run into any of those officers, if they were still there, and risk being identified as the wacky lady whose daughter died and who now, inexplicably, was looking for information about another dead girl, killed long ago. Could a private citizen even do that, go to the police and start asking questions to sate her interest? She wasn't going to find out. She realized that she knew a witness. Maybe the witness was unreliable, but she was a witness all the same. She went to find Amanda, or let Amanda find her.

Lisa Becker put her head in Ferko's office. "Did you know your friend Greg is here?"

"Greg?" The name didn't register in the context of the Riverfront Capital offices.

"Greg Fletcher," she said, "the guy from the softball game."

"Greg Fletcher is here?"

"With Prauer."

"That's . . ." Ferko searched for an original word, but when he came up empty he said, "Weird."

"I just wanted to give you a heads-up, in case he stops by." She turned, as if to leave, but then didn't.

"What are you working on?" she asked.

He shrugged. "Stuff." Truth was, things were slow. He hoped no one noticed how slow before they picked up again.

She bit her lip.

"It's a blip," he said to acknowledge her unease.

"The Grove team!" Prauer appeared over Lisa's shoulder, with Greg in tow. Lisa stepped aside, an apparent effort to evade, but was trapped by Prauer and Greg.

"My man!" Greg said, and shook Ferko's hand.

"Greg?" Ferko feigned surprise.

Greg took Lisa's hand. "We've met before. I'm Greg Fletcher."

"Hi," Lisa said, like a lovestruck teenager.

"Lisa Becker," Prauer said, completing the introduction for her.

Greg wore his sleepy look, his stoner smile.

"Greg called me. First to gloat about softball." Prauer left a pause for the laugh track, which arrived late, from Greg and Lisa. "And then to talk about the Grove deal."

"*What* Grove deal?" Ferko asked.

"So I said, 'Let's have lunch.'" Prauer leaned forward, fingertips on Ferko's desk, and loomed.

"The family's falling apart," Prauer said, addressing Ferko's premature question. "Roy was the glue holding the family together. Now that he's gone, there are elements that want out."

"There's an opportunity," Greg put in.

"The surviving Groves cut Greg's firm loose. He's on our team now."

"*Our* team?"

"Not directly, of course. That's you and Lisa. But Greg quarterbacks, which I understand he used to do quite well back in the day."

"You told him about the Punt, Pass, and Kick competition?" Ferko hoped the spectacular failure of that day would prove a belated lesson in humility for Greg, even if Prauer failed to get it.

"Greg, you didn't tell me about that. I was in awe of those kids." Prauer checked his watch. "I'll let you guys talk."

He started to leave, but then stopped in the doorway.

"Hey!" He raised a finger. "Why didn't we think of killing Roy Grove?"

This time the laugh track was timely.

"Maybe we did," Ferko said, trying to get into the spirit.

But Prauer was gone.

It was quiet for a moment. Greg occupied the spot Prauer had vacated. Lisa stood with her back to the open door, eyes wide, like a small mammal weighing escape.

"The Grove team," Greg said.

Ferko, unable to speak, waited for what would come next.

"Lisa, can I get a moment with Gil?"

"Sure." She left without looking at Ferko.

He almost stopped her to prove a point—that it was his office, and he wanted her to stay. But the truth was he wanted her to go, too.

Greg touched two fingers to the edge of the door. It swung slowly, under its own momentum, until it clicked in the doorjamb. He sat in the chair facing Ferko's desk. He opened his hands, palms up, like a plea, before leaning forward, fingers interlaced, wrists on the edge of Ferko's desk. Then he turned his hands over, fingertips touching the desktop like piano keys.

"Dude, I didn't call Bill. He called me."

He paused as though that were explanation enough.

"I think he just wants me on his softball team. Should I be flattered?"

Ferko didn't say one way or the other.

"At the same time, the Groves are all fucked up. They fired us, on the spot, because one of their cousins blew up Roy's car."

"Who did it?"

"Call the police." Greg looked past Ferko, out his window, where there was a view of a white building. Greg was resetting himself, it appeared, blinking his heavy lids, like the lights on a computer tower when the machine reboots or backs up its hard drive.

"Dude," he said again, which was probably Greg's way of not calling him Gaylord. "So, I'm really pissed off, being fired by the client like that. We all are. But I'm here in New York now, and I'm thinking I need to meet more people, so I accepted Bill's invitation to lunch."

"He took you to lunch? To recruit you for softball?"

Greg shrugged his shoulders and closed his thick eyelids. "He's really into softball."

Ferko nodded his assent.

"It's cool."

Ferko nodded again, assuming that *cool* meant *okay*, because he thought it was okay, in a certain light, that Prauer wasn't all work, that he made time for recreational pursuits, like softball, even if it was just one more competition that he had to win. After the loss to Greg's team, Prauer had taken the next two days off, apparently unable to cope.

"So I go to lunch with him and I want to *bring* him something, because, you know, he's the man. So I told him there's this one faction of the family, representing, like, thirty percent of the stock, that wants out, at any price. I mean, they're sick of the whole business. They're in mourning."

"You just told him that, unsolicited?"

"I kept it in my pocket until dessert."

Ferko looked at him.

"He's persuasive," Greg said.

Ferko knew what Greg meant. Prauer got things without having to ask.

"So, we're going to buy from these guys?"

"I tell you who to call and help you with the price."

Ferko scratched his chin. It was wrong, he knew, unethical and patently unfair. But perhaps not illegal. Not like murder, anyway. In the continuum of crimes committed by and against the Groves, this one was a blemish, possibly not even visible.

"It's a private transaction," Greg said, as though he were reading Ferko's mind.

They let it settle over them, like a beautiful piece of chamber music swelling from stereo speakers. Ferko still had the remnants of last night's dope running through his veins. He was thankful for that, and thankful, too, that he now had something tangible to work on. But he wondered what Greg's presence meant for him. He was surprised how easily he could hold his own with Greg, at least one-on-one. He wondered how long it could last, Greg treating him like a peer, with respect, before he started hitting hard-liners at him, balls he knew Ferko couldn't handle.

"Have you seen Jen lately?"

"I have." He didn't want to be more specific—say that it was last night—because here was another complication, if Greg were to become a fixture in Ferko's professional life: the dope. He had to warn Jen, though she'd likely take no heed anyway.

"Is she okay?" Greg asked.

Ferko pushed out his chin. "Yeah."

"I don't know. I finally saw her for lunch last week, and she seemed, I don't know, wound up."

"She's a little crazy," Ferko admitted. "I think that trading thing makes people get that way."

He took heart. Jen hadn't mentioned that she and Greg had had lunch, but maybe that meant she, too, recognized the importance of keeping Ferko's personal and professional lives separate.

"She said you and her are buds now."

Ferko didn't know what to say.

"That's cool," Greg concluded. He picked up a photo on Ferko's desk, a picture of Catherine, the only one Ferko kept in his office, wearing PJs, pink with hearts. Her face was pink, too, from being pressed against the breast. She smiled like she meant it, splayed on the couch after what Ferko could only guess was a particularly satisfying feeding.

"I'm sorry about your daughter," Greg said.

Ferko stared at him.

"Jen told me."

Greg touched the frame of the next photo, one of Mary Beth in a wicker chair on the front porch, not long before the accident. Even then, in those happy days, she conveyed melancholy in her silences. Ferko had snapped this picture from the doorway, when she wasn't looking. When the shutter sound clicked she'd looked up at him with an unreadable expression— peeved indifference he took to mean acceptance. He raised the lens again and she stuck her hand up, like a traffic cop signaling *stop*. He did. He stowed the camera, but got prints made of the single image he took, first in color and then in black and white. It was the latter he put in a frame and brought to the office. Mary Beth looked elegant in the photo, awakened by spring, even as her downcast eyes—looking, perhaps, at the tulips that came up every year, in spite of their neglect—betrayed her underlying sadness.

"We're going to get this thing done," Greg said. Ferko was unsure what thing. His eyes must have asked it, because Greg went on: "This Grove thing. And other things, too. We're going to be a team. We're going to make a difference. And we're going to make a lot of money."

She found Amanda straddling the fallen tree. The girl shot Mary Beth an impatient look, as though she'd been waiting for her all day.

"There you are," Mary Beth said cheerily.

"This is where I live."

She was struck by the word *live*, but kept the irony to herself. She took her place on her end of the tree. "We have a lot to talk about."

"What happens to people in the woods?" Mary Beth asked her.

"They chase boys on bikes and hit trees."

"You asked me that question the other day."

"I saw it in the library today, written on that TV."

"You *followed* me." She meant it good-naturedly, but was afraid it came out as an accusation. "I didn't see you," she said.

Amanda stared at her.

"You're a good reader," Mary Beth said.

"Just the top part."

Mary Beth retrieved the story she'd printed, and read Amanda the headline: "GIRL, 6, HITS TREE ON BIKE, DIES."

Amanda waited, as though she expected Mary Beth to read the rest of the story, and so she did. After she was through, Mary Beth studied the girl to gauge her reaction.

"I'm sorry, Amanda."

"I told you it's okay."

Mary Beth thought she might cry. In fact, she knew she should, but her medicine prevented her. That was the way she understood it, because she used to cry, before the doses were raised and raised again to a level where she could no longer do so.

Besides, the girl watching her wasn't going to cry, either.

"It didn't hurt," Amanda said.

"There's nothing here about chasing boys on bikes." Mary Beth waved the printout.

"That's the part I remember."

Mary Beth waited. She wasn't going to ask her.

"These boys came up like they always did to look at our chickens. They rode their bikes up our driveway. I was riding my bike in the front yard, kind of chasing the chickens around with my tires." Amanda paused to glance toward the side. Then she leaned forward on the tree. "My grandma didn't like that game," she whispered.

Mary Beth leaned forward, too. "I don't blame her," she whispered back.

Amanda nodded in confirmation. "I stopped my bike and I watched them and they watched me. Then the older one got out a grocery bag and grabbed a chicken and stuck it in and started riding away. I yelled for Grandma, but the boys were gone and I rode after them."

"Down here?"

"Yes."

"Is this the tree you hit?"

Amanda gave no indication one way or the other. Mary Beth remembered what Amanda had said: *It's okay. It didn't hurt.*

"You knocked it over?" Mary Beth tried a joke, but immediately regretted it.

"This is my house."

A child screamed from below, in County Park. Hot breezes swept down the ravine.

"I just wanted to get that chicken back," Amanda said. "It was our chicken."

"I know." Mary Beth tried to match the girl's flat affect, but her voice broke.

"That's all I wanted."

"I know," she said again. "Your grandma got it back. The story said so."

"Why'd he take that chicken?" the girl wanted to know.

Mary Beth was going to tell her that she didn't know. Why did people do mean things? She remembered the grandma wondering what one had to do with the other, meaning Amanda and the chicken. Mary Beth supposed no one ever figured it out.

Except the boys.

"What were their names?" she asked. "These boys."

"Felix was the older one, and Solomon was the younger one."

"What about their last names?"

"They're *brothers*."

"So?"

"So they have the same last name, silly." The girl tried on a smile, as though learning the truth and telling the truth helped.

"Of course," Mary Beth said. "Silly me. What was their last *name*?"

"I don't know."

"It looks like we're going back to the library."

"But it doesn't matter."

"I think it does."

CHAPTER SEVENTEEN

Ferko arrived home at seven thirty to a house transformed. Things were straightened and Mary Beth was cooking. Onions were sautéing in hot oil. Thick sausages sizzled in their own fat. A pot of water sat on a high flame. The fan above the stove top roared. An electric guitar spilled through the ceiling speakers that the builder had installed but they never used. A blues CD. Electric. He stood at the entrance to the kitchen and stared.

"Hi!" Mary Beth wore a smile, makeup, a sleeveless blouse, and a blue skirt with white polka dots. A salad was assembled in a wooden bowl on the counter island, a baguette sliced.

"That's a lot of food," he said.

"A pound of pasta."

"You had a good day." It could have been a question, but he made it a statement.

"I had a great day. You?"

He opened his mouth but nothing came out. He hadn't, actually. He was unnerved, in fact, by Greg Fletcher's visit to the Riverfront suite. Or maybe it was the dope he'd used the prior night, when he'd skipped out of work early and met up with Jen and she'd taken him, later, to a club where one of the Mannequins was playing with his new band and she'd stood on stage for old time's sake and posed for a song, perfectly still beneath a white spotlight for two minutes while the band and the audience thrashed. Or maybe it was the lack of dope since then, just twenty-four hours, upsetting his equilibrium, accelerating his crisis. Perhaps it was Ferko's turn in the basement and Mary Beth's turn to ascend. All it had taken was time.

His unsettled feeling mostly had to do with Greg, Ferko guessed. But he couldn't wallow in it, or dwell on it, or even consider it. Mary Beth was here, food cooking and music playing. And wine. She poured him a glass of red, which he took, clinked with hers, tipped, and swallowed. He had to tell her something, so he focused on the positive from Greg's visit:

"A project I thought was dead has been resurrected."

"That's good?"

"It's been a bit slow."

She reflected on this, an act that dulled her features, and he realized he'd never told her about his lack of projects because he was spending his downtime with Jen, getting high.

"It's good to have work," he said finally. "Puts bread on the table." He grabbed a hunk of the baguette she'd sliced and bit it.

The turnaround came in the blues progression, and she actually shook her hips before stirring the skillet with the onions and sausages.

Upstairs, in their bedroom, he changed into shorts and a T-shirt, then lingered. He should have been downstairs with Mary Beth. The table was set. The good linen napkins they used only when they had company. It was a lifetime ago—company. But this was something. Treating him as such. She'd cut blooms from the vines that climbed the fence out back, that choked the azaleas and hydrangeas they'd planted, then neglected. They were weeds, these vines, but she was the sort of gardener who kept a crowded bed, who let things go, even when she wasn't neglectful. Plus, she was a sucker for blue flowers. These opened in the hottest weeks. Like this one. Now the flowers stood on their submerged tendrils, propped by petals on the lip of the vase, a narrow glass vessel the shape of a test tube.

She was trying, maybe too hard, and he didn't know what to do or say. Had he ever? It was a vexing question. His social skills, when it came to Mary Beth, had atrophied. He heard her footfalls in the dining room, smelled the tang of sautéed garlic. He took the stairs down as she was bringing out the serving dishes to the table—the pasta, sauce, and salad. He helped with the bread and wine.

They sat in their places. He served himself pasta in a bowl, a sausage, a ladle of tomato sauce, while she tossed then served herself salad. They traded serving dishes and repeated, and he still didn't know what to say. She watched him, her eyes too bright in the waning daylight.

"I called Chris today," she said finally.

"Oh?" Christiana was Mary Beth's older sister, who lived in Charlottesville with her husband, Matt, a commercial banker, the sort that joined the local chamber of commerce and took customers—the second- and third-generation executive officers of family-owned business-es—to Virginia football games on Saturday afternoons. They lived an exceedingly comfortable, if unspectacular,

life, with three kids—one each in high school, middle
school, and elementary school—in a newish development west of downtown. The house was more than twice
the size of the Ferkos' for less than half the price. There
were thirteen windows on its brick front. From each
hung, beginning Thanksgiving weekend through the end
of January, a plastic Christmas wreath to match the real
deal on the front door. Chris embodied a certain type of
small-town American opulence, born of stuff purchased
in ridiculous quantities from enormous discount retail-
ers. She couldn't brook others not wanting what she had.

When Catherine died, Chris got churchy—platitudes about angels and God's will and such, judgments
that deepened Mary Beth's profound regret and hard-
ened Ferko's dull anger. Chris couldn't, or wouldn't,
turn it off. She was *there* for them, whether the Ferkos
wanted her to be or not. And they didn't. So Mary
Beth shut her sister off—a conscious avoidance that
must have been noted and felt hurtful, though Ferko
wasn't aware they'd ever received such feedback, either
directly from Chris or indirectly from Mary Beth's parents or her younger sister, Lucy. The rest of the family
still lived near Richmond, an hour from Chris and her
brick-front palace. It wasn't a long drive, yet they kept
their distance, too, and Chris accepted their snubs with

an air of superiority and the delusion, Ferko suspected, that her family was envious.

"She said Lucy had a boyfriend."

"Really!" Lucy was thirty-two. At eighteen she'd left home for college, like her sisters had. Lucy's choice was Clemson. But she'd suffered some sort of breakdown freshman year, come home, and never left.

"Some guy from work."

She was a cashier at a clothing boutique. Her actual title was sales associate. The job had done great things for her—paycheck, self-esteem, and now this: boyfriend.

"But they broke up," Mary Beth said, deflating the cheer she'd conjured. She made air quotes: "He wasn't who she thought he was."

"What does that mean?"

"Chris's words."

"Sounds ominous."

"I called Lucy to get the scoop. I left her a message."

"She doesn't return calls."

"I'll call her again tomorrow."

"What else is up with Chris?" he asked, a question that elicited an update on everyone *but* Chris: Mary Beth's mom and dad, Chris's husband and each of their three kids. They were practicing, Ferko figured—Mary

Beth and Chris on the phone earlier today, and Mary Beth and Ferko now—by talking about everyone but themselves. It was still momentous, Mary Beth calling Chris and then preparing an elaborate dinner. It was preseason warm-ups for some later date when they'd talk again about things that mattered. And Ferko was relieved—even as Mary Beth went on about a trip to Hawaii that Matt and Chris had taken this spring, even as Ferko contemplated what Mary Beth could have possibly told Chris about Ferko and what *he'd* been up to— that tonight wasn't that night. Grief was a clock, with hands that moved if you waited long enough. Ferko suspected he'd cheated grief, with its linear qualities, its inflexible rhythms. He'd discovered a shortcut, somehow, that took him to a place he wasn't supposed to go.

Was that it? He had a bowl of food, a glass of wine, and yet he felt empty. His house was too new, too clean. He crinkled his nose, flared his nostrils, and sniffed. Was this his life now? Was he a junkie? It was a small urge, and it passed, but he was conscious of it again, and he awaited its return, as if it were something in the ocean, a clump of seaweed floating in the surf, ebbing, touching his skin, washing over him from time to time.

Mary Beth went on—Matt and Chris and their children. Ferko thought of Mary Beth's prescriptions, all those combinations the doctors had tried. He'd studied their names—both brand and chemical—looking for patterns. The doctors were guessing, throwing darts at a wall. Had one hit the target?

She stood and he stood with her. He stacked their plates, but she blocked his path to the kitchen.

"These dishes aren't going to wash themselves," he said.

"Shouldn't they?" Her eyes beamed. "Isn't this the twenty-first century? Aren't we supposed to have a robot maid?" She took the plates from him and set them back on the table.

"I felt strong enough to call Chris." She looked at him until he looked away. Then she touched his wrist, encircled it with her fingers, and pulled him toward her. They fell into an embrace that felt at once familiar and new. Their bodies fit together in a reassuring way. Her hair smelled like oranges and her skin like clay. He knew he should tell her he loved her. Such a response should be automatic, something he learned in the intro course, Husband 101, or even in its prerequisite, Advanced Boyfriend. But he didn't tell her, or couldn't, and the moment passed and they let each other go, cleared the table, and moved everything into the kitchen in silence.

He ran the faucet and began rinsing. Mary Beth loaded the dishes he stacked on the counter, and dried the pot and skillets he washed by hand. She wiped the counters, and set the dishwasher to run overnight. He looked at e-mail in the study, but there was nothing of consequence. Everyone was taking the summer off, it seemed, or they were lost, like Ferko, and didn't know what to do. Greg had quit his job, Ferko had heard from Lisa, who'd heard from Cosler, who'd presumably heard from Prauer. They called it *gardening leave*, when a banker put in his notice, was told to go home, but remained on the payroll. Greg actually *did* have the summer off. He wasn't officially able to start at Riverfront until September. Yet Ferko imagined that Greg's e-mail inbox and sent folders told a different story, that he was working some obscure angle, even now, in exchange for a promised future payoff, the magnitude of which Ferko could only guess.

Gardening leave. Ferko's garden had been overrun by weeds. Perhaps he and Mary Beth were ready to reclaim it. He shut the computer down and killed the downstairs lights.

She was waiting for him on the upstairs landing, standing beside the girl with the pigtails. Ferko paused on the second stair from the top, unsure of what it meant that they were together and whether or not he wanted to know. They watched him, together and separately, with moony faces, each with her arms at her sides. Then the girl took Mary Beth's hand in hers.

"Gil, this is Amanda."

"I know Amanda." Ferko took the last two stairs, and faced them on the landing. "But not by name."

Amanda looked up at Mary Beth and whispered, loud enough so he could hear, "We've never actually met." It was the voice of a child, a *real* child.

"Not properly." Ferko stepped forward, his hand extended, which the girl took in hers. It was a real hand, with flesh and bones, a *child's* hand, and it conveyed, in that first touch, a single pulse of energy that shot through his fingers and hand and wrist and arm, down into his chest and pelvis and buttocks and legs. It threatened to overwhelm him, to knock him backward, down the stairs, the way a jolt of electricity could knock a man down. But then it receded into a pleasant buzz that lasted a beat or two before it disappeared completely. "How do you do?" he said, and released her hand. He stepped back, restoring the gap between them, and waited for what would happen next.

Mary Beth grinned like she'd just handed him a huge box wrapped in pretty paper.

"So?" he asked.

"So, I met Amanda a few weeks ago at the School on the Ridge."

"But Amanda doesn't go to school there."

"No, she doesn't."

"I used to," Amanda offered.

"She used to." Mary Beth's smile turned grim.

"When I was alive."

"Ahhh," Ferko said, "when she was *alive.*" He quashed the urge to say that that made sense, because schools didn't, as a practice, enroll dead children. He realized he was talking around the girl as though she weren't there, which was true in a way. He chanced a look at her. She was just a girl who needed a bath. He didn't mean to be impolite.

Mary Beth said, "You didn't tell me you knew Amanda."

The girl tugged at Mary Beth's sleeve. "He *didn't* know me."

"Knew *of* Amanda," Mary Beth corrected herself.

"You didn't tell me you knew her, either."

"We don't talk."

He had no response to that. They were finally speaking directly. He should have welcomed it. Instead it made him uneasy, here with the girl, who was—what? He looked at Amanda. "What's your story?"

He regretted that the question sounded harsh. He was about to take it back, or apologize, but the girl's face, unfazed, looked up at Mary Beth's, as though asking permission to tell him, and Mary Beth was digging in her skirt pocket, then unfolding a square of paper into an eight-and-a-half-by-eleven-inch sheet.

She handed him the page. "Here's the story."

It was an article from 1983, the *Bergen Crier*, about a six-year-old girl who died in the woods near County Park when her bike fell down a ravine and hit a tree. The girl's name was Amanda Russo.

"Her house was right here," Mary Beth said. "I found it on an old map. It was here, Gil, where we're standing."

Ferko stared at the page, read the words, the individual words—*girl, chicken, bicycle, grandmother*—but couldn't put them together in any way that made sense. He recognized the School on the Ridge. He recognized County Park. It was an accident, involving a child in Glen Wood Ridge? *That* was the connection to Catherine? He wasn't sure how to ask. He didn't wish to blame Mary Beth again for the baby's death.

"This is Amanda," he said instead.

Mary Beth and the girl looked at each other. Then they nodded.

"You don't look blown away," Mary Beth said, with a tinge of hurt.

"I'm just confused."

"It's a lot to digest," Mary Beth admitted.

Ferko studied the girl. She looked at him coolly. She'd been a benign presence, a curiosity, something he looked forward to, even if their encounters were fleeting and infrequent. Perhaps she'd been here from the start. He had a sense that she had, though he'd seen her only since Catherine died. But now the girl was *really* here, with a name and a story. What did she *want*? Ferko handed the page back to Mary Beth with a shrug. Her face showed disappointment, and he guessed his did, too. Her smile was gone, replaced by creases that formed at the corners of her mouth, at the junctions of lips, cheeks, and chin, crushed, as they were, by the ruinous combination of earth's gravity and metaphorical weight.

"What does this have to do with Catherine?" He surprised himself with the question.

A shadow descended on Mary Beth's face. "*This?*"

"The news story." He indicated the printout Mary Beth clutched in her fingers. "The girl." He realized he was talking around her again, and that was rude. But he couldn't think of her as an actual being with feelings. She played a role. That was all. He remembered Dr. Yoder's theory—collective burden. Whose burden was Amanda?

She spoke for herself: "I didn't know Catherine."

Of course not, Ferko thought, and maybe what the girl wanted from them was irrelevant, because they had wants of their own. Wasn't that the way the world worked? You gave and received, roughly in equal amounts. The cynics like Prauer would say you bought and sold, that it didn't count unless it was quantifiable in some form of accepted currency—money or tickets or wins and losses. But Ferko knew better. He had a mission, which, in an instant, dwarfed Prauer's empire. Mary Beth looked wounded and helpless, holding the girl's hand. Ferko stepped toward them and covered their hands with his. "There's a connection," he said, meaning Amanda's presence and the grief that swamped them in the wake of Catherine's absence, but he realized, too, that the connection began here, with their palms and fingers touching, now interlocked, warm blood pulsing through fingertips, his pulse meeting Mary Beth's and whatever facsimile Amanda's apparition produced. He let the connection be what it would to each. Their hands were warm. The distress on Mary Beth's face vanished, was replaced by a placid air of contentment that mirrored the girl's, that perhaps mirrored his own. He remembered all those times the girl had vanished when he'd tried to get close. Now she was here, and he held her hand. It was a real hand, a child's hand. Was that the connection? Could it be so simple? He wished to know, and they did, too, it seemed, for they remained joined at the top of the stairs for some time; it wasn't clear how long.

PART III
AUGUST 2007

CHAPTER EIGHTEEN

Year after year, August signaled an end. The signal was stronger when you were young and summer meant freedom and blooming daylight that stretched into hours one associated with nighttime. But then the daylight waned, first in imperceptible increments, which crept like shadows, accelerated, until you couldn't help but notice. One could see the horizon clearly then, the lip at the edge of the canyon. The school year. Fourth grade, fifth grade, sixth.

For adults, summer was different—flatter, the way everything became flatter when you grew old, like the hills you once sledded and stood on your pedals to climb, like the Christmases and birthdays you once anticipated, even after you discovered they disappointed, again and again, until you became numb to their disappointment.

But still: temperatures rose and fell, in the quicker frequencies of night and day and the longer frequencies of seasons, while each wave—both short and long—gathered speed and blurred. Years were a collection of months, months a collection of days, days a collection of hours. Rain turned to snow, water to ice until ice melted and color returned to the landscape. April was a red balloon, flaccid in an open, pink palm. June was a red balloon, inflated and knotted and bopped by a knuckle on a warm current of air. August was a red balloon forgotten and collapsing in a dusty corner.

Mary Beth hadn't been back to the woods in weeks, not since Amanda had shown herself at home, an event that, at the time, seemed momentous. It still was, even as it had become inscrutable in the weeks that followed.

The girl had not appeared again, though her presence lingered at the top of the stairs. Mary Beth sensed it when she came in from outside, when she climbed the stairs, when she slid into her sheets at night and woke in the morning—a warm, settled feeling that started beneath her breastbone, in the vicinity of her beating heart, and radiated down into her stomach and out into her shoulders and neck, the muscles and bones in her upper arms. It was like a drug, this feeling, euphoria grounded in contentment. She could take a hit just by breathing the air in her house. She asked Gil if he felt it, too, and he said that he did, that he'd always felt it, and she eyed him suspiciously, because he wasn't a euphoria-grounded-in-contentment kind of guy; rather, he was a restlessness-grounded-in-exhaustion kind of guy. Melancholic, too, but who was she to judge? There was no reason to doubt him, with the proverbial cat (in the form of Amanda) out of the bag. But where *was* she, since the night those weeks ago with Gil at the top of the stairs?

Last night, Friday, he'd called. It was three weeks to the day since Amanda had shown herself to them. Gil wasn't coming home. Mary Beth was used to this sort of thing. It went with the bonuses, the size of which sometimes staggered her. So she understood, or said she did. But when she woke this morning, Saturday, alone, it was too much like it was before. Like Amanda had never happened. She called for Amanda but there was no Amanda. Of course there wasn't. So she got up and got dressed and packed her water bottle and left the house.

The air was gray and close, the sun behind banks of dark clouds. Nothing moved, except Mary Beth

trudging up the sidewalk and the occasional car rolling up or down Amos Avenue. Nearly everyone, it appeared, was out of town. She lifted the hair off her
neck and tied it in a ponytail.

The heat swelled in the woods beyond the empty
field. There was no shade since there was no sun—just
a darker, denser place, the leaves a blanket containing
the cumulative heat of summer. She started down the
slope to the felled tree. She sat and looked around,
wondering what would happen next. She was as still
as the air. Sweat blossomed at her hairline. She wiped
it with the palm of her hand. She uncapped her water
bottle and took a swig. Then she poured a splash into
her cupped hand and brought it across her brow. Water streamed down her face like rain. It had been a dry
summer. Maybe rain was where the day was leading.
And now she hoped for Amanda but she also hoped
for rain.

But the heavy air wouldn't budge, and the sweat
came again. She thought of her neighbors, all those
nameless shapes and shadows, who'd escaped to the
ocean or a lake in New York, upstate. Better yet,
Maine. Maybe Canada.

She'd found the boys' names—Felix and Solomon
DeGrass—in the library, in a community directory

circa 1982, the year before Amanda had hit the tree on her bicycle and died. *This tree?* Mary Beth wondered. She dug her fingertips into the grooves of the bark. Felix, the older brother, was dead. MAN, 30, PLUNGES FROM CHELSEA ROOF, DIES. The article in the *New York Times* implied something sinister—an unidentified woman the police wished to question. But there was no follow-up, at least not in the *Times* or any other news source Mary Beth could find. It was as though the story had died with Felix, and it occurred to Mary Beth that Felix's death was like Amanda's, like Catherine's—no one knew the truth. Maybe someone did, but they weren't telling. Mary Beth imagined Felix De-Grass haunting the rooftop and sidewalks and streets around the building where he fell. Or jumped. Or was pushed.

Amanda had said that it was okay, that it didn't matter why. When you were dead, you were dead. *Why* wouldn't change it.

"Amanda," Mary Beth called to the woods now. "I need to ask you a question."

She hadn't actually worked out the question. Something to the effect of *Doesn't the truth matter?* But she thought she already knew the answer. She just needed to *prove* the answer, like a scientist with a hypothesis.

"Amanda!"

The crickets went silent for a moment before resuming their song.

Solomon DeGrass knew the truth about Amanda. He guarded it in Princeton, New Jersey. What was required of Mary Beth, she realized, was a journey, a confrontation of sorts, truth-to-truth, with or without Amanda. She waited for the girl now, but the girl didn't show, and after a time Mary Beth became aware of something above her—the whisper of fingertips, the creasing and crinkling of paper. It was rain, which grew steady, drummed a patter on the leaves on the treetops. When she felt the first drop she'd go, walk up the dirt incline and out into the open field and past the school and down Amos Avenue home. It wouldn't matter that she got wet. In fact, she wished to do so, the way children wished to run through a rainstorm or the spray of a hose.

But until then she stayed beneath the patter. It was as though she were inside a tent or some manufactured rainforest habitat at the zoo, where the warm spray from jets creates humidity and a plastic dome protects the fake elements from the real ones.

The rain fell harder, and the leaves on the trees applauded. Yet she stayed dry, hoping for release, hoping that Amanda would appear.

But the woods were an umbrella, and Amanda
didn't show. Was this storm the beginning of the end of
summer? A raindrop touched her arm. Then another.
Shafts of rain had breached the leaf canopy. Rain fell
in her hair, on her shoulders, on her toes through the
nylon web of her sandals. Raindrops stained the hard
earth. She climbed the rise and followed the trail at the
top. The rain became one with the vertical landscape.
By the time she reached the open field her skin was
soaked.

CHAPTER NINETEEN

The sky contained no blue, just a gray haze that hung close to the tops of buildings, obscuring those elements one associated with sky—color and clouds and planes and the contrails they left, which, perhaps, were all one now, subsumed by the haze—though the sun's outline was visible where the haze brightened, a pop fly, a softball that Ferko would have dropped if he were in right field instead of gazing out the conference room window of the Riverfront suite. Inside: more haze. Lisa Becker sat at the table before a laptop, scrolling through a spreadsheet, while Greg Fletcher studied his screen. They were surrounded by Styrofoam and cardboard boxes, plastic forks and crumpled napkins, the wreckage of takeout. They'd worked late last night. Ferko had slept on a couch in reception. Now he was unshaven and ripe in his Friday clothes. It was Saturday afternoon. He was still unsure of his role. He was a sounding board for Greg's ideas and theories. Or maybe Greg was waiting for the opportune time to expose Ferko's irrelevance to Prauer. Greg's technical skills were surprisingly sound. Some guys could bullshit so well it was impossible to prove them wrong. Greg could support his conclusions with numbers. He had his own way, though, and it was hard to predict his answer.

And Prauer, back from vacation, two weeks fishing in Alaska, wanted an answer—the value of Grove Department Stores. He wanted to know the price at which he should start the negotiation and the price at which he should go no higher. Greg's theory still held—that certain family members wished to sell. But now, Greg believed, the family was more unified, and they all might sell at the right price—a number Greg, conveniently, claimed to be ignorant of.

He clicked keys. An e-mail? Ferko felt the urge to wander past and peek over Greg's shoulder, but he felt a deeper urge, too, emanating from some indeterminate place, where bone and tissue joined, and this latter urge was the stronger one, and it swept him from the room, thumbs to phone, redialing Jen Yoder's cell, which rang and rang and rolled to her voice mail, where she instructed the caller, in a calm voice that belied her feral nature, to leave a detailed message and she'd get back to them as soon as she could. She'd told him once she'd wanted to be an actor. Perhaps she really was one, and her voice mail greeting was Jen playing a woman with her shit together.

But Ferko had left a message earlier, something about being in the city, at work, and hoping to cop. He'd winced when he said *cop*. He was in the business of buying and selling. He understood things in those terms. But you bought milk and copped dope. Language was precise. If you used the right verb you didn't need the noun. Now he didn't wish to sound desperate, when, in fact, he was getting there—a combination of a poor night's sleep, insecurity, and proximity. Manhattan now *tasted* like dope. He felt its tug each time he boarded the PATH in Hoboken and the brake was released and the train began to coast into the tunnel that took him under the Hudson. Then the train accelerated, as though the drug itself were the engine turning the wheels, along with the benign and mundane—electricity, coal, job, paycheck. Heroin was close, even if he didn't know how to find it. He was a child, playing the game where someone hides an object, then navigates for the seeker—hot and cold. But Jen was the navigator, and she wasn't answering. He cut off the voice mail before the beep, before he substituted *hoping* in his previous message with *needing* now.

He stared at the phone. If he only knew the right keys in the right order, he'd be in business. Everything had a password—computers and accounts, records and files, encrypted e-mails.

And drug markets. They were amorphous. They appeared and disappeared like Amanda at the top of the stairs. Could he find one on his own? He could take a cab to Jen's, give her one last try via phone, buzz her door, send a *where r u?* text, and, failing all that, wander the streets, searching for the corner dance, the hand-to-hand. It was desperate and doomed, inefficient, physically and legally perilous. But, excepting disaster—a mugging or an arrest—it was a desperation he could endure alone. At least he'd be doing *some*thing.

He poked his head in the doorway of the conference room. The gray sky had darkened, it appeared, in the minute he'd stepped out to call Jen, wrapping the room and its contents—its people and paper, furniture and gadgets, wall covering and carpet, even its stale air—in a veil of fatigue.

"I've got to go," Ferko said.

Greg glanced up from the screen, raised his eyebrows in an are-you-sure? expression, even as his fingers didn't break stride on his laptop keys. Then he gave Ferko his sideways smile that said nothing.

Lisa kept her head down, where, on her screen, there were a thousand ends to fuse, Ferko imagined, cells to tie, worksheets to link. She couldn't be bothered with Ferko's crisis, which she might have imagined was existential rather than physical. Ferko supposed it was both. Or perhaps she had plans, and the faster she worked the faster she got out. Or perhaps hers was the burden of the technically proficient. Or perhaps it was more prosaic—she was doing her job to the best of her ability, proving her worth to Prauer, indirectly, through Greg, her new meal ticket. She'd managed to stay relevant even as Ferko hadn't. He gave her that.

"Call me if you need me."

"We're good." Greg fluttered his fingers before resting them on his keys.

Lisa glanced at him, then at Ferko. Then she sighed.

"Stay close," Greg said through his crooked smile.

He'd been dismissed too easily. He remained in the doorway an awkward moment, then shouldered his bag and left, imagining Greg and Lisa exchanging

meaningful looks before lowering their eyes to their
laptops and the tasks at hand.

Outside, the air was close. Tourists slogged up and
down Sixth Avenue with plastic shopping bags and a
veneer of exhaustion and dazed curiosity. Ferko passed
them with purpose, crossed Sixth and descended the
stairs to the subway station at Forty-Seventh, where the
F was pulling in. He boarded the train. There were seats,
but he stood. He was a predator, stalking the aisle with
his eyes. The passengers were the usual collection of the
down-on-their-luck, the just getting-by. Someone on
this train probably knew where to cop. Maybe they had
a Baggie in their pocket now, one they were willing to
part with for two or three times what they'd paid. Ferko
searched their faces for the friend-of-Jen hipster type,
for the hustling immigrant, the desperate. It was Saturday afternoon. Anyone into dope was probably high or
sleeping it off. The stubble on Ferko's beard grew. His
hair frizzed. The pores on his skin opened and emp-
tied. Nothing had prepared him for this. Even the past
couple of years, with Catherine gone and Mary Beth
descending. Now it was Ferko's turn. Best to descend in
a subway downtown, where no one knew him or paid
him any mind, even as he scrutinized their faces for any
glimmer of recognition, of shared purpose.

It was spitting rain when he emerged onto Second Avenue. Still nothing on his phone. He called Jen, and again got her voice mail and hung up before she finished speaking. He was a dozen blocks from her place. He could feel its pull, like some new form of gravity he'd only now sensed. The air felt different, more languid. The people looked looser, somehow, in the way that they walked and sat on benches, one knee draped over the other. If Ferko ever belonged here it was now. Yet their contented eyes refused to meet his, even while they met one another's. He wondered if he were a ghost, his spirit wandering the East Village like Amanda's wandering Glen Wood Ridge. He climbed five concrete stairs and ducked through an open doorway.

It was dark inside the Sand Bar. The TV was off. Speakers mounted on brackets high up in the corners played a chant, a soprano wailing over bursts of men's voices like a rough sea of percussion. Heaven's choir, he thought. He recognized the bartender from when he was once here with Jen. A group of college kids sat in the corner playing cards. He took a stool at the bar by himself and read the names and examined the logos on the taps. But the barman ignored him, stood, grinning in the corner, watching the kids with nostalgia, it seemed, as though watching a clip of himself and his then-friends fifteen years ago projected like some 3-D home movie recorded before they'd gotten jobs that had become careers, paired off, and married. Before responsibility and the apex that marked the end of youth and the slow, tedious descent toward death.

Ferko sat on a stool, rapping his knuckles against the bar top. Maybe this was eternity, hooked on heroin and unable even to get a beer, like Tantalus with the clear pools of water and the ripe fruit on trees. What had Ferko done to deserve the gods' wrath?

But then the bartender looked at him and said, "My man."

Ferko nodded, as though such a gesture told the bartender all he needed to know: the patron was looking for Jen Yoder, purveyor of dope. Ferko pointed to a black arm at the cluster of taps, and the bartender filled a glass with a reddish ale and set it in front of Ferko. He wrapped his hand around the base of the glass. He took a swig. Then another. Two swallows and the glass was half gone. It helped. The beer. It gave his body something to do other than register the lack of dope. He tipped the glass and swallowed the rest.

"Thirsty?" The bartender refilled the glass. Weren't bartenders supposed to be clever? Ferko sipped the fresh beer. The bartender watched him from his station by the cash register, where liquor bottles stood in a straight line like soldiers in battles centuries ago. He was in his late thirties, like Ferko, with wrinkles around his eyes freighting what was left of his youth. Ferko wasn't sure how long he could last with Prauer, in private equity, until he was exposed as a fraud. Was this Ferko's future, standing in a dark bar on a Saturday afternoon in god-awful August, pouring beers for the full-of-promise and the downward-spiraled? No wonder the guy had nothing to say.

"You know Jen Yoder." Ferko realized, as soon as he'd breathed the statement, that it was forced and desperate. He never could schmooze, even in the best circumstances. Never mind that it was near the top of the banker-adviser skill set. But now his veins were vacant, crushing from withdrawal.

The bartender squinched his face. "Who?"

Ferko slugged his beer, which he'd already hoisted by the time the bartender had asked his question. There was no need, really, to wait. He wasn't sure when he'd ever drunk a beer that tasted so good.

"Jen." He licked his lips. "Yoder. She comes in here sometimes."

The bartender waited for more, but there was no more. "A lot of people come in here," he said.

Ferko made a show of glancing around, at the empty stools and tables, at the empty chairs. Even the card game in the corner had been put on hiatus in favor of low conversation.

"*Sometimes,*" the bartender said.

Maybe he was clever after all. And maybe Ferko was, too. And would be, always, through his association with Jen.

"You know her," Ferko said. "She makes her presence known."

The bartender watched him, expecting, perhaps, a physical description. But providing one would have made Ferko sound like a detective on a bad TV show. Or a stalker.

"Why don't you call her?" the bartender asked. His eyes danced in the dim light.

"I have."

Ferko looked away. He knew the bartender's next line—*Maybe she doesn't want to be found.* Ferko didn't want to hear it. He drained his beer and slapped a twenty on the bar and hopped off the stool, dizzy with fatigue and withdrawal and two glasses of beer drunk in rapid succession.

"If I happen to see this Jen Yoder," the bartender called after him, "who should I say was looking for her?"

The kids in the corner looked up. They were Fer-ko's past; he was their future. He pushed open the glass door and ducked beneath the low, leaden sky.

Jen powered on her phone. Then she thumbed her dad's number with one hand while she covered the screen with the other. "I don't feel well," she said when he picked up.

"Well, hello to you, too."

An obvious response eluded her.

"Headache?"

"Uh-huh."

"What else?"

"Chills." She left out nausea.

"Fever?"

"I don't know," she said, which was true.

"You're not going to come and see me," he said.

"I'm sorry."

"When you were in kindergarten you got the flu on picture day."

She remembered the event, and she knew the story, which he'd told her, directly or indirectly, dozens of times since. She tightened her blanket around her shoulders and put her head on a pillow while her body shuddered.

"We sent you to school anyway," he continued. "Your mom dressed you in the clothes she'd picked out. A pink-and-white dress."

"And white tights," she said. "And black shoes."

"I don't know about those."

"Dad, I know the story." A wave of nausea rose up inside her, then stilled. She needed the call to end.

"Oh, you do?" he asked. "So, what's the point?"

A month later the picture had come. Jen looked like a ball with the air let out—miserable and defeated. The doctor and his wife had made their sick daughter go to school on picture day, and here was the proof. It had sat on the desk in her dad's study, like some kind of warning, propped against the cup that held the sharpened pencils. It was probably still in the study somewhere.

"They have picture makeup days," she said.

"They do?"

"Of course."

"I don't know about that."

She waited for him to say more. She lacked the energy herself.

"The point is to stay home, rest, and drink plenty of fluids."

"Okay."

"Clear fluids. And I don't mean gin or vodka."

"Ugh."

"You take care. I'll call you tomorrow."

The earpiece clicked, and she powered off her phone and set it facedown on top of her nightstand, then thought better, the phone being too great a temptation within arm's reach, so she mustered the energy to walk the phone to her bureau and bury it deep in the sock drawer. Then she flopped back down on her futon, spread-eagle, in her shorts and T-shirt. The air conditioner rattled in the window. A car horn honked from the street. She considered turning on the radio, something talky, but decided against it. Best not to let in any signals. Thus, the phone off and buried in the sock drawer. The shades were drawn and the lights were out. How long could one last like this? She had food in the fridge and the cupboard, toilet paper in the closet. The postman delivered her mail, and when her box was full he'd slip in a note to let her know they were collecting the rest, which she could pick up by presenting the note and a government-issued picture identification to the clerk at the post office.

She'd call in to work this week. The flu. She had some sick time.

Eventually, someone would worry. All those unanswered texts and messages. Someone would come by. It was nearly Saturday night. It could happen at any moment. Someone like Amy or Nick or Larry or Gordon—it didn't matter who—would wander by and buzz her from downstairs, maybe even piggyback in and start banging on her door and calling her name, and, despite her best efforts to check the signal, the signal would have found her, and she'd have to ignore it in a more active way.

There was a reason people fled town to kick. Everything here was a habit. The frequency, for instance, with which she checked her laptop and her phone. The texts she sent, the food she ate, and the beer she drank. The dope she copped.

Even the dogs on their leashes peed on the same trees and poles, day after day, around the block, clockwise or counter, at the whim of the walker. Jen had done her share of dog walking. Rectangles were best— four left turns or four right being the only variable.

Now she concentrated on the sound made by the window unit. How many times, she wondered, did its fan turn in a second, a minute, an hour? Each revolution was a milestone, an accomplishment, because each revolution consumed some increment of time. Her quest was monk-like—stay put. She'd succeeded for sixty-eight hours. She figured by ninety-six the worst would be over. Thus far, the pull had been steadily stronger. She felt it wash over her now until she concentrated again on the sound of the fan in the window unit, spinning fast enough, she imagined, to appear transparent without its casing. It stirred the air in her monk's cell.

Queenie still hadn't called, but Solomon DeGrass had updated his home page. New office hours, links to the four courses he was teaching this semester. It was time, Jen had told herself. First kick, then confront, then call Queenie. She liked the alliteration, the aggression imbued in the *k* and the hard *c*, in the active nature explicit in the verbs themselves. She'd written them in large capital letters on blank sheets of printer paper and taped them to the back of her closed door. Then she'd numbered them:

1. *KICK*
2. *CONFRONT*
3. *CALL QUEENIE*

It was a get-your-shit-together call to action. She had food enough, an air conditioner, electricity. When Monday morning came, she could turn on her phone long enough to call in sick.

Kick, confront, call Queenie. Jen controlled her own destiny.

The buzzer sounded, jerking her upright. It sounded again. Someone was downstairs on the sidewalk wanting to party. She'd done the same thing herself. It was Nick or Amy or Larry or Gordon. Maybe Jane. Jen had to get the word out. She needed a confidant. She wasn't looking to party. Nor was she blue-lipped on her couch. She'd *under*dosed. It wasn't a bad word. It made her think *underfed*, and she realized she'd skipped lunch.

The buzzer buzzed, insistent. She put her pillow over her head, and braced herself for the next call.

Ferko stood in front of Jen's place, finger on the gray button. He pressed it and held it. Let it go. Pressed it again, and waited. Fat raindrops fell, half-dollars on the sidewalk. Jen's entry had no cover. He could find one that did—some narrow vestibule—within eyeshot of her place. It was like a stakeout, but more desperate. Now the sky opened, and he had no choice but to sprint down Twelfth Street. He ducked under an awning, from which rain ran in a single blurry sheet and splashed the cuffs of his khakis. The window told him it was a sewing machine repair shop. Could such a business still exist? Maybe it was a front for a drug dealer. But the place was dark. The sign on the door said it had closed at one, and wouldn't reopen until ten on Monday morning.

The rain fell, and sent up a roar, like an adoring crowd after the last note had rung. He enjoyed live music. He wished to hear some tonight—with Jen and a head full of dope. Rain slapped the asphalt and concrete. It puddled and formed rivulets. It beat the canvas awning under which he stood. Even the occasional car coasting down Twelfth Street was hushed by the notes ringing off its rooftop and hood. One rolled past now, a steel drum, its music mixed with new notes, familiar ones that had him reflexively reaching for the phone in his pocket.

It was ringing.

Two-one-two, but not Jen's. Still, he tasted the cool drip of dope in the back of his throat.

"Hello."

"Gil."

"Lisa."

"Don't sound so disappointed."

"I was expecting someone else."

"Next stop, Ho-Ho-Kus?"

It was a name she liked to say. The town had a pub he and Mary Beth used to go to. A deli. A Chinese restaurant. No dope.

"I'm still downtown."

"Prauer's on his way."

Ferko tried to process this information. To his surprise, he found he could. "How much?" he asked, meaning, how much did Greg think Prauer should pay for Grove.

"A billion-one."

"That's a lot," Ferko said, because it seemed like a conclusion he could make. He hadn't been paying much attention to the details, though.

The rain fell harder now, if that was possible. Lisa said nothing, unless he missed it in the roar.

"It's pouring," he said, to fill the void. It felt comfortable to backpedal, to talk about something as obvious as the weather.

"It's dry up here in the clouds," she said.

The sky flashed, and thunder pealed off the sides of apartments as if off the walls of canyons.

"Whoa. Seriously, it's doing nothing here. Are you under cover?"

"Kind of."

"Get a cab and get back here."

"It's pouring," he repeated, meaning that any prowling cab had been hailed by now. It didn't help, of course, that he was east of First, in front of a closed sewing machine repair shop. But he wasn't going to tell her that.

"Call a car," Lisa said.

When he didn't answer, she said, "Do you want me to call one?"

"No."

It was a betrayal—Greg calling Prauer. Yet Ferko could marshal none of the requisite outrage. He stood under the awning, soaked and indifferent, contemplating his next move, knowing it had nothing to do with Lisa Becker or Greg Fletcher or Bill Prauer or Grove Department Stores. Sometime later—maybe days or weeks or months or years—he'd blame drugs for this lapse, for going out in absentia instead of in a blaze of fucked-up glory, complete with technical errors and social gaffes. He'd always imagined his undoing would be to lose Prauer a ton of money. The truth was more tedious: Ferko had been pushed aside and didn't care. Grove had led Greg to Ferko; Greg had led Ferko to Jen. Things had been heading here since the first meeting with Grove two months ago, when Greg had sat across the conference table from Ferko, the way he might have in sixth grade, at the long lunch tables in the Edgefield cafeteria. Ferko wondered whether the seed of this betrayal had been planted then.

"Gil," Lisa said.

"I'm here."

"Well, we're *here.*"

Ferko remembered, or tried to, the point he'd made to Jen about fate weeks before at Café Ivy. He'd been high. He'd made sense. So much so that his chest had swelled—in concert with his heady arguments and the dope in his blood—with a warm flush of invincibility. Now he tried to summon a similar case, to justify, if only in his head, his indifference. He was missing the dope, of course, if not the logic. He wasn't always this morose.

"Hold on," Lisa said now, "here's Greg."

"Dude," Greg said, "get back here. We're a team. I take that seriously."

Rain drummed the awning over Ferko's head.

"We're in this together," Greg pleaded. He actually pleaded, and, while Ferko processed what it meant that Greg Fletcher was pleading for his return, a memory seized him. He was on the blacktop, in this memory, at his elementary school in Edgefield, before the morning bell. All around, kids ran in flocks, while Ferko and Greg Fletcher faced each other, talking about something of rapt interest to Ferko—television, probably. Ferko looked up at Greg, who was always taller. Then other boys joined them, flanked Greg and Ferko, though not actually part of the conversation. More and more boys, a sea of faces, a who's who of fourth grade. Then, just as Ferko was about to say something to move the conversation forward, to make a point, to express a like or dislike, Greg stepped forward and pushed Ferko over the back of another boy, who'd sneaked up behind Ferko and gotten down on all fours. Ferko fell. The boys ran. The bell rang. Later, in the boys' room, he pinched a disc of dried blood the size of a quarter from the hair on the back of his head.

"This is your deal," Greg said now. "Prauer will be here in an hour. You're presenting."

"I'm *presenting*?"

There was movement on the other end—fierce and quick, the phone conveyed from room to room. "I did this for *you*." Greg's voice held an urgency Ferko had never imagined Greg could muster. Maybe in the huddle on fourth and ten, but Ferko had never been in that huddle.

"For *me*?" Lightning flashed. He braced for a thunderclap that never came.

"Prauer will be here in an hour. What do you want me to tell him?"

He considered a smart-ass reply, but coming up with one was beyond his mental, emotional, and physical capacity.

"I don't feel well," he said, which had the advantage of being true enough.

A couple across the street caught his eye. They were small, thin, walking with a singular purpose, without umbrellas or raincoats, their hands stuffed into front pockets of black jeans. They wore T-shirts and sneakers, black or soaked black by rain. The landscape was colorless—wet asphalt and gray concrete and stone, the rain that filled the gray sky—except for the couple's hair. There was a glint of red in the woman's and purple in the man's. They were friends of Jen's, the couple who'd joined them at Ivy's once, a few weeks before.

He hung up and stowed his phone and leaped over the gutter, where rainwater collected from the streets and sidewalks and flowed toward the river. There were no cars. The couple on the other side stopped and turned. All he could think of to say was "Hey!" He couldn't remember their names.

"Hey," they said in unison, without a glint of recognition, unfazed, it appeared, by the pounding rain, by the water that dripped from their chins and noses and the knobby bones protruding from their wrists.

"You're Jen's friends," he said with a surplus of hope, enough, perhaps, to turn a dead-end statement into a question awaiting reply. "Jen Yoder," he added, conscious of landing the last syllable. He tapped his toe on the pavement to add a period.

"Yeah," the guy said anyway, answering the question that hadn't been asked. His hair was black with a purple stripe. Matted and soaked, he looked like a sad pet with a distinctive mark. His name was Dave, Ferko remembered. And the girl was Tina.

"Ferko!" she said. Her eyes flashed in the gloom.

"Have you seen our girl?" Ferko glanced across the street toward Jen's building, the steel door, the rusted mailboxes and buzzers flanking it.

Dave's eyes raked the building's face. His long lashes blinked in the deluge. "Her lights are out," he said.

"It's daytime," Tina said.

"It's raining."

"It's pouring."

"The old man is . . . " Dave sang.

She turned to Ferko. "Text her."

". . . snoring."

"I have," Ferko said. "Texted, called, buzzed."

"Napping," Dave said.

"We're copping," Tina said. "You in?"

Ferko's gait matched theirs, stride for stride, hands in front pockets. He remembered he had an umbrella, one that folded and telescoped—an amazing feat of engineering—into a baton in his bag, but he left it there. Best to follow Tina and Dave's lead. They walked east, then south, then east, block after block. Ferko's blue shirt turned translucent. "Cop spot," Dave said at one corner, and Ferko followed his eyes to a form in a black poncho under an awning across the street, but they turned the corner and walked east. By Tenth Street the deluge had tempered. By Ninth it had nearly stopped. Drops fell into puddles and made tiny wakes, like stones lobbed from the shore of a still lake.

They came across a guy in a red anorak, a hood pulled over his head. Tina stopped. Dave and Ferko with her. This was the first person they'd seen since the guy in the poncho, and Ferko realized they were the only ones out in the rain. Buyers and sellers. It was that easy.

"Hey," Tina said.

"Hey." The guy studied the three of them. He had a red beard that looked a few days old. A freckled face. A disinterested gaze.

"Ferko," Tina said, "how much do we have?"

"What do you—" Ferko started to ask, but then thought better. "I don't know," he said. It occurred to him she was asking about money. He knew what he had—a little more than a hundred—but he didn't know what she or Dave had.

"Do we have sixty?" she asked, and Ferko got it. His heart beat harder and filled his arteries. He felt grateful. With Greg and Lisa in the Riverfront conference room, Ferko had had no role. So he'd bailed. Now he had one, an important one, a role he knew how to fulfill. He was *buying*. For the three of them. It was a magnanimous gesture, their bringing him here. It was Ferko's turn to reciprocate.

"Yeah," he said.

"Pay Red, then."

Ferko fished three twenties out of his wallet, then folded and wedged them between the knuckles of his first and second fingers, like a magician with a handkerchief, some sort of sleight of hand, and Red produced a handful of glassine bags, each with a portion of white powder, from the unzipped pouch of his anorak. He exchanged the money for the bags in a single, fluid motion. Ferko closed his fist. Then opened it.

"Stow it," Tina said. "Someplace dry." They turned to go, to continue east, the way they'd been walking. Ferko stuffed the bags into his front pocket. It was a dilemma he hadn't anticipated, keeping the stuff dry. His shoulder bag was soaked. Was it dry inside? Maybe in the zippered pocket where he kept his thumb drive and ibuprofen? He'd find out soon. They'd go someplace, perhaps around the corner, and divvy up the dope and then use. He cupped the bags in his dry palm. The sky brightened. Red was gone, vanished down the alley. Dave and Tina hustled across Ninth Street, holding hands. Ferko turned to follow, but two guys were converging on him from the east and west. They were youngish guys dressed in blue-and-black tracksuits and white running shoes with various curvy stripes. They walked toward him, with cautious sideways steps, hands behind their backs. A car glided down the street, its lights flashing, and braked. The passenger door opened. Then the driver's door. Uniformed officers stood behind them. "Hold on, sir," one said, which, for a brief moment, presented a false note of hope. The police, after all, served and protected. But then one of the tracksuit guys was on him. "Turn around," he barked. "Spread your feet and put your hands against the wall."

They frog-marched him, flanked by the guys in tracksuits, to the precinct, which, it turned out, was just around the corner from the cop spot. Red was either an idiot or a genius. But he wasn't here to cower or boast. Ferko wondered whether he'd been set up. Bad luck. Ferko luck. They took his photo. They measured his height and weight. They took his blood pressure. It was like going through intake at the hospital (complete with the ID bracelet) except no one expected him to answer the questions the clerks asked, which ranged from the mundane—reading from his driver's license: "Are you still at 4540 Woodberry Road in Glen Wood Ridge, New Jersey?"—to the sarcastic—"Bad day, huh?" All the while the shorter of the two tracksuit officers stood behind him and guided him from station to station, from clerk to clerk. Ferko wasn't cuffed. He wasn't even under arrest, as best he could tell. He kept his mouth shut, was as compliant as silence allowed. The hallway opened to a room, a bullpen with desks and chairs. Activity swirled. Uniforms. Computers and printers. Ringing phones. Fried chicken and lo mein. English and Spanish. Cops who looked like crooks, and crooks who looked like cops. Firearms strapped to hips and ribs. Bursts of laughter like automatic weapons. A flat-screen on a wall showing the Yankees. Someplace sunny. Oakland. Posada up. One on, one out.

And Ferko looked—what? Stricken, he imagined. Maybe he wasn't the good guy or the bad guy. Maybe he was the victim. Maybe he was the witness. They

didn't stop Dave or Tina, even as they'd walked hand
in hand in front of the squad car. With Ferko against
the wall, his back facing Ninth Street, he'd sensed them
watching the proceedings from a safe distance. And no
one ran down the alley after Red, either. They took Ferko's wallet, his phone and keys and a receipt for a milk
shake he'd bought hours earlier, hoping the winning
combination of fat and sugar would ward off his need
for dope. They found that, too, and asked, "What's
this?" like in the movies. Then they went through his
shoulder bag, with its notes from meetings, presenta-
tions never filed, papers he'd been carrying for months,
since before Jen, before dope, before Greg and Grove,
and all the while the search was happening, while his
legs were spread and his hands were against the wall,
prostrate, he remembered the times with Jen, how
she'd handled everything—the money, the dope, each
aspect of the wordless transactions. He'd gone with her
only twice. Mostly, by the time he arrived, she'd already
copped. He could tell by the settled look in her eyes,
by the serene angles at the corners of her mouth. She'd
protected him. So much that Ferko never really felt
he owned it, even if it was his money she used. Now
he owned it, and even this seemed somehow okay. He
remembered before, and there was nothing there but

thick walls. Isolation. His and Mary Beth's. All that had been razed. By Jen. By Amanda. Not by dope. He couldn't remember ever wanting it.

When the clerks were done with their questions, the tracksuit guy led him into a room with gray walls and a door with a small, square window, head-high. There was nothing on the walls but scuff marks and dirt. A laminated table stood in the center, surrounded by three chairs—one on each of the long ends and another pushed against the wall farthest from the door. The tracksuit guy paused in the doorway, looked at Ferko, and sniffed. Then he shut the door, and Ferko was alone.

He didn't know how long it had been. They'd taken his watch and phone, and there was no clock. He could mark time by watching the heads go back and forth in the hall beyond the door. He wasn't even sure if the door was locked, but he wasn't going to try it, either.

Years ago, before they were married, Ferko and Mary Beth had taken a trip to a spa out west, with mineral baths and hot springs, and they'd paid extra for a hot wrap, where you were placed in a windowed room heated by the baths, and wrapped in hot towels, head to toe, so that only your nose was exposed. Then the spa people left you there, all wrapped up, but you weren't allowed to talk in the spa, so no one explained to Ferko that he should get up when he'd had enough, that no one was coming back to tap him on the shoulder and let him know that it was time. So he'd lain there and waited, feeling claustrophobic, trying to decide how much time had gone by. When he couldn't stand it any longer, he sat up and unwrapped the towels. Mary Beth was gone. He found her in one of the pools outside. "How'd you like it?" she'd asked.

"It was awful."

Ferko and Mary Beth hadn't gone away in a long time. It was a simple thing to travel. You chose a place and made arrangements and booked a flight and packed a bag. There were lots of places to go.

The door groaned, and the two cops in the tracksuits filled the opening. The smaller cop held a red file folder and a pen, followed by the taller cop with a single sheet of paper, folded once. "My name is Officer Thompson," the taller one said, "and this is Officer Henry." He unfolded the piece of paper in his hand. "Gilbert S. Ferko of Glen Wood Ridge, New Jersey. Have you ever been to Glen Wood Ridge, Officer Henry?"

"Can't say I have." His voice was thin, unsure, conveying inexperience in its upper registers.

Good cop, bad cop, Ferko thought. Smart cop, dumb cop. The bankers and the lawyers played the same games in conference rooms uptown.

"Me, neither," Thompson said. He dragged a chair from the far end of the table, twisted it around and placed one running shoe on its seat and leaned an elbow on his knee. Henry stayed by the door.

"The tests came back on that stuff you were holding. Do you know what they showed?"

Ferko knew enough not to say anything, but it seemed impolite to ignore the question completely. He shook his head.

"Of course you don't." Thompson's smile showed his teeth, which were remarkably white. "You're not going to talk to us, are you, Gilbert?" He left a pause, and Ferko found himself in a staring contest he couldn't possibly win. Thompson's eyes were mapped with red lines. He looked as though he hadn't slept in days, the bulk of the hours spent winning staring contests with the weak and famished, with addicts in withdrawal.

Ferko blinked and glanced toward the door, where the window revealed heads passing by at an impressive clip and frequency. The pull of heroin had been replaced by a satisfying numbness that occupied his entire core.

"That's good," Thompson's voice boomed. He removed his foot from the seat of the chair, draped his fingers across the back, and stood on his toes. "Because we haven't read you your rights. Seems that stuff you were holding was heroin, Gilbert. Low-grade, which I applaud." Thompson winked. "Saves lives." He took a breath, and paused. It was Ferko's turn to speak, to defend the product's quality, safety, and value. When he didn't, Thompson continued:

"You're under arrest for criminal possession of a controlled substance in the seventh degree, an A misdemeanor in New York State."

He stepped back and Henry stepped forward, a simple bit of choreography that, Ferko imagined, the two had executed hundreds of times.

"You have the right to remain silent," Henry said. "Anything you say can and will be used against you in a court of law. You have the right to speak to an attorney, and to have an attorney present during any questioning. If you cannot afford a lawyer, one will be provided for you at government expense."

He stepped back, and the two officers beamed at each other and then at Ferko. A phone rang. Thompson's. He put it to his ear. "Yeah?" A sound like a mouse from the earpiece. "Yeah?" He screwed up his face, his eyes focused on the far wall. "Ye-ah?" he drawled, two syllables. Then he spun on his heels and pulled the doorknob and left the room. "Who?" he asked, as the door closed behind him.

"Ruh-roh," Henry said, bobbing on his toes.

"What now?" Ferko asked, inexplicably emboldened by Thompson's hasty exit and Henry's Scooby-Doo reference.

"We"—he hesitated—"wait for Officer Thompson."

"No, I mean in the big picture. What can I expect next?" He had questions, but he was also looking for an advantage. Sometimes the less experienced adversaries would tell you things they shouldn't. "I get a call, right?"

"You watch too much television."

"We all do," Ferko said. Actually, he watched very little, but he used to watch more, which was how he knew about the phone call. "My wife is probably worried. I want to tell her I'm safe in police custody, and not dead in some alley."

Ferko left silence to see if Henry would fill it. But he didn't, and the room stayed quiet—Ferko in his chair and Henry on his feet—for a full minute before the door opened and Thompson, still on his phone, filled the entry. He stood, hunched, and squinted at

the far wall, as though whoever was on the other end
were actually a tiny figure projected there, and the
harder Thompson squinted the better he could hear.
Foot traffic blurred behind him, left and right.

"Yes, sir," he said, and crooked a finger at his partner, and Henry, ever obedient, stepped in to receive
the message whispered in his ear. They looked at each
other, shared a conspiratorial nod, before Thompson
turned and exited. The door groaned and shut.

"Someone important?" Ferko asked. He had the
sense that it was just him and Officer Inexperience
from here forward.

"Oh, yeah," Henry said, drawing out the syllables
to maximum effect.

Ferko considered the hierarchy: precinct chief to
district chief to police chief to mayor. Was it that flat?
Bill Prauer was friends with the mayor, and Ferko entertained a brief fantasy in which Prauer, concerned
by Ferko's absence at Riverfront and unsatisfied with
Greg's answers on Grove, had hunted Ferko down, put
out an APB and tracked him here and demanded his
release. But then he remembered waking up this morning on the couch in the Riverfront lobby. It felt like
weeks ago, days since he'd left Greg and Lisa in the Riverfront conference room. Ferko imagined them now,

presenting their case to Prauer. Or maybe that meeting was done—mission accomplished—and Prauer was on the phone now with Roy Grove's lawyer, Horowitz, with belated condolences over the death of his client. Yuk, yuk, yuk. Then pitching a meeting with the surviving Groves. Could Horowitz make that happen? Prauer could be impetuous like that. He turned on a dime, made unpredictable bets that made millions. It was part of his mystique.

"You want to call your wife," Henry said.

Actually, Ferko wanted to call Jen, but said, "She's going to wonder what the hell happened."

"She looking to party, too?" Henry asked.

"What's with you guys?"

Henry shrugged. All the time in the world.

CHAPTER TWENTY

It was Monday morning before she called her dad again. He answered hello with a rushed anxiousness, followed by animated relief once she said hi.

"What's wrong?" she asked. It wasn't like him to worry about her.

"I've been trying to call."

"I turned my phone off. I wasn't feeling well, remember?"

She expected him to ask if she was drinking enough water. It was where he usually started, with her and with his patients when he'd been in practice. *Hydrated organs are happy organs,* he liked to say, and she'd always pictured hers as pink, slippery fish, writhing in the clean pools that filled her body's cavities, because she heeded his advice and drank lots of water. She expected that her organs *were* happy organs; though less so lately, with the substances—powdered and liquid—she'd been consuming. But she was clean, four days and drinking lots of water. She opened the fridge and grabbed a bottle, along with a stick of butter and some crackers—also in the fridge, to keep from the roaches. He sometimes asked her about eating, too, and she realized she hadn't been all that good on that front.

When he didn't answer, she said, "I'm feeling a little better," to assure him.

"Sometimes I don't know what you're up to."

She felt the weight of withdrawal then, a flush of nausea, something solid pressed against her, a concrete wall. The morning had gone well. She'd managed to sleep. She put the butter and the crackers on the dining table, and twisted open the top of the water bottle. "You're not supposed to," she said, recovering. She took a swig. "I'm thirty-eight."

"I got a call yesterday from Ferko. He says he can't reach you and thought maybe you were staying with me. So I try to call you. It goes straight to voice mail. I try you later. Same thing. Last night. Same thing. I couldn't sleep, imagining the worst."

"Dad." Jen felt it now—something had attached itself to the place in the pit of her stomach where the butterflies flapped their wings. But this something was solid, weighted, and it told her she wasn't getting off dope. In fact, it told her that right now a line of dope would be good; it was close, available, and wasn't it great that she had a day off from work to get a bag and get herself right again?

"Then, this morning, I still can't reach you. I tried your office but you're not there. Then some guy named Nick calls. Do I know him?"

"Nick?"

"Says he's your friend."

She sighed into the mouthpiece.

"Nice kid," her dad said. "He hasn't been able to reach you since Saturday."

"You don't know him," she said, answering the question he'd asked but had since moved on from.

"Why's he calling?"

She thought she detected accusation in his tone. It wasn't like him to judge her.

"Then I hang up with Nick, and guess who calls me in the next instant?" Her dad didn't give her a chance to guess. "Ferko, asking if I've heard anything."

The thing in the pit of her stomach swelled. She'd assumed she was on her own. She realized now she wasn't.

"I'm sorry, Dad."

"I was about to call the police."

"It was a bad idea to turn off my phone," she said, but she didn't believe it. She hadn't gone about it in the right way, was all. She should have issued a warning.

"Well, I'm relieved," he said, with the sort of finality that indicated that the difficult portion of the conversation was over.

"It was a misunderstanding," she said.

She waited, but so did her dad.

"It was unnerving," he said after a while. "I couldn't find you."

"I'm fine," she said.

He gasped. Was he crying?

"Dad?"

"Tell me you're okay," he said after another moment.

"I'm okay. I'm sick, but I'm getting better."

"You call me. If you don't, I'll call you. Leave your ringer on. You'd better answer."

The text messages scrolled in a long, unbroken string, symbols bunched together and piled up. She didn't think she could face them. She didn't think she could follow the tiny letters that formed the indiscernible words. There were phone calls, too. New messages waiting. She wondered whether she'd need to toss the phone and get a new number in order to stay clean. She clicked on Ferko's two-oh-one, the first number she saw. He answered on the first ring.

"You called?" she asked.

"Hey!" he nearly shouted. "Are you pissed at me?"

"For what?"

"Oh, thank *God.*"

"For what?" Then she said, "I've been sick," which, quite suddenly, felt like a lie, self-inflicted as her condition was. When you're hungover, you don't say you're sick. You say you feel awful.

"I'm not feeling well," she said.

"Where've you been?"

"At home."

"I stopped by Saturday. You weren't home."

When she didn't answer, he said, "We got busted."

"Who?"

"Me, Tina, and Dave. Except they skated and watched me do the perp thing from a safe distance across the street. It was like Paramus all over again."

"I didn't stick around and watch."

"You skated."

"*I* was holding," she said. "You weren't."

"This time I was."

"Oh, shit."

"I've never had more than a speeding ticket. Now I'm in databases. I'm probably on the no-fly list."

She took it as a good sign he could make jokes, if those were jokes. They sounded like jokes. She took it as a good sign she could talk to Ferko about his misadventures without impulse blossoming inside her. The sliver of sky through her window was blue. The sun reflected off the dull surface of her parquet floor.

"What do you have, a cold? The flu?"

"I guess."

"You know that sewing machine repair shop?"

"Which one?"

"How many are there? The one on your street. It's never open."

"It is sometimes. It's kind of random."

"Is it legit?"

"They're Bulgarians. I don't sew."

"It says it's open from ten to four. It's not open."

"Where *are* you?"

"I'm here. On Twelfth Street."

"Me too," she said.

"Small world. Get down here. Let's go."

She kept her foot in the open door and leaned out the entryway and breathed the outdoors for the first time in days. It felt like fall. Not cool, exactly, but not hot, either. The humidity, which had been a near-constant presence since late June, was gone. An actual breeze stirred, had pushed out the bad in favor of the good, thick arrows copied and pasted onto the meteorologist's map, the jet stream a roller coaster, pushing high into Canada, along the shores of lakes where French speakers camped and moose lapped water from shallow pools, and down into New England and the Mid-Atlantic and America's largest city. Ferko was still a few doors down. He wore gray shorts and a white T-shirt with blue piping at the neckline and cuffs around his biceps, which, Jen noted with surprise, revealed definition. He hadn't shaved in days; his hair was a shock. She supposed hers looked worse. When she'd last checked beneath the dim bulb in her bathroom her complexion was pallid, her eyes sallow. Ferko looked well enough, despite having been busted two days earlier. Had he scored, after all? His pupils said no. The smile pasted above his scruffy chin infected his face with optimism. He opened his arms, oblivious to (or at least unalarmed by) her appearance, and enfolded her in them and squeezed. She let him, like a patient dog. When he let her go, his fingers encircled the braided vine inked on her wrist. "Your shoes," he said.

She looked at her bare feet.

"Where are your shoes?"

"Upstairs."

He waited.

"I'm sick." There, she said it again. That little lie. She'd have to tell him, about kicking at least. He expected to get high. She knew that much.

"Come on," she said, and he followed her into the dark hall, practically black when the door shut behind them, and up the stairs to her apartment. She let him in

"I wasn't expecting company."

"It's okay." He glanced about, at the remnants of her breakfast on the coffee table, a spot of cereal and milk in the bottom of a bowl, cracker crumbs on a napkin, empty glasses from yesterday and the day before. She lay on the sofa, and Ferko took the futon. The TV played soundlessly, a commercial for a cleaning product. She reached for the remote and switched it off.

She closed her eyes. Then opened them. He was watching her. "Have you quit your job?" she asked.

"I called in sick."

"Copycat," she joked. "What happened Saturday?"

He shrugged, and looked around the apartment as though he'd misplaced something. Then he told her how he'd been at work Saturday, how he needed to score and couldn't reach her, so he left work and took the subway down, and still couldn't reach her but he ran into Tina and Dave, looking to cop, and Ferko tagged along with them. They bought from some white guy on Ninth, right by the precinct, it turned out. An idiotic cop spot. A black-and-white pulled up and two guys in tracksuits descended.

"Tracksuits?" she asked.

"Who wears tracksuits, right? My parents in the seventies."

"Undercover cops in the aughts."

"That's just weird," he said. "*The aughts*. A hundred years ago they didn't say *the aughts*. They said *the nineteen hundreds*."

"Did they?" She considered it. "You can't say *twenty hundreds*. That sounds stupid."

"And *the aughts* doesn't?" He smiled.

"You're in a surprisingly good mood."

He shrugged. "I'm glad to see you."

She, too, felt decidedly better, cocooned rather than imprisoned, no longer isolated. The back-and-forth with Ferko helped. Her heart beat faster, her blood infused with adrenaline. She felt merely hungover. It reminded her of college on weekend mornings, rehashing the prior

night's events with her roommates and the residents on
her hall, when the coincidences piled one on top of the
other and she was starting to see how the world worked,
that there were consequences for bad behavior, but these
consequences were tempered by youth and contained
by the self-selecting microcosm of the Columbia campus. The strongest substance she'd used then was vodka.
Now she swigged from her water bottle.

"It's a misdemeanor," he said. "I got a desk appearance ticket." He made air quotes. "I need to appear in
September. If I don't I'm fucked."

"Did you post bail?"

"Not required."

"That's efficient," she said.

"I can't believe you don't know this stuff."

She'd always wondered about the process, but was
never curious enough to figure it out. The risk seemed
that remote.

"You have a lawyer?" she asked.

"Bob."

"Bob the lawyer," she said.

"He came up on the search engine."

"That's how you got a lawyer?"

"Criminal possession, controlled substance, seventh
degree." He paused a second, then added, "Manhattan."

"That's the search that produced Bob," she concluded.

He pointed at her, a single downward motion with his index finger. A checkmark.

"I'm surprised there's not a printout taped to the wall in the perp lounge," she said. "Or a bullpen of lawyers, queued up for well-heeled users like you."

"Bob says disorderly conduct. Noncriminal for a first offense. They'll send me to counseling. He says it would be good to start early. That's why I'm here."

"For counseling?"

"Bob's office is at Second and Fourteenth. I just met with him. But that's not a bad idea. Counsel me."

"Say no to drugs?"

"Platitudes!" he said.

The sign on the back of her door—kick, confront, call Queenie—was in plain sight. She was glad that Ferko hadn't noticed or asked about it. It was clear she'd need to tell him about kicking, though it seemed impossible to explain Felix DeGrass and his brother Solomon and the possible audition with Queenie. Suddenly Jen's plan seemed overly ambitious and complicated. If one piece didn't work, none would. A wave of nausea coursed through her and she shuddered. She hoped it didn't show.

"I'm past due," she said. "I've been lucky. Too lucky. I've used up my luck."

"What does *that* mean?"

When she didn't answer, he said, "Let's go."

"No."

"You're not that sick."

"Apparently you are, though."

He straightened his legs, crossed one ankle over the other. He had all day.

"You haven't told her."

He studied Jen

"Mrs. Ferko," she said, "about your arrest."

When he shrugged, she said, "You *do* need counseling. Or therapy."

"You've got the couch."

She rolled on her side and brought her knees toward her stomach, placed her hands beneath her head on top of the pillow. She waited. That was what therapists did. They waited, then passed the tissues. She had a box in front of her on the coffee table. Jen waited, but Ferko did, too. She closed her eyes. When she opened them, she said, "You blew off work, for what—to get high?"

"I had to meet Bob."

"*Tell* her," Jen said, meaning Mary Beth. She'd grown weary, quite suddenly, of *Mrs. Ferko*. Yet *Mary*

Beth seemed too intimate for someone she'd never met.

His shrug conveyed an air of indifference.

"You're an asshole."

"You like to call people assholes. It's your go-to."

"There are a lot of assholes." She looked in his eyes in what she hoped was a meaningful way.

"How about dumbshits? Or pantloads? Or jerk-offs?"

"I'm kicking." There, she said it. "That's what this is about."

She'd never before thought of her apartment as quiet. There were noises in the hallway. In the units upstairs and down. Cars on the street. Even in the middle of the night, when she woke at odd hours. Now there was nothing. She watched him.

"Like, quitting?" he asked.

She nodded.

"Why?"

"Because I want to."

"But why do you want to?"

"I can't tell you why." It was true enough. The story of Felix DeGrass was hers alone. It would soon be the brother's. She wasn't sure how that would go. Maybe then she could tell others. Maybe Ferko. "It's really going to happen this time," she added.

He squinched his eyes. "You've tried before?"

"Sort of."

He crossed his arms. "You said you could quit anytime you wanted."

"Yeah, and I never really wanted to before."

Years ago, of course, she'd made the link between Felix's death and the dope she used. But it had taken all this time to make the link in reverse: if she could get clean, she could come clean. It was that simple. She sat up, the blanket wrapped around her legs, and tapped out a cigarette from the open pack on the coffee table. She turned the top toward him. He raised his open palm—pass. She struck a match. The tip sparked and flared. She brought the smoke into her mouth, her throat, deep into her lungs, then exhaled toward the ceiling.

He stood. "Can I get a glass of water?"

"There's a bottle in the fridge."

"I don't want the pure stuff. I'm counting on trace amounts of drugs in the city water." Still, she heard him rooting in the refrigerator.

She was having fun, she realized. Was it the nicotine talking? And what if it was? She'd spent the weekend denying her dependence. She'd set a goal and achieved that goal—alone—and emerged intact on a sunny Monday morning. She could add a new goal, up the stakes, and drag from the drug world the last person she'd dragged in. She didn't know the twelve steps, but she knew enough people who did. They were *noble gestures*. That was all. This one surely qualified. Plus, Jen liked its symmetry. Plus, the target was here, joking and drinking nothing harder than bottled water.

"Can you open the window?" she asked when he returned.

"Oh, thank God." He set the bottle on the dining table, parted the thin curtains, and opened the sash.

A stereo played from a car coasting past. A dog barked. A breeze blew the curtains, which unfurled like flags.

"Remember that scene in *The Exorcist*?" Ferko asked.

Jen shook her head.

"A breeze blows through an open window and moves the curtains in the little girl's room. The audience understands that this is the moment when the girl becomes possessed."

"Regan," Jen said. "That's a scary movie."

"We're afraid of the outdoors. That's what that means."

"I'm not."

"You've been hiding in your apartment for days."

"You've no idea what I'm going through."

"I think I do."

Jen guessed he meant his own withdrawal—the need to score, the chances taken, the arrest. But then she remembered the mythical Mary Beth, at home with the windows closed and the shades drawn. Jen pulled the blanket tight around her and lay on her side.

"Your dad's ghosts inhabit buildings," Ferko said. "They don't fly in through open windows."

She closed her eyes.

"They've got reasons to be there," he said.

"You should talk to him about it."

"But they're not really scary, are they? Not like the devil that blows in through Regan's window."

It was the thing she'd asked as a girl, listening to her father's stories. *Aren't ghosts scary?* She'd wanted to know against her better judgment. He'd told Jen he understood why people were curious about ghosts. Scary was part of their attraction. The unknown frightened people. Indeed, as a boy, he'd been taken by the stories of the Hurlingham ghost on his block in Washington Heights. People told ghost stories, sought ghost stories, for the charge that came from the inexplicable, the phenomena unexplained by the Einsteins and Edisons and Newtons. Gravity, sure, but apparitions? Traveling through walls? He explained all this to Jen, when she was a child, when she asked whether ghosts were supposed to be scary. But he was a doctor, a man of reason, of science. And he also told her that phenomena could be explained, through biology, chemistry, and physics. Ghosts, perhaps, were surges of energy. It had disappointed her then, and it wasn't until later, when the books were published and Jen read them, that she realized the truth, according to her father, lay somewhere in the vast spectrum bridging the explicable with the baffling. But between her dad's initial explanation and her reading and understanding of the books' narratives, her mother got sick. Then her mother died. Jen was twelve, on the cusp of puberty. All she had was a father, a doctor, who knew all about girls' bodies, women's bodies, but couldn't even braid hair. And the things her father wasn't, or wasn't able to do, became as tangible as the mother and the things the mother had been able to do. This, to Jen, became a ghost: a presence gone, a vacancy. Years later, at Columbia, she studied drawing, and learned about negative space. She studied script writing, and learned the power of silence. But before she did, her mother appeared in Jen's dreams.

This dream mother was the mother at the end—the gravely ill one, the one with the wig, the hair too dark and straight. As time passed, as the dreams became less frequent, her mother's presence in them faded. The outlines were there, as was the wig, but the colors were washed out, the voice weak, a hoarse whisper that said inconsequential things. This, too, became a ghost. And now, years later, the dreams were even less frequent, but still they came, and her father, who hadn't been blind when Jen's mother was alive, now was, in Jen's dreams. Everything had aged but the house and the mother, and the mother, Jen realized, had become a part of the house, a thing left on the floor, an obstacle to step around as Jen went from room to room or up the stairs to the bedroom her parents once shared.

"We've got a ghost at home," Ferko was saying now. "Amanda."

Jen couldn't shake the image of her mother inhabiting the Edgefield house in her dreams.

"You don't believe me," he said.

"I do. Tell me."

"She comes and goes at the top of the stairs. Appears and disappears." He crossed his legs at the ankles. "But it's not scary. One moment she's there and the next she's not. Like film edits."

"Sounds jarring."

Ferko shrugged. "She's just a girl."

"Like those twins in *The Shining*?"

"Umm, no."

"The Hollywood version of ghosts," Jen said.

"Tell your dad."

"*You* tell him."

"I have questions."

"Ask him."

The white curtains billowed from a breeze that dipped from the rooftops.

"Seriously," she said, "he'd get a kick out of it."

"She's an infrequent visitor," Ferko said. He was haggard, unshaven, awaiting his court appearance, missing work. For all she knew, he was unemployed. He could have interrupted himself at any moment, said, *Let's go* or *Let's score*, but the way he was sitting, sneaker heels on the coffee table, told her he wouldn't. Instead he said, "Mary Beth sees her a lot."

It was Monday, noon, the middle of August. Ferko had a ghost. Jen felt better, clean. The weather had turned and pointed toward the next season.

CHAPTER TWENTY-ONE

He left in the afternoon, expecting traffic but encountering little. He drove crosstown on Fourteenth, then uptown on Eighth. He stuck an elbow out the open window. Something had altered during the course of the day, hanging out with Jen with the front window open, the white curtains waving. Some great weight had been lifted. Perhaps it was her suggestion—demand?—that he tell Mary Beth. Everything. He imagined the conversation, and it didn't bring dread. It hadn't been a mistake. The dope or the arrest. There was nothing to apologize for. It was another way to grieve, like Mary Beth in bed with the curtains drawn. It wasn't over. He could have zipped home now, confronted her absence instead of her presence, as he had

on all those other days and nights since the collision
that took Catherine. He still wanted dope. It wasn't
over. Maybe it never would be. Maybe it was an urge he
would need to manage from here on out, in certain set-
tings, in certain weather, in certain moods. He needed
to be *mindful.* That's what the therapist had advised
Ferko and Mary Beth way back when, the month they
went together, when they tried that. *Mindful.* It was
that simple, Ferko had understood. He didn't know
why you needed an advanced degree to dispense com-
mon sense. He could manage his urge. He managed it
now up Eighth Avenue, past apartment buildings and
dry cleaners and pizza joints that lined the street. Past
hipsters with hair falling in their eyes. Past art galleries, the Chelsea Hotel. How much dope in the past
fifty years had been shot or snorted or smoked on this
one block alone? The buildings blurred. He could head
north, then bang a right—east—on the next one-way.
He could be at Riverfront's offices in five minutes. It
was another world, one he couldn't manage. *Mindful*
was no use. Once Mary Beth couldn't manage. Now
she could. He hoped.

He turned left, where the sign pointed him toward
the Lincoln Tunnel, and he followed the other cars
down the ramp. Lanes narrowed, then disappeared.

Cars slowed in the bottleneck but didn't stop. They were sucked into the tunnel's dark, open mouth, then spat onto the Jersey side, back in the bright sunshine.

She was sitting on the front porch, the top step, in the sunlight, when he pulled into the driveway. A white cat with gray spots lay on its side on the second step beside her. It lifted its head, and turned indifferently when Ferko emerged from the car.

"Who's that?" he asked, and closed the car door.

"Her collar says Daisy."

"Who's Daisy?"

Mary Beth shrugged. "My friend?"

"You don't like cats."

She shrugged again.

Daisy stretched a paw and shielded her eyes from the sun. He sat next to them.

"What's with the beard?" she said. "And the clothes."

"I had an appointment."

"With the homeless?"

"I called in sick."

"Okay." Mary Beth waited, prescient. Maybe Amanda, in her sleuthy omnipotence, had ratted him out.

"Where's our ghost?" he asked.

Mary Beth flattened her mouth, raised her eyebrows and the tips of her shoulders for a full second before returning his gaze. Two girls on bicycles pedaled past on the sidewalk, followed by a mom, running with a dog, and a gust that rustled the leaves on the young trees. In two months they'd turn and drop. Daisy flicked her tail. Mary Beth awaited an explanation.

"Heroin," he said. "Dope. I've been using."

She narrowed her eyes, and he told her about Jen, about everything—the bike accident, buying dope, snorting dope, and the mall thing, complete with the mannequin act, the mall cop who stopped him and let him go. It was a story that defied logic, he realized now, that held no connective tissue between its juxtaposed events, comprised no causality. But he told it, and when he'd gotten through that first night he paused.

"What are you saying?" she asked.

"I got busted. This past Saturday. In the city. Real cops. I was charged with possession."

A breeze stirred her hair, the ringlets she favored now that it had grown longer, now that she cared how it looked.

"What else are you saying?" she asked.

"I don't know. Isn't that enough?"

"If that's all there is."

He tried to gauge where this was going. A car trundled past, too slow, it seemed. Ferko wondered if the driver had braked to get a gander at the actual residents of the blue house with the white trim, outside in the actual sunshine. When he and Mary Beth had moved here, he'd assumed they'd know their neighbors. Then they never did.

"I expected that you'd leave me," she said. "First I prepared myself. Then I waited for it to happen."

Her clear eyes gazed into his.

"Did you hear what I said?" he asked. "I got busted for possession of heroin."

"What's it like?"

"Getting busted?"

"Heroin."

He considered what to say.

"You didn't shoot it?"

"I snorted it."

She waited. Then she said, "That's good."

Daisy stood and stretched, then turned around once and lay on the concrete walk that met the porch stairs. She rolled on her side.

"It's a feeling like a flood," he said. "Well, that's not right." Then he changed his mind: "Yes it is."

Mary Beth squinted.

"It's like a flood in that it's got a current, a strong pull. It fills you and empties you at the same time. Puts in the good and takes out the bad." He'd nailed it, he realized. He let his words sit like that. A commuter train rumbled from the direction of the Glen. A horn sounded. Then another word came to him, and he couldn't help but say it: "Numb."

"Numb," she said, though it could have been a question. She stared ahead, beyond their yard.

"Numb doesn't sound good."

"Numb sounds good."

"A good numb," he said. He smelled roasted garlic from someone's kitchen. The train engine growled.

"Will you go to jail?"

"You're not real upset by this."

"I actually want to cry."

He waited for the punch line.

"I wish I could."

"I won't go to jail."

She nodded.

"I need to appear in September. A first offense. I'll probably just get counseling and no criminal charge."

"You have a lawyer?"

"Bob."

"Bob? That's a funny name for a lawyer," she said.

"It's a good name for a mechanic."

"That'd be Bobby."

He put his arm around her, and she scooted her butt against his.

"You'd think," she said, "if one's husband had a lawyer, his wife would know the lawyer's name."

"Now you do."

"Did you know I haven't cried in over a year?"

"That's good or not?"

"Not," she said. "I've got to get off these pills."

"Did you talk to your doctor?"

"Did you talk to *yours*? Did he write you a prescription for smack? Did your insurance cover it?"

"*Smack*?" he said.

"*Horse*?"

"*Dope*," he said. "No one says *smack* or *horse*. Everyone says *dope*. And I've stopped."

"*Kicked*?" she asked.

"Yeah, and so should you. Call your pusher."

"Dr. Levin?"

"That's him."

She put her head on his shoulder.

"Do we know how to have fun?" Ferko asked.

"Yeah. Popping pills and shooting up."

"Snorting lines!" he corrected her.

The girls on bikes rode back down the sidewalk, in the opposite direction. They looked to be Amanda's age, six, when she rode off into the woods. But these girls were real, alive, no one's collective burden.

"Does the bully know?"

"No," Ferko said.

She meant Prauer. She'd met him once, on a Friday afternoon approaching Christmas. She'd brought Catherine into the city and stopped by the office. There was a Christmas party that night on the Upper West Side, a friend of Mary Beth's from childhood. She met Ferko at the office and took the tour. Prauer was attentive, genuinely tender. He held the baby and walked her around the suite, then brought her to the big windows facing Sixth Avenue and pointed out the twinkling lights in the dusk. And Mary Beth had somehow observed in this bullying behavior. Ferko was never sure how. Prauer was, of course, a bully. He wasn't big physically. Just personally, emotionally, financially.

"Did you," Mary Beth started, then paused, "consider leaving?"

"I might not have a choice."

"What does that mean?" Her voice turned sharp.

"I screwed up the other day, when I got busted. They might not want me back."

"I meant *me*." Their bodies had separated, he noticed now. "Did you consider leaving *me*?"

"We were talking about Prauer. I missed that segue."

"Keep up."

He remembered what she'd said—that she'd expected he'd leave her.

"Well?" She waited.

"No," he said.

"Why not?"

"Because I wouldn't. Because I love you."

She held his gaze. Her eyes glistened for a single moment, reflected the afternoon sun.

"You really want to cry," he said.

"I'm sorry."

It occurred to him that she was sorry for a lot of things. So was he. He thought about fate, about those things you could affect and those things that affected you, but it was a circular reference, a self-referential loop, the concept too complicated. Philosophers asked questions they didn't have answers to.

"I messed up," she said.

His first instinct was to deny it, but he couldn't bring himself to do so.

She gasped and buried her face on the sleeve of his T-shirt. She breathed. When she was done his shirtsleeve was dry. So were her eyes. Then she smiled in a way that made her look sad. "You're crying," she said.

It was true, he realized, and the tears came at once, flooded his eyes and ran down his cheeks. He did that sometimes—cried—even before Catherine, before Mary Beth. She touched a finger to his cheek and sniffed a tear.

"I've made a mess of it," she said.

"Look at us." He held his hands out, pink palms toward the blue sky. "This isn't a mess." He supposed his face was red, tear-streaked. He supposed it really was a mess. But maybe that was the point. Because they were outside, on the front porch, with a cat named Daisy, instead of inside, hidden in the bedroom behind the drawn shades. It was a start, getting to know the neighbor's cat, even if they didn't know which neighbor the cat belonged to.

"Yeah," she said, "a couple of junkies."

"A couple of *recovering* junkies."

"A mess," she said.

"A *good* mess."

"Optimist."

"Optimist?" He lifted his shirt and wiped his face. "*I'm* the one crying."

"Can you take Friday off?"

"Sure. Though I might not have a job to take off from."

She squinted at him.

He blinked.

"I can," he said finally. "What's Friday?"

"We're going to Princeton."

"Princeton?" he said. "What's there?"

CHAPTER TWENTY-TWO

It was Wednesday, and he hadn't been back to the Riverfront suite since Saturday. *Not feeling well,* went his e-mail to Lisa Becker on Monday morning. *How's Greg? How are the Groves?* But Ferko knew from the e-mail traffic how the Groves were: Prauer's binding term sheet committed a billion-one. The Groves were rich. Not distressed-retail-department-store rich. They were cash rich. They were out, too, could spend the rest of their lives on the Florida beach of their choice, nursing their millions. Each article on Grove Department Stores—and Ferko received them all through his e-mail alerts—touched on Roy's murder, possible motives, possible suspects. Most focused on the youngest son, Kyle, who had arrests for possession of cocaine and ecstasy, and one incident, widely reported, in which he'd thrown Roy off his yacht into the Gulf of Mexico. In the end Roy had declined to press charges. The article yesterday—in the *Journal*, which reported the agreement in principle between Riverfront and Grove—rehashed the family dynamics, and then quantified, based on unspecified family sources, how much Kyle stood to gain from Roy's murder. Twenty million dollars. Ferko figured the entire Grove clan was better off with Roy gone. Except Roy, of course.

Ferko poked his head into Lisa's office. "Hey!" he said.

"Welcome back!"

He continued to the kitchen for coffee and food.

Greg's office was dark. Weeks ago, when he arrived—first to visit, then to occupy (in a temporary, unofficial capacity, with office and laptop)—the alchemy at Riverfront shifted. Any sense of complacency that had previously existed was gone. Props were knocked down. Floors fell away. Ferko walked on joists, the footing treacherous, while George Cosler and Greg Fletcher formed a team. A basketball team. They went to the gym at lunch and played pickup, two on two, while Prauer went on vacation—to Alaska, some river a four-hour flight from Anchorage. The plane brought arriving campers and food and supplies once a week, and picked up departing campers and their refuse. There were cabins, a freestanding dining room and kitchen, outhouses. The camp was open four months a year. And yet there was a signal—maybe even a tower—and Prauer kept in touch the way he would on some diligence trip to Shanghai. His e-mails came at odd hours, even taking into account the time difference. It never got dark, of course, and Ferko imagined Prauer, his boundless energy, catching fish, eating fish, and never sleeping, fixated on Grove Department Stores from his remote and ever-sunny corner of America. The e-mails came to Ferko, Greg, and Lisa, in that order, and Cosler and Greg would come back from basketball, showered and shining, and log back in. Sometimes Greg proclaimed, "Whoa!" if Prauer attached photos, as he often did, of fish, hip-high, held by their gills by straining men in waders, behind whom stood strange trees and green hills, blue sky, water, preternatural colors, a landscape from another planet. Then Greg tapped his keys—the guy could type fast—and fired off a response to Prauer that wasn't copied to Ferko or Lisa. By the second week, the e-mails were coming to Greg, Ferko, and Lisa, in that order. Ferko had been passed that quickly.

He found Lisa in the breakout room, where she'd opened her laptop and stacked her Grove files. She'd put meetings on his calendar: ten o'clock with Greg, eleven o'clock with Greg and Prauer. Despite everything, they still expected Ferko to do things.

She glanced at his food—a bagel with cream cheese and a hunk of Prauer's salmon. Another filet—smoked and salted, garnished with capers and served with bagels and cream cheese—sat in the kitchen, largely ignored by the overindulged Riverfront staff. Since Prauer's vacation, the salmon—his trophies—appeared a couple of mornings a week. At first their appearance was met with unreserved enthusiasm. Then the novelty wore off, and more fish meant less eaten. It would sit in the kitchen, slabs like human thighs with forkfuls missing, until someone tossed it by the end of the day. If Prauer paid attention, he'd have diverted the fish to a shelter or food bank. As unpredictable as he was with his investment decisions, he was equally unimaginative with his magnanimity.

"You're better?" Lisa asked Ferko.

"In the pink," he said, lifting the top of his bagel to reveal the fish beneath.

She made a sour face.

"Better," he said. He capped the bagel and took a bite. This morning, in the mirror, he'd looked a bit gaunt. It was good to eat. He swallowed.

"What're we doing?" he asked.

She raised her eyebrows and waited.

"We have meetings," he said.

"You're reporting on financing."

"What does Prauer expect?"

"Seven fifty."

"No fucking way."

"At least," she said. "You should've stuck around Saturday. Greg said it was possible."

Ferko imagined it now—Greg, in Ferko's absence, swagging seven fifty, minimum, perhaps even suggesting it was Ferko's number, raising Prauer's expectations so that he'd accept the billion-plus price tag while still meeting his hurdle. The more debt Riverfront raised against the Grove assets, the better the return on investment. Worse, with a seven-fifty floor, Prauer would expect more debt—eight hundred or eight fifty. Each dollar of incremental debt was a dollar less he'd need to invest from Riverfront's funds, boosting returns. Ferko was being set up to fail. He supposed he deserved it.

"Fuck Greg," Ferko said.

"I suggest you tell him that directly"—she glanced at her watch—"in twenty minutes."

"No one's going to lend Grove five hundred. Four hundred's a stretch. The leveraged loan market is done. Prauer knows that. Even dickhead Greg knows that."

She tsked him, stared at him with her hard eyes until they softened.

"Did I ever tell you," she asked, "I wanted to be a schoolteacher?"

He put his elbows on the table and folded his hands. "I don't believe you have."

"All growing up. Until my junior year of college."

"What happened?"

"Money happened."

Ferko pushed his chin forward and nodded. Money had happened to him, too. After college. The stock market was rising. The math wasn't difficult. Twenty percent returns meant you could double your money every four or five years. It worked until it didn't. Guys like Prauer succeeded through optimism and swagger and the uncanny ability to spot a bargain. When things got bad they put their heads down and kept buying. That was the value they added: determination and guts and the ability to convince rich people to trust them. The theory was dodgy—something bought at a given price today would be worth more tomorrow.

"You know what's nice?" she asked, but she didn't give Ferko a chance to answer. "There are teachers everywhere. You can be in New York or Wisconsin. I always imagined myself someplace north, a town on a river that freezes every winter." She paused as though allowing herself to imagine it. "Not a city, but a town," she said. "Maybe even a village. And the people who live there skate the river, from one town to the next. I think I read that in a book once."

"Or heard it in a Joni Mitchell song." It was an obscure reference, but it didn't faze her. He took another bite of his bagel and wiped his mouth with a napkin.

"*Village* makes it sound like there's no central heat," he said. "Just a wood-burning stove. Or maybe you'd use coal. You could shovel coal into your potbelly stove."

"Coal's dirty," she said.

He nodded his agreement. "And there'd be no school system, no salary. You'd teach the village elders' children in exchange for beads and baskets and fish." He removed the top of his bagel to reveal what was left of his salmon.

"Okay, a town, not a village. Someplace with historic buildings. But not *too* historic."

"Sounds quaint."

"And a Starbucks," she said.

"The historic Starbucks?"

"They *love* those properties."

"Why are you telling me this?"

She paused to shrug. "Exit strategy?" It was more question than statement.

"But *I'm* the one who's about to get thrown out on his ear," he said.

Greg didn't show for their ten o'clock. Lisa walked Ferko through the deal.

"Financing contingency omitted," she said.

"*Nice*," Ferko said, but it wasn't a surprise. It was Prauer's MO, to allow himself no outs. It gave him an edge, which he used, even in a case like Grove, where the competition for the assets was thin.

After a time they had nothing left to say. Ferko stuck his head out into the hallway. Still no Greg. His office lights were out. They were equipped with motion sensors, which meant that no one had been there for a while.

"Maybe he's hanging out with Kyle Grove," Lisa said.

"The murderer?"

"The Grove family bad boy."

She pulled up an image on her laptop. Kyle Grove's blond hair fell past his collar. He wore a scruffy beard, black sunglasses. He looked like he belonged in Hollywood.

"You're obsessed with him, aren't you?" Ferko asked.

She shrugged. "Kyle and Greg are hanging together, growing their hair, getting tan on Daddy's yacht."

"Dead Daddy's yacht," Ferko said.

"Taking full advantage," she said.

Greg finally appeared, on Bill Prauer's heels, in the conference room at five after eleven. Prauer had a pad of paper and a pen, and he sat at the head of the table. Greg had a file folder. He set it down and took the chair next to Lisa, at Prauer's right elbow. Greg swept the hair from his eyes, which displayed their usual indifference.

"Where are we?" Prauer asked.

Greg pushed his chair back, rested his elbows on his armrests, and made a tent with his fingers. He waited, with Prauer, for an answer, though there was nothing in Prauer's question or demeanor that indicated the question wasn't directed at Greg. In fact, it was Greg's question to answer. It was his deal. Yet he waited, and the longer he waited the longer the silence dragged. Seconds passed. Prauer raised his eyebrows and glanced at Ferko, when Lisa jumped in:

"We've designated Funds IV and V as buyers on a fifty-fifty—"

"I'm aware," Prauer interrupted at a startling volume, "which funds we've committed."

Silence, several moments' worth, after which Prauer said, "Financing," at a more reasonable level. "We're
here to talk about financing."

There was another beat of silence before Ferko spoke:

"Can we take a step back?" His voice was weak,
the cumulative weight of the past few days—the lack
of drugs and the search for drugs, the arrest and the
recovery. He imagined that he looked thin, pale, sitting
alone on the window side of the conference table. "I've
been out the past couple of days and I want to make
sure I understand the expectation."

"The expectation is we'll raise as much debt as
possible on the best terms possible from third-party
sources using the assets of the newly acquired company." Prauer folded his hands on the table. "It's called
a *leveraged* buyout."

"The money's not there."

"Bullshit. Money's pouring into our funds."

"No one's lending. It's all sitting. Or flowing into
equity."

"Bullshit," Prauer said again. "Who've you called?"

When Ferko didn't answer, Prauer said, "Who?"
They stared at each other as if there were no one else
in the room.

"I'll call," Ferko said after a moment.

"People owe us. They want our deals. They pant like dogs. They beg for bones. We've got red meat."

"The dogs aren't hungry." It was a bold thing to say, and it surprised Ferko that it had come from him.

"Who. Have. You. Called?" Prauer turned up the volume and left a beat between each word. "Citadel?" he asked.

"I'll call them," Ferko said.

"Dimension?"

"I'll call them." There was a hint of defiance in his voice. Again, a surprise.

"Damn right." Prauer slid his phone across the tabletop. Ferko stopped it with the heel of his hand, and everyone—even Greg—watched the phone expectantly, as though it might activate on its own, start calling lenders, sharing data, and producing commitments.

"I said I'll call them." Ferko pushed the phone back. It stopped in a spot roughly between the two, and Prauer picked it up and waved it at Ferko.

These sorts of flare-ups occurred more often than they should have. Ferko had been on the receiving end a few times. He'd survived them before. He doubted he would this time. Prauer stood and exited without a word—a goodbye or a so long or even a demand for an update by a fixed time. Silence swelled in his wake. Lisa stared at the keys of her laptop. Greg was as amused as his perma-smirk allowed.

"Don't be an asshole, Greg," Ferko said.

"Great metaphor, Gil. Mrs. Wall would be proud." He glanced Lisa's way. "Seventh-grade English," he said, by way of explanation.

"Ahhhh, we were just talking about teachers," she said.

"How much did you tell him we could finance?" Ferko asked.

"Relax," Greg said. "Bill's a big boy. He writes these deals with no financing outs because he's prepared to finance them himself."

"He hasn't had to yet." Ferko looked to Lisa, as though for confirmation, and she nodded.

"I haven't seen it."

"The market's turned," Ferko said.

"It's not that bad," Greg said.

Silence filled the room. He looked sheepish, an expression that elicited—somehow, and against Ferko's better judgment—sympathy.

"There's a price for everything," Greg said. "He pays more. Maybe the funds guarantee."

Lisa closed her laptop, stood, and collected her paper files.

"I hope you know what you're doing," Ferko said.

"Who have you called?" Greg asked. It was the same question Prauer had asked, but there was no malice in Greg's inflection.

Ferko didn't answer. Was Greg mocking him?

"I need to know so that we don't call the same people."

Ferko collected his notepad and the random pieces of paper he'd printed to comprise his file.

"Let's get this done," Greg said, the way he might have as a quarterback in a huddle.

Ferko stood, and Greg did, too. Taller, of course.

"I'm bringing you along," Greg said, "whether you want to come or not."

CHAPTER TWENTY-THREE

Gil and Mary Beth drove past strip malls anchored by big-box stores, set behind acres of asphalt and cars parked in rows like crops. The highway was four lanes on each side, and Gil stuck to the right-middle, driving too slow for safety—fifty-five (the speed limit), and even less—while the North Jersey warriors in their luxury cars and SUVs sped past on either side. They were housewives, back-to-school shopping with kids in tow. They were sales types, late for appointments in the vast business parks concealed behind the few stands of trees.

Mary Beth had pages on her lap, directions from the Internet—Glen Wood Ridge to Princeton—north out of town, then west, then south on the interstate to some state highway that went straight to campus. An hour-twenty, according to the printout. They had plenty of time to make their two o'clock appointment. Gil could drive as slow as he wished.

Too often the pace here frightened her, and she blamed it, sometimes (and only in her mind), for Catherine's death. But just as often, and usually more, she remembered the moments before the accident, when the front wheel of the jogging stroller rolled down the sloped curb to the asphalt on Lyttondale Avenue. The wheels were like those of a bicycle, sixteen inches, with a rim and spokes and a tire with a tube that inflated with a pump. She'd grown up in a newish development with cul-de-sacs and curved streets that connected at right angles. She'd had a bike, a five-speed with a banana seat. She was something of a tomboy. She rode alone, up and down the sloped curbs, standing on her pedals. She'd loved the sensation, and she'd imagined Catherine did, too, when the front wheel fell suddenly and the stroller's nose dipped or when the front wheel lifted—a wheelie—followed by the back wheels rolling up the curb, and Mary Beth would let out a high-pitched *Whoops!* regardless of the direction—up or down—and, though it was impossible in those moments to see Catherine's expression, she always imagined one of agreeable surprise—eyes wide, cheeks pink.

They'd been conditioned to drive, even from their house on Woodberry Road to the Glen. Gil drove his car there every morning and parked in the municipal lot next to the train station. It wasn't even a mile. She'd measured it once, at the end of her run, on a morning when she'd finally made it up Amos Avenue without having to walk. She'd felt exhilarated. She undid the baby's harness and held her against her sweaty tank top and glistening neck and collarbone. Then she unlocked the car and placed the baby in her car seat—rear-facing—buckled this harness, and left the stroller on the front walk and retraced her route, noting the mileage on the odometer. It was three and a half miles in all, including 0.9 from the train station in the Glen. She understood, of course, why Gil drove. It was fifteen minutes to walk each way and five to drive; he saved twenty minutes each day he drove. But since this past winter, when she'd begun to leave the house again, she'd done so on foot, walking *up* Amos Avenue instead of *down*. It was a form of exercise, a new way to grieve. She had the time and the need. Not everyone did. She saw it now as a blessing, as the cars sped past on either side. She actually felt sorry for their drivers, the ones with jobs and families and normal lives that kept them hustling, just as she felt sorry for the man who'd caught the front wheel of the stroller on Lyttondale Avenue and tipped it and dragged it, only to stop and free himself and steer around the obstacle and speed off. The shadow behind the wheel of the blue car was a man. She'd always known this, though she couldn't say how. Even in the first numb interview with the police, she'd called the driver *he*. "He?" the policeman had asked. He wore a uniform and a mustache. She had to explain that she hadn't actually seen the driver (or the license plate or, for that matter, the car itself, except to identify its color), but she was sure the driver was a man. The officer wrote that down. She was told later she'd been in shock. She didn't know what that meant, and she still didn't after looking it up on the Internet. She doubted such a condition existed. She'd merely been numb, ambivalent in a way that made *numb* feel *hollow*—ambivalent toward the man driving the car and ambivalent toward her own culpability, until the threads of anger weaved something harder and larger, the way cells turned cancerous and spread. And she'd welcomed this anger, which was, at least, a real emotion, even if it was only directed inward and made her withdraw from the world, with its sun and sky and clouds and rain, from the lawns and streets and sidewalks and curbs. She'd pulled her shades, unable to blame or accept blame. Until—now she felt sympathy. Was that it? She remembered sympathy. Did sympathy encompass forgiveness? Could she include herself?

It was a blessing to be unhurried, and Gil, it turned out, was the type of hero who drove slowly, who didn't ask a lot of questions, whose patience exceeded reason. For most of two years she'd wondered why he hadn't left her. It turned on this: driving to Princeton, New Jersey, for a meeting with Solomon DeGrass, who, years ago, as a boy, might have stolen a chicken from a woman named Dorothy Miller and her granddaughter, Amanda. It sounded like a crime from 1883 instead of 1983, but Mary Beth had sent the alleged perpetrator an e-mail, pretending to be a student, and made an appointment. It wasn't hard to do. The semester hadn't yet started. It was the middle of August, and schedules weren't set. Dr. DeGrass was probably her age. Amanda, if she'd lived, would now be thirty, a contemporary, one of the young mothers pushing a stroller in Glen Wood Ridge, like Mary Beth just a few years ago. Maybe the old house—Amanda's farmhouse—would still be there, and Mary Beth's wouldn't. Maybe Mary

Beth and Gil would live in the Glen or on the Ridge or in some other town without a Lyttondale Avenue. With Catherine. It made her head swim.

She'd brought the article from the *Crier*, folded in her pocket, but she hoped not to use props. She trusted that she'd know what to say when the time came. This journey was for Amanda, she'd told Gil, even as she knew it was for herself and Catherine and Gil. Cars passed on the left and right, and Gil let them, his hands on the wheel at ten and two like a kid with a learner's permit.

Jen had arrived late to Penn Station and missed the ten o'clock, which meant she missed the connection at Princeton Junction and had a half-hour wait for the train to campus. None of this portended well for her new life as a sober non-fuck-up, but she'd thought too late to print out a map of the town and the campus so she'd know how to get from the train station to wherever she was going, and this small act of non-planning had started a cascade of lateness that landed her two miles from Solomon's office ten minutes before her appointment. The old Jen might have hoofed it with her thumb out in case a generous soul would give her a lift. The old Jen wouldn't have even thought to call

Solomon to warn him she was running late. But this new Jen let her city instincts take over: she went looking for a cab and, of course, this being a train station, she found one, spent the dollars she would have spent on dope only two weeks before, and made it to the arts center, where Solomon held office hours, with three minutes to spare.

His office door was closed, though. She checked the number against the info she'd copied from his web page. She took a breath. Then she knocked.

But there was no answer.

She knocked again. She examined the seams, where the door fit the frame. No light came from inside the office. She opened her phone and dialed the number she'd copied, and the phone rang from the other side of the door. It rang and rang. Then a recording kicked on: "This is Solomon—" She hung up. She remembered her professors at Columbia. They advertised office hours they never seemed to keep. It was a joke, she'd decided, so she caught them after class.

Now she leaned her back against the tile wall and slid to the floor. A piano played behind a door farther down the hall, a jaunty tune, like one from a scene in a costume drama, a party in a grand ballroom within a lavish estate, where the gentlemen bow in their tights and powdered wigs and the ladies curtsy in their gowns and then are led by their delicate fingers to a single square on the marble floor. They turn to face their partners. Eyes meet. Then the dance commences, a human wheel that turns as one, like the wheels of the coaches that carried the guests to the party. Now the coaches rest outside with the horses that pulled them. The animals are watered and brushed and stand together, black eyes reflecting the flame of the gaslight and the cold stars in the sky. Their drivers have moved to the galley for talk and tobacco.

Jen closed her eyes. The piano notes, muted by the closed door—by wood and distance—floated like dust in the empty hall. She belonged outside with the horses, she realized, or in the galley with the help. But not in the stuffy party. She wasn't sure why. She wasn't sure how she knew this, but she always had, even when she was young and popular, still unspoiled, standing in front of the full bleachers at an Edgefield football or basketball game, chanting those incessant cheers, even when she rode that ridiculous lap around the track that ringed the football field on the back of Jonathan Fahey's vintage convertible with an armful of lilies, waving to her subjects, the queen who'd been crowned.

"Ms. Yoder?"

She opened her eyes.

Solomon DeGrass wore his hair to his collar. It was brown, light enough at the tips to be called blond. Chlorine-damaged, perhaps, though his pallor did not suggest a summer spent outdoors. He brushed his bangs from his eyes and reached down and took her hand and shook it, and she allowed herself to be helped up. He was taller than Felix. Thinner. The younger brother, though older than Felix had been on the one night she'd known him. So was Jen. She gazed into his eyes, and a memory swamped her—Felix on the rooftop, the distant lights from the taller buildings shaping his eyes like question marks, infusing them with wonder. And Solomon, now, in the dim hallway, his eyes as curious as a child's.

"Dr. DeGrass," she said.

"Solomon."

They stood there for a moment, her hand in his. He'd been expecting someone younger. The piano had gone silent.

"Please." He tried one key from a ring, then a second. The door opened and he flipped on a light. The room was windowless, a square, seven by seven, made smaller by the books that lined the walls. There was a metal desk, eighties-issue, too big for the space, like an old Lincoln parked in an alley. A closed laptop with a light blinking sat on top, surrounded by paper. Solomon sat in the desk chair and swiveled it and then stood when he realized that more papers were piled in the seat of the second chair, next to the door. He removed these and set them on the floor in the corner, beneath a framed photo of a woman with two babies in a double stroller and a second with two kids—a boy and a girl, maybe four—in adjacent swings on a playground.

"Twins," he said, when he saw her looking at them. "Molly and Felix."

She blinked at the name, but Solomon didn't seem to notice.

"Do you have children, Ms. Yoder?"

"No." It wasn't a question she'd ever been asked before. She was glad for that. She didn't hang out with a crowd that had children or thought much about them. She wondered who she'd hang out with if she were to stay clean. "Call me Jen."

"If you ever do, Jen, have twins. Gets it over with—bam! One of each. You can't draw it up any better."

He sat in his seat, so she sat in hers. The piano commenced again, a slower piece in a minor key. "Do you mind if I close the door?" she asked, and Solomon opened his palm, a be-my-guest gesture. She stood and shut the door.

He waited. Seconds passed, and it became clear he had no more pleasantries to fill them with. There was nothing else to say, so she cleared her throat and swallowed. "I knew Felix."

"Oh?"

She glanced at the photo of the twins. The boy had fine hair. The girl's was curly. "Your brother, Felix."

"Yes." Solomon straightened his back and crossed his legs. His chair creaked. "Of course," he said, an invitation to continue.

"I was with him the night he died," she said.

Solomon tilted his head. His mouth fell slack. He studied an indeterminate point in the middle of her face—the tip of her nose, perhaps. "Are you—" he started, but lost his way. "There was a woman he was with. He left the bar with her. Are you—*her*?"

"I am."

"She had dark hair."

"That's me," she said. A wave of relief washed over her. It was only a first step, but she'd taken it.

"The police were looking for you," he said.

"I suppose so."

"You *suppose* so?"

"I've never told anyone this. You're the first."

His smooth face was pinched, folded in on itself.

"I met Felix late. He'd been celebrating his play."

"This was at Staub's?"

"Yes. Were you there?"

"Not that night."

"He was at the upstairs bar. There were lots of people. People he knew—collaborators and friends, actors and writers, but he was somehow alone."

"He was moody."

"Yeah?" she said.

"Like a character in his own play. He was difficult to draw out."

"I found him easy to talk to." She hoped it didn't sound like a boast. She paused a beat before she continued: "Eventually, my friends left. And then *his* friends left. We stayed at the bar and talked until they turned on the lights and we had to leave."

Solomon waited. The next part was the cab to his place, but instead she went back: "We talked about ghosts."

"*Ghosts?*"

"His play," she said, "was about a dead girl and her ghost."

"Go on." He winced, or appeared to.

"That's all I know."

"You were at the reading—"

"No," she interrupted. "I only met Felix afterward, at the bar."

He grimaced, an expression of frustration.

"It seemed quite important," she said, "that he tell the story. Have you read it?"

When Solomon didn't respond, she said, "The play."

"No. It got lost."

The overhead light hummed. She only now noticed.

"Someone must have a copy," she said. "What about the company that put on the reading?"

"That's not why you're here?" His voice sharpened. Had she imagined it? "To give me a copy of my brother's play?"

"No." She'd gotten stuck. She wasn't here to talk about a play she hadn't seen. She was here to tell her story, Felix's story. It was as important to her as Felix telling the story of the dead girl and her ghost. She imagined she was an actor in a play. The scene: a small office in the theater department of a university.

WOMAN

We took a cab to his place. He wanted to celebrate more. There was a deck on his roof, and it was a nice night. We stopped at his apartment on the way up. I waited in the hall. I thought he'd ditched me, or maybe forgotten me. I thought he went to bed, and I was wondering if I should knock or just take a cab home. Then the door opened and he came out with two glasses, an ice tray, and a bottle of Scotch. It was still dark when we got to the roof. There was a deck with tables and chairs, but Felix took me beyond there, onto the gravel of the roof-top, to the edge, where there was a little raised part of the roof, hip-high. We rested our drinks there. We leaned against the ledge. He sat on it. We were looking north. You could see the glow of Times Square. Then the sky brightened in the east. Then the tall buildings, and it was morning. Then Felix was standing on the ledge.

BROTHER

Why did Felix . . .

WOMAN

I don't know why. He jumped onto the ledge. I don't remember. One moment he was standing there, and the next he was gone. I thought maybe he was hiding, or had gone off to pee behind the equipment on the roof. I looked over the ledge and saw him on the sidewalk.

(Brother looks stricken)

I ran to the stairwell, and then down—I don't know how many flights. Back and forth. I was out of breath and dizzy and disoriented when I got to the lobby. Once outside, I went left when I should've gone right. I got to the corner and turned and there was no one there, and for a moment I thought I'd imagined the whole thing. Then I heard someone scream. It was from the next block up, and I threw up on the curb. There were people there, I suppose, across the street or on the sidewalk. Another drunk on a Sunday morning.

(Pauses)

I got up after some time. I don't know how long, but there were still no sirens. I wouldn't hear those until I was a few blocks east. I don't know that they were for Felix, but I suspect they were. I lived on Fourteenth then, east of Broadway. I kept walking until I was home.

She wanted to stand, to walk, but there was no place to go in the small space. There was nothing to do but await the brother's response. She'd told the story as best she could. Relief flooded her. She'd *told* it. There was only one more thing to say, and she said that, too: "I'm sorry."

She looked at her hands, folded in her lap, the tiled floor beyond them, with its stacks of paper to be tossed, filed, or ignored—stepped around or over—until he tripped and the papers spilled and he had to restack them in some haphazard way to deal with later. She chanced a look into his eyes. He seemed older than when they'd started, when she'd met him in the hall.

"Why?" he asked, but there were too many *whys*. Why did Felix climb onto the ledge? Why did he fall? Why did she leave? Why had she kept silent all these years? Why was she sorry? She'd told Solomon *what* had happened, but the questions that mattered most were *why*. And she didn't know why, couldn't begin to fathom the questions, much less the answers. They overwhelmed her, in fact. She hadn't cried in years. Maybe since the days after Felix died. Had she cried then? Why? She hadn't asked the right questions.

Nor could she cry now. She wiped her dry eyes with the heel of her hand, which blackened. The junkie look, she called it—the late nights, looking like death, her skin pale, her lashes thick with mascara, her eyes drawn with liner, made dramatic when her pupils narrowed. It was a look—until you rubbed your eyes and things started to smear. Then it was a different look, though no less striking. She wiped her hand on her jeans.

"Why are you here?" he asked.

She let the question hang between them.

"Forgiveness?" he asked.

She shook her head.

"Friendship?"

She shook her head again. The truth was she didn't know why. She was an empty vessel—pure. She let her silence say it. She didn't trust herself with words.

"Why did Felix jump onto the ledge?"

"I don't know."

"You were there."

"I was, but I don't know why. I told you."

"Did he jump?"

"I don't know."

"Was he despondent?"

"No." She searched for the right words, then found them: "Manic. Drunk."

"Were you fighting?"

"No."

"Why did you run?"

"I don't know."

He studied her. Seconds passed. She couldn't bring herself to meet his eyes. Instead, she watched a pile of papers placed on the floor by a metal filing cabinet.

"How can I reach you?"

Now she looked at him.

He pushed a pad of paper and a pen toward her. She wrote her name and number and e-mail address, and slid the pad with the pen back to him.

He tilted his head to study it.

"That's my cell." She was surprised her voice was clear. "I live in the city."

"My parents may call you."

"I can talk with them." She swallowed. It was just the beginning. "Where do they live?"

"Glen Wood Ridge."

Ferko! she thought. She wondered if he knew them. Maybe the brothers grew up there. She imagined them wandering the aisles of the Grand Union that used to be ten minutes between Glen Wood Ridge and Edgefield.

"My dad lives in Edgefield," she said.

He exhaled through his nose, an affectation connoting humor.

"I had family there," he said. "The Fletchers."

"*Greg* Fletcher?"

"My cousin."

"He's back East."

His eyes got big. "Oh, I know."

He had more to say, and she waited for it.

"Do you know the circumstances of his move back here?" he asked.

"No."

Solomon smirked.

"A job?" she asked.

"You're his friend?"

"In seventh grade!"

His lips flattened. He opened his mouth, then closed it, and tucked his hair behind his ear. "He stayed in my parents' basement when he first moved back. Slept on the couch even though they had spare bedrooms upstairs. Then they went to Europe for three weeks. When they got home Greg was gone and so was their car. He left the plates on the kitchen table and a check for $25,000 for a new car. He'd moved into the city. My dad pressed him, and Greg finally admitted that he'd wrecked the car in a construction zone on 17. Hit a Jersey barrier. He apologized. Charming guy. They haven't heard from him since."

Solomon swiveled his chair.

"I looked him up," he said. "He bought a place for three million in the city. Why sleep on your uncle's couch when you have that much money?"

Jen considered the question, though she didn't think it was one Solomon expected she would answer.

"That's a weird story," she said.

"Your friend's a weird guy."

"So's your cousin."

"True."

Solomon stood. The meeting was over. Her confession was inconsequential. It had landed with a thud. But now something else was happening. Something important. She had to press:

"Do you know the Ferkos? They live in Glen Wood Ridge."

"No—Ferko?"

She nodded.

"That's a funny name." He opened the door.

She stood. "You have my number."

He showed her the pad.

"I put my e-mail there, too."

"Thanks for coming," he said, though there was nothing thankful in his voice.

It felt like a date that was ending badly. She'd never hear from him again. She might have felt relieved, but instead she felt sad. She shrugged and said, "Thanks," then turned to go.

The door swung shut behind her. The piano down the dark hall played a sprightly tune. She remembered her daydream about the party where she didn't belong, her self-banishment to the kitchen with the help and the drivers of the coaches.

Kick. Check. *Confront.* She'd tried. She wasn't yet ready to call Queenie. Jen was empty now. She had nothing left. But that emptiness, curiously, gave her hope.

The Lewis Center for the Arts was on the north edge of campus. Gil found a parking spot down a side street with no meters. There were houses here, painted white and yellow. On the corner stood a restaurant and coffee shop, the sort of streetscape you'd expect to find adjacent to an Ivy League school. Cars cruised past, north and south. Mary Beth and Gil waited for the walk sign, and, as they waited, Mary Beth noticed a woman beside a hedge on a sidewalk that curved from the entrance of the arts center toward the back and the expanse of the Princeton campus. She had dark hair and dark eyes that seemed to be watching her, watching them, and there was something about the woman's face—watching, waiting, *searching*, distant across the trafficked two-lane and the green demarcating campus from town—that reminded Mary Beth of Amanda across the field at the School on the Ridge, at the edge of the woods that led to County Park, that first time, with the anonymous mothers on the playground. They'd been oblivious, Mary Beth had assumed then, of all children except their own. Now she glanced at Gil. He was watching the traffic, the façade of the arts building, the vermilion lights of the don't-walk sign. What did people do while they waited for lights to change? He was reliving his highs on heroin, perhaps. He was out of sorts, accompanying Mary Beth on the proverbial wild-goose chase, while the bully, William Prauer, was making millions at someone else's expense. Maybe Gil's. She tapped his elbow to get his attention, to point out the woman across the street, but once she did the woman was gone, the way Amanda was gone when she slipped into the woods. Or simply vanished when Mary Beth blinked.

"What?" Gil asked.

"Nothing."

The light had changed. The walk sign flashed white, pulled her across the street with Gil, between the stopped cars, toward the entrance of the arts center.

She glanced toward the hedge and the sidewalk that disappeared behind it, but there was no one there.

Solomon's office was on a quiet hallway on the second floor. The door was closed, the room marked by a number, which corresponded to the office number on his web page. She paused and sighed.

"Are you ready for this?" Gil's voice was a near whisper. He was a good sport, having never challenged her or even quizzed her about what *this* was. She'd explained it as best she could: the professor, when he was a child, had stolen Amanda's chicken, leading to the bicycle crash reported in the *Crier*, the one in which Amanda had died. Gil accepted all this without asking how she knew.

She knocked and the door opened a crack. A youngish face filled it, an expression lacking recognition or even acknowledgment that someone might be calling during office hours. His green eyes behind round lenses darted from Mary Beth to Gil, then back to Mary Beth.

"Dr. DeGrass," she said.

The door opened farther and he stood in the space. He was the right age—in his thirties. She'd brought Gil for support and protection, if needed. Now, seeing

Solomon's slender frame, the protection part didn't seem necessary.

"I'm Mary Beth. I made an appointment." When Solomon made no gesture to step aside and invite them in, she added, "For two o'clock?"

He turned his thin wrist, but it had no watch. He kept himself in front of the gap between the door and the frame.

"We're a few minutes early," she said, though she didn't believe this to be true. "Do you want us to wait?"

"No." He cleared his throat. "I was expecting a student. That's not you, I don't think."

"No, that's not us."

He turned sideways and opened the door and she stepped through.

"This is my husband, Gil."

They stood in the small space, facing one another. "May I?" Mary Beth asked, indicating the empty chair next to his desk.

"Of course!" He closed the door, which gave them more room. "I don't have a third chair." He looked at Gil, who'd taken up residence leaning against a metal filing cabinet in the corner.

"He's fine," Mary Beth said, as though he were nothing more than a henchman, someone whose job was limited to doing Mary Beth's bidding. He played it well, imparting no greeting—oral or physical—when introduced. He stood in stony silence, his face blank, his expression unreadable. She marveled at his perceptiveness. They were involved in a transaction of sorts, she realized, an exchange. Transactions were where Gil thrived. She could count on him to play his part.

"This is a strange day for appointments," Solomon said, taking his chair after Mary Beth had taken hers. "I don't even know the nature of yours. I was expecting a student about my midcentury course this fall."

"I misled you in my e-mail," Mary Beth said. "I'm sorry about that."

Solomon glanced at Gil. There was music playing from the small speakers that flanked his computer screen. It could have been static—just bits of drums and bass that didn't mesh in any way that made sense. It could have been jazz. It could have been something conventional, playing at a volume too low to hear properly.

"You grew up in Glen Wood Ridge," Mary Beth said.

"Do I know you?"

"No, but I think you knew a friend of mine." She considered leaving a pause, but determined there was no advantage to doing so. "Amanda Russo."

Solomon blinked.

"Maybe you didn't know her name," Mary Beth said. "She wasn't there long. She lived with her grandmother, Mrs. Miller, in the house with the chickens on Amos Avenue, between the Glen and the Ridge."

He emitted something audible in his exhale—something akin to suffering. "Who are you?" he demanded.

"I told you," Mary Beth said. "I'm Mary Beth, and this is Gil."

"*Who*!" Solomon said. "I didn't ask your names. I asked *who* you are."

"We're friends of Amanda's. I told you that."

"Amanda's dead."

"You *knew* her?"

"The Miller place and the chickens—yes, I remember her. She died. I was nine. It was a big deal. I'd never known anyone who'd died. An uncle, maybe. But she was a kid, younger than me."

"Kids aren't supposed to die," Mary Beth said. Something caught in her throat. She tried to stay composed.

"It was a long time ago."

"That's why we're here," she said.

Solomon waited. A horn blared through the static on the computer's speakers. Jazz.

"You left her," Mary Beth said.

"*What?*"

"Kids aren't supposed to die, but you let her because you stole a chicken and you thought you were going to get in trouble."

"Who told you that?"

"You let the chicken go and rode your bikes home and promised to never tell."

"Who told you?"

"Amanda."

"Impossible." He looked at his computer screen, as though it might provide an answer. "Did she put you up to it? The woman who was here?"

"What woman?"

He picked up a pad of paper on his desk. "Jen," he read.

"Jen who?" Gil asked from his perch in the corner.

"She's got the script. *You've* got the script."

"When someone's hurt," Mary Beth said, "you help."

"What's it called?" Solomon asked.

"What's *what* called?" Gil demanded.

"The play," Solomon said. "Felix's play."

"Who's Felix?" Gil asked.

"The brother," Mary Beth jumped in.

"He's dead," Solomon said. "Do you know him, too?"

The conversation had been derailed. She wished to put it back on track.

"Of course you do," Solomon said. "You know *her*."

"Who?" Gil said.

"The woman who was here—Jen."

"Jen who?" Gil asked again.

"Jen!" Solomon waved a pad of sticky notes and threw it on the desk among the other papers and magazines.

"You either stay and help," Mary Beth said, "or you go get help."

"How *dare* you? Get out of my office." He stood. It was good, now, that Gil was here.

"Get out!" he said again. "You people are sick. Get out before I call security."

She stood. Whatever happened was long ago, when Solomon was a boy. Now he was a cipher. She saw that. She'd come all this way for a simple insight. It would have to do.

She opened the door, and Gil followed. They were ten steps down the hall when Solomon called out: "Who are you?"

They turned. He was standing in the doorway, backlit like a rock star.

"Ghosts," she said.

Some lies were truer than some truths. But with this one told, she'd never felt more alive.

The train trestled over swamps. Lower Manhattan gleamed though the window with too much blue sky, the empty space where the towers once stood. It was Friday, payday. If Jen had gone to work, she'd be off now, preparing for the weekend. People left Manhattan in August. They went to beaches on Long Island or the shore in New Jersey. Or they quit completely and traveled the globe. Jen preferred an empty city to a crowded beach. She felt the pull of the old routines. A couple clicks on her phone and she'd score. But there was no signal here, in the swamps beneath the electrical right-of-way. She couldn't go back now, anyhow.

It had been unnerving, seeing Ferko. Had he followed her? It had seemed possible, as she trailed him back inside the arts center and up the stairs to the second floor and the quiet hallway to Solomon's office. She'd kept her distance as the woman—Mary Beth—knocked on Solomon's door, and he let them in after some discussion and closed the door. It had seemed possible later, after raised voices, when the door opened again, and Ferko and Mary Beth emerged from the office, and Solomon called out a question so basic—"Who are you?"—she wondered if the interaction were occurring in reverse, if this were the *coming* rather than the *going*. Jen couldn't hear the answer, yet she could have stepped from the shadows and provided her own. *Who* was easy. *Why* was the question. Yet she couldn't ask. Not yet. Solomon closed his office door, and Jen followed Ferko and Mary Beth from a safe distance. Had she been following all along? They walked quickly, bounced down the steps like undergrads. She remembered the dead baby and the grief they carried. It wasn't evident. She followed them through the front door and blinked in the bright sunshine. She lowered her sunglasses. They crossed the street to the corner where Jen had first spotted them, and continued on. Still, Jen followed—dodged traffic and peered around the corner of the coffee shop, as they climbed into a hatchback, Ferko in the driver seat, Mary Beth in the passenger seat, pulled out, and drove away.

Which meant, of course, that they *hadn't* followed her, that they'd come on their own. Which meant *what*?

Now she checked her phone. It was a mile or two, as the gull flies, to Battery Park. Yet there was no signal. It astounded her. She'd received texts all week from friends asking what was up. She'd answered each with a single word: *kicking*, to which her friends responded: *?* or *!* or *?!?*. The pace of those texts had slowed, but now, with Friday night looming, they'd picked up again, before she'd lost her signal. The new entreaties were more cautious: *drink?* But Jen knew, too well, the laws of gravity, how drinks with certain friends in old haunts would lead to using. She wished to call her dad, but now she'd have to wait until she cleared the power lines, perhaps the tunnel into Penn Station. She'd buy a pack of cigarettes and a ticket to Edgefield, a Friday commute with unknown adults. She didn't know what to make of Ferko in Princeton. Shapes had drifted like floaters in her eyes since Greg Fletcher had reentered her life and Ferko had followed with his enigmatic wife and dead baby. Had she made any progress connecting them? She was clean. She'd made the pilgrimage to Princeton and Felix's brother. She'd confronted that part of it. But there was more. It wasn't over. Ferko and Mary Beth's presence today told her that. First she'd call her dad. Then discover what was next. Maybe one day, even one day soon, she'd use again, but she couldn't yet, before she'd even had a chance to begin not to.

CHAPTER TWENTY-FOUR

It didn't take Ferko long, leaning against the metal filing cabinet in the tiny office in Princeton, to recognize that Mary Beth was grilling Dr. DeGrass the way Jen had once urged Ferko—when they were at Ivy's on Houston Street after snorting dope in the unisex bathroom upstairs—to imagine grilling the driver of the blue car. And in that instant, when he recognized that Mary Beth was substituting Dr. DeGrass for the driver of the blue car, Ferko realized that the questions he'd posed to Jen those weeks ago at Ivy's were the wrong questions. He'd wanted to know the circumstances that led the driver to the right turn from Amos Avenue to Lyttondale Avenue in the Glen at precisely the moment when Mary Beth pushed the stroller into the street. He'd wanted to know where the driver was coming from and where he was going. Now it felt like what he'd wanted was a cop-out, an excuse to collect useless information. Because fate—at least Ferko's theory about fate—worked only to a certain point, after which you had to play the hand you were dealt. Fate was no longer part of it. And that was what Mary Beth was doing, in that moment, in Solomon DeGrass's office. She was *owning* it, taking control. There were things you could control and things you couldn't. Fate went only so far. Ferko remembered his conclusion—the driver's leaving was a decision, and that decision was wrong.

And it mattered.

But the questions he'd asked Mary Beth a dozen different times in a dozen different ways in the last two years didn't. *Why*, went one version, *push a stroller on a street when there's a sidewalk, buffered from the traffic by a curb and a stripe of grass?* But he saw now how that was like asking Amanda why she was riding her bike in the woods. It was obvious why, which led him to another question: Why hadn't he recognized that before?

He still felt Amanda's presence in the house, even if her presence was less tangible, less apparent. When he'd asked Mary Beth about Amanda today, on the way to Dr. Yoder's, she'd confirmed his sense of things.

What about the woods below the School on the Ridge, Ferko had asked. Mary Beth had abandoned them because Amanda had, too. "I miss her," Mary Beth had said, "but she's not really gone."

Now they sat at a round table, four of them—Dr. Yoder, Jen, Ferko, and Mary Beth—on the deck beside the pool in Dr. Yoder's backyard. The table was metal, and the chairs were, too, with enough heft that they wouldn't blow over in a storm. The table had a hole in the center, where an umbrella could go, but there wasn't one. Perhaps it had worn out over the years. Perhaps it was unneeded, given the shade provided by the tall trees at the edge of Dr. Yoder's property. The table was in the shade. Half the pool was.

The water was clean, its surface skimmed of debris, even though the occasional leaf high up turned and fell. A few yellow ones had collected where the patio met the stone wall on which the faceless couples had sat in the shadows and made out at the high school graduation party Ferko had attended twenty years ago. There was beer then. Now he drank lemonade with ice poured from a glass pitcher. The cold front from a week ago was gone. The heat and humidity had crept up, as they tended to do in summer after fronts had passed and the clockwise circulation allowed the sultry air from the south to be carried again up the coast. They hadn't brought their swimsuits.

"Why not?" Dr. Yoder looked wounded.

"Come on, Dad," Jen said.

"She hasn't been in the pool in ten years."

"Ummm. Actually, it's been fifteen."

"You used to love it."

"When I was a kid!"

Dr. Yoder shrugged. "I like to swim."

Jen refilled her glass. Her eyes were unreadable behind her sunglasses. She hadn't yet made it clear why she'd asked them over, why it was paramount that Mary Beth, whom Jen and Dr. Yoder had never met before, accompany Ferko. Jen had called the night before with the invitation.

"What'd you do today?" she'd asked.

Ferko, who didn't wish to explain the trip to Princeton, said, "Nothing." Then, "What about you?"

"Same."

Now Jen pushed out her chair and stepped onto the stone wall and over it, onto the grass abutting it. "Tell my dad about your ghost." She retrieved a pack of cigarettes from her pocket and a book of matches. "He's an expert."

"Enthusiast," Dr. Yoder said, "not expert."

"I read your story," Mary Beth told him, "about the boy in the basement in Washington Heights."

"The first ghost story I ever heard," he said.

Jen struck a match.

Dr. Yoder turned his head like a squirrel. "Cigarettes."

She lit the tip and shook out the match and pointed it at her dad. "He used to smoke." She exhaled.

"When I was young."

"He misses it."

"Nostalgia."

"How about that?" She took a drag. "A doctor who smoked."

"We all did." His useless eyes appeared fixed on Ferko's shoulder. "I could tell you we didn't know any better, but we actually did."

There was a pause. Ferko smelled the tang of Jen's cigarette and felt its subtle pull, fingers tugging a loose thread beneath his chest. He felt he could unravel, the sensation no longer urgent but chronic.

"Tell me about your ghost," Dr. Yoder said.

"Amanda," Mary Beth said.

"Amanda."

"She was six when she died."

"So young."

"In 1983."

"And recent."

Jen held her pose—elbow bent, cigarette wedged between her first two fingers, empty fist on her hip. Ferko remembered her description of her punk band, the Mannequins, how she'd hold poses with a lit cigarette wedged between her fingers while the musicians and audience thrashed about. But now she brought the cigarette to her mouth, inhaled and exhaled, before resuming her pose. She was listening, that was all—her entire body leaning in the direction of the table where Ferko sat with Mary Beth and Dr. Yoder, less like a mannequin than a flower whose stalk leaned toward the sun, its petals opening—as Mary Beth told Dr. Yoder the circumstances of Amanda's death.

"You've got *details*." He sounded impressed.

"Library research," Mary Beth said.

"Excellent!"

Ferko hoped to steer the conversation, eventually, toward *collective burden*. Whose was Amanda? The De-Grass brothers', certainly. Possibly the grandmother's. But then Amanda's spirit had stayed, even as Solomon had grown and left town and landed in Princeton, even as his brother had died, even as Amanda's grandmother had died, too, her estate settled, the property sold, the house razed, the trees cleared, the earth shaped, a curved stripe of paved asphalt named Woodberry Road, lined with a few dozen houses built from four models, including the Belvedere, a Cape Cod with fiber-cement siding and dormers. A blue one on the parcel that would become 4540 Woodberry was purchased by Gil and Mary Beth Ferko. Was Amanda a presence then, when they first moved in? Her presence became prominent only after the woman gave birth to a baby girl and after the baby girl was killed. And whose collective burden was Amanda then? There was a connection between the baby's death and Amanda's presence in their lives. Collective burden was larger, somehow, than Ferko understood. Perhaps larger than Dr. Yoder understood.

Mary Beth was telling the story of first meeting Amanda, how she was just another girl on a crowded playground on the last day of school. But something was missing—a parent or caregiver. Then she ran across the field and into the woods, and Mary Beth followed. Dr. Yoder cocked his ear. Jen stepped closer on the grass side of the stone wall.

In sunny Florida, Ferko imagined, the collective burden at Grove headquarters had become fierce. This was the price for profiting from another's death. At Riverfront, too, where Greg had pitched (and Prauer had accepted) a switch from seller to buyer, where Greg had arrived with the other side's intel and come up with a too-high price. And Ferko realized, quite suddenly, that his value to Prauer all these years was skepticism and cynicism. Prauer was paying too much for Grove. The lenders agreed. There was no other way to prove it until Prauer lost his shirt.

Now the e-mail stream from Riverfront had been stanched, even from Lisa, Ferko's last ally. He was out, possibly fired, a ghost himself, a name in random files.

"You spoke to Amanda?" Dr. Yoder was asking.

"Every day," Mary Beth said.

"Amazing."

"She lived with her grandmother in a house that preceded the developments up the hill, on the Ridge. It was the 1980s, and the grandmother still kept chickens in her front yard. The house was set back from the road a good distance. The house and the chickens were a curiosity. Kids came by to see them. Up on the Ridge they lived in ranch houses that were built in the sixties. You can see the city from up there."

"On a clear day," Ferko interjected.

"I remember," Dr. Yoder said, "catching a glimpse of Midtown, occasionally, driving north of here. It was a surprise even when you expected it."

"These kids," Mary Beth said, "could see the skyline, then ride their bikes down the hill to check out the chickens pecking in the dirt around Amanda's house. It was like going back in time."

Jen crushed her cigarette with her sandal, and stepped over the stone wall and back onto the pool deck.

"There were two boys—brothers—who came to Amanda's house one day. The older brother, Felix, grabbed a chicken and rode off."

"Felix," Jen said.

"Amanda chased them into the woods on her bike. She lost control down a ravine and crashed into a tree." Mary Beth dipped her head. "That's how she died."

Dr. Yoder pursed his lips. Jen appeared placid, indifferent. Ferko imagined a thousand needs raging behind her dark lenses.

"Felix who?" she asked.

"DeGrass," Mary Beth said. "We met the brother, Solomon, yesterday."

Jen lifted her sunglasses and balanced them on top of her head. She wasn't high—her pupils were too wide—but something was wild and desperate there. She was still trying to kick, perhaps.

"When Amanda hit the tree," Mary Beth continued, "they rode home and left her, and never told anyone."

"Fascinating." Dr. Yoder cocked his head. "Jen, will you get my tape recorder from the study?"

But she stayed, her hands at her sides, the book of matches wedged between two fingers like a cigarette. She might have been staring at Mary Beth. Or her father. It was impossible to tell.

"What did the brother tell you?" Dr. Yoder asked.

"Not much," Mary Beth said.

"He showed us the door," Ferko said.

"And he ranted about a script," Mary Beth said.

"A script?" Dr. Yoder asked.

"Like we'd read a play, or seen a movie." She looked at Ferko, but he had nothing to add. He'd been baffled by the notion of a script. "He didn't believe we knew Amanda," she said.

"How could he?" Dr. Yoder asked. "Jen, the tape recorder, *please*."

It was noon, the middle of August. Everything was still—the hot air, the leaves in the trees, the water glassed on the pool's surface. And Jen Yoder, the mannequin, who didn't move or even blink.

But only in that moment. In the next she was running toward the house. Mary Beth glanced up. Dr. Yoder tipped his head toward the retreating thwacks of Jen's sandals on the slate patio.

She pushed open the back door and disappeared.

Dr. Yoder shrugged. Ferko had a notion to go to her. He hesitated, but then did, and found her in the kitchen, sitting on a stool, elbows on the counter, a phone pressed to her ear. In a moment she pulled the phone back, checked its screen, then placed it on a folded piece of paper.

"Jen."

Her shoulders twitched, but she didn't turn around.

"What if I told you," she said, "that I was driving the car that killed your baby?"

Ferko watched her.

"What are you—" he started.

"Would you forgive me?"

"But you weren't."

"But what if I was, hypothetically?"

"Why are you—"

"Hypothetically," she said.

"Hypothetically, I'd ask you why you left." He moved to the other side of the counter to face her.

"Because I was scared."

"Scared of what?"

"Of what I'd find. Of my role in the whole fucked-up business."

"I don't know what you're saying."

She unfolded the piece of paper that lay beneath the phone and handed it to him. It took him a moment to process what it was. Then he recognized the name and the room number from the Lewis Center for the Arts.

"He's not in today," she said. "Or he's not answering calls from stalkers."

Ferko waited for what would come next.

"I was in Princeton yesterday, too," she said. "I saw you there. I thought you'd followed me, but now I wonder whether I followed you."

"I don't get it."

"Neither do I."

They found her father's cassette recorder on the desk next to his computer. It was black, with a scratched plastic case, a built-in mic, and five buttons, each as big as a thumb. Ferko supposed it had been here, in this study, for decades. It had been here the night of Jen's graduation party, and further back, too, when Ferko was a boy, trailing Greg Fletcher around the ball fields behind their elementary school.

Now Ferko trailed Jen outside, to the patio, where Dr. Yoder was asking Mary Beth when she'd last seen Amanda.

"It's been a few weeks," Mary Beth said. She shot Ferko a look that asked him where the hell he'd been.

Jen placed the cassette deck on the table between them, along with the power cord. "There's no place to plug it in."

"The battery's good." Dr. Yoder patted the machine with his fingers splayed. Then, in one deft motion, he pressed the REC and PLAY buttons simultaneously. A red light lit and the wheels turned the cassette tape. "See?" he asked.

He faced the machine, as though addressing it: "August 18, 2007. Interview with Mary Beth and Gil Ferko, regarding a ghost, a six-year-old girl named Amanda who died in 1983 in Glen Wood Ridge, New Jersey. Amanda once lived in a house, since razed, in the approximate spot of the Ferkos' house, which was built in . . ." Dr. Yoder paused for an answer.

"In 2004," Mary Beth said.

"Thank you," Dr. Yoder said. He turned his face in her direction. "What I don't understand is—" he started. "What did the ghost—I mean, *why* did the ghost seek you out?"

"The ghost lives in our house," Ferko said.

"But Mary Beth first encountered her at the elementary school," Dr. Yoder said.

"Amanda followed me to the elementary school," Mary Beth said, "but sometimes I wonder whether I followed her."

Ferko's head swam. Jen lowered her sunglasses over her eyes.

"Tell me," Dr. Yoder said.

"I'd been inside for a year and a half. I was grieving."

A shadow darkened Dr. Yoder's face.

"When I went out again, I went up the hill instead of down. I wanted to avoid down. I still do."

"I don't understand," Dr. Yoder said.

Mary Beth glanced at Ferko, her expression serene.

"We lost a child," Ferko said. "A girl. There was an accident." He imagined the blue car, the green stroller, the cruel impact.

"I'm sorry to hear that."

The tape turned in its wheels. A breeze bent the thinnest limbs on the trees. Ferko was starting to see something now: a thread, at first fuzzy, then distinct, in the deep recesses of his mind, the place where puzzles were solved. He'd never been good at puzzles—jigsaws or Rubik's cubes or crosswords. But now a thread grew visible, thin and tenuous, but black, as tangible as night, connecting, somehow, Amanda to Catherine.

Jen pulled her chair closer to the tape recorder and its built-in mic. She sat, then sighed. The lenses on her sunglasses were as dark as the face of the tape deck, which she now addressed: "Guess who else went to Princeton yesterday to meet with Solomon DeGrass?" The question was rhetorical, answered in her next breath: "Me."

Mary Beth blinked. Ferko waited. The thread connecting Catherine to Amanda thickened and grew shoots, like the spindly legs of spiders or the webs they spun.

And Jen told the story again. She'd had a dry run only the day before, but it was harder now, with her dad in the audience. Solomon had judged her, of course, but she didn't care about Solomon DeGrass. Her father's presence made her voice quaver. Yesterday she'd pretended to be an actor in a play. Today she hid behind sunglasses and studied the moving parts visible through the plastic housing of the cassette deck—the wheels and white sprockets that turned the tape. Computers and MP3 players didn't have moving parts. It seemed a shame. Inside and up the stairs, in the bedroom that was once hers, that was still hers on those days and nights when she slept here, was a ceiling fan. How many times had she lain on her back and studied it, counting its revolutions? Now the cassette's wheels marked time, and each revolution advanced the tape, while the story progressed—the bar, the cab, the roof, home. When she got there she chanced a look at her dad, whose face was a mask of thought, beneath which the wheels turned, like the wheels on the tape deck. And now another memory swamped her—a party at Paula McDonough's house to celebrate the end of seventh grade. It was Jen's first boy-girl party—a real one, with music and dancing. Paula had a stereo in her finished basement, with a cassette player and a bunch of mixtapes she'd made for the party from records her brothers owned. It was summer; the day was long. No one bothered to turn on the lights when the sun went down. Kids danced. Jen danced. Greg Fletcher kissed her, and she kissed him back. Her mom was dead, less than six months gone, and she was kissing a boy. And then the boy left. And not just the party. He *left* left. He moved to California.

Now her dad said, "It means something."

Of course it did: Greg's move back East, his relationship to the DeGrass family, the car he borrowed and wrecked and never returned, his obsession with Ferko.

"Greg Fletcher was driving the car that hit your baby," she said.

"Greg Fletcher," Mary Beth said.

"Jen," Ferko started, but she waved him off.

"No, I don't know for sure." She opened her phone and dialed his number. She didn't know what she'd say if he answered. But then he did.

"Jen!" he said. "Long time!"

She stood, then quashed the urge to turn her back and retreat for privacy, the automatic response signaled by that part of her brain where manners ruled.

"What are you doing today?" she asked. "Ferko and I are hanging out."

"Ferko's MIA."

"Not anymore."

"Put him on."

She met Ferko's eyes. "He's not here. I'm meeting him."

"Where?"

She was running out of lies.

"There's a place called Ivy's on Houston." Old habits in old haunts.

"Houston where?" he said.

"First. South side." She turned her wrist to check the imaginary time on her imaginary watch. "Five thirty."

"It's twelve now," he complained.

"I just got up," she said.

Disappointment packed his silence. "Okay," he said after several moments, "tell Ferko he fucked up, but I'll make it right. Also, tell him I'm buying."

CHAPTER TWENTY-FIVE

"I never liked that kid," Dr. Yoder said, meaning Greg Fletcher.

"You loved him, Dad. Everyone did."

"*I* didn't," Ferko protested.

"Yes, you did."

"He used to beat the crap out of me." This wasn't exactly accurate, but it was more tenable than the truth—that Ferko had somehow allowed Greg's superior athletic skills and outsize popularity to cut a deep, permanent wound inside Ferko's head and heart, both together.

"But you wanted to *be* him," Jen said, revealing, in an instant, the truth it had taken Ferko thirty years to resolve: he'd disliked himself more than he'd disliked Greg Fletcher.

Even Dr. Yoder nodded. He was shirtless and shoeless, misshapen and yellow, wearing only black swim trunks and goggles, extra eyes on the wide expanse of forehead, which ranged from his eyebrows to the thin wisps combed over the crown of his head. He looked like a large insect dropped from a tree to the exposed pool deck.

They said their goodbyes, and Dr. Yoder pressed the goggles over his eyes and sat on the lip of the pool with his feet in the water. "Good luck," he called, then took a breath and went under, pushed off the side and swam, no more than a few strokes from one side to the other. He emerged, took a breath, and pushed off again.

They'd made a plan. They ensconced Mary Beth in a coffee shop around the corner, and found Greg in Ivy's, standing at the bar with a glass of beer. He was wearing an ironed blue button-down with long sleeves rolled up to the elbows, red shorts with green checks and a rope belt, blue flip-flops. It was too much color, really. It hurt Ferko's eyes in the dim light. Ivy's patrons showed their colors with tattoos and hair. But now there were none. Only Greg, looking like a lost tourist. And Jen and Ferko, looking like what?

"I came by early and the place was closed. I guess they don't do a good lunch business."

"They don't have a kitchen, Fletcher."

"She knows the coolest places." He kissed her cheek.

Ferko pointed a thumb toward the second booth, the one he and Jen had once shared after snorting dope in the windowless water closet upstairs. They took their respective benches, and Greg slid in next to Jen. He raked his tanned fingers through the hair that fell in his eyes, flashed the peace sign. "Two more of these?" he called to the bartender. Greg glanced at Jen, then Ferko. "Cool?"

"Absolutely," Ferko said. It was a word that had come into favor uptown, overused by the overpaid. It managed at once to convey competence and insincerity. He smiled.

Greg's face lit up. "Where ya been, man?" He opened his hand, which Ferko took but wound up grasping only Greg's thumb, a sausage link joined to a palm, fingers wrapped in a soul-brother shake.

"I been around," Ferko said, in spite of himself. It was an awkward gesture, an even more awkward exchange. The bartender loomed with a tray and two pints of beer.

"Hey, Jen." He placed the beers on the table.

"Manny."

"It's been a while." His sideburns reached his chin. He held the tray like a Frisbee. "You've got new friends."

"I've always got new friends, but these are old friends. Edgefield, New Jersey."

"I forgot you're from New Jersey."

"Everyone's from somewhere," Jen said. "Ferko and Fletcher, this is Manny."

"From LA." He gave Ferko his free thumb, another soul-brother shake. Then he opened his hand to Greg, who ignored it. "Don't leave me hanging, bro," Manny said. But Greg did. He sipped his beer.

"Seriously, dude," he said, once Manny had left. "What *happened* to you?"

Ferko revived his phone with a single touch. The screen illuminated, symbols he didn't try to decipher. He placed it on the tabletop next to his beer. Then took a swig. "I got a lot going on," he said.

"We all do."

"No," Jen said, "he does."

Ferko made a show of reading his screen. Mary Beth had sent a text with a dozen question marks.

"I'm trying to make him rich," Greg said.

"Who asked you to make me rich?" Ferko lifted his eyes. Greg's face opened like a flower, a wondrous expression typically reserved for the recently converted, the born again.

"Why don't you make me rich?" Jen chimed in. "No

offense, Ferko, but you're already there." She turned to Greg. "He's got a house in Glen Wood Ridge."

"New construction," Ferko said, then added, "2004."

"Edgefield's rich cousin," Jen said.

Ferko pressed his eyebrows together and studied her. They both did.

"That's what my dad calls Glen Wood Ridge— Edgefield's rich cousin."

"Cousin!" Ferko said, appreciating the analogy, the connection to their mission. He turned his attention back to the phone, according to the script they'd constructed.

"Stop with that, man!" Greg swatted the phone, which spun twice before stopping in more or less the same spot.

"Dude!" Ferko said, getting in the spirit of Greg Fletcher.

"That's rude," he said. "You're like George Cosler."

"Don't say that."

"Always checks his phone."

"Leave him alone, Greg."

Ferko scrolled down. "Sorry," he said. "I'm a bit distracted." In his head he counted from one to ten. Then his eyes found Greg's. "The police think they found the car that hit my baby."

"*Really?*" Greg's reply was immediate.

"They're running tests."

"Tests."

"They said they might have the results today. But it might be next week." Ferko's senses were heightened. His blood pumped. A bead of perspiration licked his temple.

Now Greg was silent, but not indifferent. He was colorless. His mouth formed his lopsided smile, but it seemed directed inward instead of outward. Everything about his face was sunken, collapsed.

"What kind of tests?" he asked finally.

"There's evidence." Ferko paused a beat. "Or potential evidence."

"Evidence?"

"Don't make him say it," Jen jumped in. "There's *evidence*."

"I'm trying to understand."

"The car hit a stroller," Jen said. "They've got a bumper. There's evidence on the bumper."

"Potential evidence," Ferko put in, sticking with the story.

"Do they have the whole car?"

Ferko shrugged. "I guess." He glanced at his phone as though an affirmation were imminent.

Greg exhaled, a balloon deflating. "Where?"

"I'm waiting for details." Ferko tapped a key on his phone.

"Where's the men's room?" Greg squinted toward the far end.

"Up the stairs." Ferko pointed toward the back with his chin.

Greg slid out of the booth, an expression on his face that Ferko couldn't read.

"What do you think?" he asked, after Greg took the stairs two at a time with his long stride.

"It's him," Jen said. "It's got to be, right?"

"I don't know."

The front door opened and Jen looked up. Two guys walked past—friend-of-Jen types, wearing jeans in spite of the weather. Tattoos peeked from the collars and cuffs of their T-shirts. The closer guy gave Jen a Boy Scout salute, three fingers together at the line where his spiky hair met his forehead. They went straight for the back and up the stairs to the hallway and the sink and the single doorway labeled TOILET, which was locked. They withdrew to barstools downstairs.

"What do we do?" Jen asked Ferko.

"Wait to see what happens when he comes back?"

"Did you text Mary Beth?"

"I don't know what to say."

Jen looked up again, past Ferko's shoulder, as the front door opened. Two friends of Jen's. "She's back," said a woman, who put an arm around Jen's neck and kissed the top of her head.

"Are you?" the guy asked. "Are you back?" They were younger, and reminded Ferko of Tina and Dave. Maybe those two would walk in next. They'd all relive Ferko's arrest.

"I'm *here*," Jen said.

"Fair enough," the woman said, and she turned toward the back, with its stairs and hallway and door with a lock and its private space to cut lines and snort dope. Her braided pigtails bounced as she walked. Her friend followed, but the guys sitting at the bar stopped them and they waited in the queue.

Ferko glanced up the stairs. Still no Greg. "Why did you choose here?" he asked her. "Why Ivy's?"

"It was the first place I thought of."

Ferko waited for more.

"I was on the spot," she said.

He sighed. "Who are your friends?"

"Her name is Corina." Jen didn't turn around. "Her boyfriend is Jared."

"What about the other guys?"

"The one guy's Tony. I don't know the other guy. At least I don't think I do."

"You're like the mayor of Ivy's."

She bit the tip of her finger.

"Have you talked to Tina and Dave?" he asked.

She nodded.

"Did they ask about me?"

She nodded again.

"And?"

"I told them you were kicking, like me."

"Are you?"

"So far."

Greg was on the stairs, taking his time. The two guys in the dope queue—Tony and his friend—stood and waited for Greg to complete his descent. His hair was mussed, like he'd run water over it, like he'd splashed some on his face. He walked slowly. Jen made room, but Greg stood, steadied himself with his strong hands on the worn tabletop.

"I'm not feeling well," he announced.

Ferko met Jen's eyes.

"I'm sorry," Greg said, without saying what he was sorry for, and he turned to leave.

"Greg, wait." Ferko slid out of the booth and stood. He was off-script now. "What's wrong?"

Greg stepped back.

"You can tell me." Ferko laced his voice with mock empathy, but took no pleasure in being the aggressor. Greg once could outrun anyone. But not now.

"Don't leave, Greg," Ferko said. "Don't make that mistake again."

"What the *fuck*?" Greg glanced at Jen, still parked in the booth.

Ferko texted Mary Beth: *It's him*, but when she arrived a minute later, breathless, her face flushed, Greg Fletcher was gone.

Mary Beth and Ferko collected themselves in the booth while Jen found a blank card in her bag. She retrieved a pen from an unzipped pocket. She looked at them and waited. Together they wrote a note:

To the Glen Wood Ridge Police Department:
On September 14, 2005, there was a hit-and-run at the corner of Lyttondale and Amos. A child in a stroller died. The case remains unsolved.
I have reason to believe that Greg Fletcher, a current resident of Manhattan, was involved.
At the time, Mr. Fletcher was staying at the home of his relatives, Mr. and Mrs. DeGrass, who

own a house in GWR. Mr. Fletcher had use of the DeGrass's family car, which I believe was the car involved. The DeGrass family was traveling out of the country at the time of the accident, and is likely not aware of the open police investigation. Mr. Fletcher told Mr. DeGrass that the car was totaled in a single-car accident, and then paid cash to compensate Mr. DeGrass for the vehicle. Mr. Fletcher can tell you how he disposed of the vehicle. Mr. Fletcher is affiliated with a firm called River-front Capital, with offices at 1151 Sixth Avenue in Manhattan. His cell phone is 405-339-4990.

Thank you for looking into this.

They left the card unsigned, and Jen addressed the envelope without a return address. Then she retrieved a book of stamps from her bag, peeled one off, placed it on the sealed envelope, and gave the card to Mary Beth to mail later.

Now they looked at each other, and there was nothing left to say. Jen finished her beer. (As she'd penned the card she'd also, somehow, made respectable progress on her glass.) Ferko's was still half-full. Greg's was barely touched, growing warm and flat, and Jen wrapped her fingers around the abandoned glass and claimed it.

There were more people inside Ivy's. The light outside had changed. Ivy's was somehow brighter and darker, both at once, and the new light made the shapes sharper, the noises crueler. Ferko imagined the trip home tonight, a long walk across town to the PATH station in the fading light. Then one train. Then another. By the time he and Mary Beth arrived in Glen Wood Ridge it would be fully dark, even as two months ago, in June, when he'd first met Jen, eight thirty would still have been daylight. And these insights produced a wave of sadness, an isolating loneliness that overwhelmed Ferko for a moment. Summer was ending. The days would get short. Then they'd get cold. They had one easy act left—mailing the anonymous card. Then it got hard—the waiting. Ferko wasn't convinced the card would work. If it didn't, they'd try again. He was through at Riverfront. He'd go home with Mary Beth, and settle into some new routine that would define who they'd become next.

But Jen knew her next move, Ferko supposed. Her face took on a new glow, as though the low sun behind the buildings had somehow found her. She sat on her side of the booth, her phone on the table in front of her, a narrow slip of paper tented on top. Ferko could see numbers written there. Numbers and dashes. A phone number. Digits she'd use to score. Her eyes met his, and she smiled, a look of contentment he'd never seen in her before. Patrons streamed through Ivy's front door in groups of twos and threes. Some acknowledged Jen with a "Hey" or a nod or a vague gesture involving their open hands. Not all, but enough. They had lumps in their pockets where they stashed their dope. Behind her was a world of possibility, of perfection and bliss. All she had to do was wait the Ferkos out to enter it.

And that was what she'd do. Because the silence they now shared wasn't hers, Ferko knew. It belonged to him and it belonged to Mary Beth and it belonged to the dark house in New Jersey with a child's things and a different child's ghost. But no actual child. The silence swallowed them. He sat in the booth and hoped it hadn't. He hoped he'd mistaken calm for silence. He hoped its true nature would be revealed. But now it was time. Mary Beth stood, and Ferko did, too. They said their goodbyes, and took their silence with them when they left.

ACKNOWLEDGMENTS

Writing and publishing a novel is an achievement that some writers accomplish many times in their lives. I'm in awe of these writers. I'm fifty-four years old and this is my first novel, written through years of late nights and early mornings, sitting alone at my dining table with an overhead light and a laptop. Writing is a solitary act, but not entirely so. Completing this book also required generous amounts of love, support, and belief from a small army of family, friends, teachers, mentors, and publishing professionals.

I'm blessed to work with a wonderful group of writers—Madelyn Rosenberg, Jim Beane, Catherine Bell, Carmelinda Blagg, Christina Kovac, James Mathews, and Kathleen Wheaton—who read the unsteady early drafts and helped me form the characters and find the story. Their unfailing honesty, generosity, and talents were crucial to the successful completion of this book.

I've had many teachers over the years who generously shared their talents and experiences and continue to offer their support. Among them are Jessica Neely, Roberta Murphy, Mary Kay Zuravleff, Leslie Pietrzyk, Mark Farrington, and William Loizeaux. I try to emulate these teachers in my interactions with other writers.

When I first set out to write a novel about characters who use heroin, I had a difficult time getting past the junkie stereotype. Then I read Ann Marlowe's memoir, *How to Stop Time: Heroin from A to Z*, where I found fully functioning people who happened to use heroin. I was on my way.

I wrote large sections of the novel's first draft and final revisions during residencies at the Virginia Center for the Creative Arts, and I'm indebted to its staff and supporters for the time, space, sustenance, and community they offer.

My agent, Mark Falkin, took a chance on an unknown writer because of his belief in this book. I'm grateful for his instincts, diligence, and composure.

I owe many thanks to the folks at Tin House for their belief in me, and for converting my three-hundred-page manuscript into this book. Designer Jakob Vala came up with a striking cover that was true to the story, and publicists Nanci McCloskey and Meg Cassidy got the book from the start and helped it stand out. I especially owe a huge debt of gratitude to my editor, Meg Storey, who championed my novel and pushed me in ways that didn't always feel comfortable but always proved right.

Finally, this book wouldn't exist without my biggest supporters—Alice, Brigit, and Travis. While writing occurs in a place of solitude, it succeeds in a place of love. My family's faith in me exceeds reason. They also come up with some pretty good ideas for stories and endings.

© BRIGIT CANN

DANA CANN's short stories have been published in *The Sun*, the *Massachusetts Review*, the *Gettysburg Review*, *Fifth Wednesday Journal*, the *Florida Review*, and *Blackbird*, among other journals. He has received a Pushcart nomination and fellowships from the Virginia Center for the Creative Arts and the Mid Atlantic Arts Foundation. Cann earned his MA in Writing from Johns Hopkins University, and he teaches fiction workshops at the Writer's Center in Bethesda, Maryland. *Ghosts of Bergen County* is his debut novel.